SMITHEREENS

The Story of Annie D.
Harmony
Dancing on Glass

SMITHEREENS

SUSAN TAYLOR
CHEHAK

DOUBLEDAY

New York London Toronto Sydney Auckland

PUBLISHED BY DOUBLEDAY
a division of Bantam Doubleday Dell Publishing Group, Inc.
1540 Broadway, New York, New York 10036

DOUBLEDAY *and the portrayal of an anchor with a dolphin are*
trademarks of Doubleday, a division of Bantam Doubleday Dell
Publishing Group, Inc.

Book design by Terry Karydes

Library of Congress Cataloging-in-Publication Data

Chehak, Susan Taylor.
    Smithereens : a novel / Susan Taylor Chehak. — 1st ed.
       p.   cm.
      1. Foster home care—United States—Fiction.   2. Teenage girls—
    United States—Fiction.   3. Murder—United States—Fiction.
    I. Title.
PS3553.H34875S65   1995
813'.54—dc20

                                                    94-23218
                                                      CIP

ISBN 0-385-47788-0

For Cindy Morehead
and
In Memory of Sam

I was a girl, and my dreams were of Death. In my mind he was tall and pale and handsome, a man with greased black hair and softened lips and drowsy eyes. I thought maybe I recognized his shadowed figure—it reminded me of something, of someone—and when he called to me, I wanted to answer him; when he beckoned, I did my best, I tried to comply. I was tempted to follow along after him; I didn't care exactly where. Anything would be better than this, I thought. Anyplace would be better than here.

I found him beautiful. It felt dramatic. It seemed to be clearly real.

A handful of aspirin, chalky white tablets, cupped in the pale soft pucker of my palm.

Wind surging through an open bedroom window.

Shingles that lapped down from the rooftop's steep peak; gutters filled with a slime of wet leaves. Dainty girl's feet—in white socks trimmed in a tangle of sweet

*lace, in shiny black gleaming patent leather Mary Janes
—they scrambled, scrabbled, and slid.*

*Beyond the bridge's railing, the river rushing past; a
dizzying flow of black water, empty, cold and deep.*

Or fire. Or rope. Or a gun.

*I was toying with Death, and he gazed back at me,
enthralled. My smile was coy. I thought I understood
who he was. I believed that I recognized something
about what he wanted me to do. But I was only teasing
him; I was leading him on. He knew it, and he loved it.
He followed along after me, pleased by my game.*

I giggled; I howled.

*I was a child, a young girl, just a kid, a teen. I was a
colt, a kitten, a pup—I could be playful and foolish, and
I was flirting, innocently, ignorantly, with Death.*

*It was a game. Hide and seek. Child's play. I'm It,
you're It. It was touch me, don't touch. Red light, green
light. Advance and retreat. I took two steps forward
toward him; then, heated, I gave myself another,
longer, step back.*

*I pursed my lips for him; I blew my sweetest kisses
his way. I batted my squinty eyes. I gave him all the
sass and back talk that he seemed to be asking for, with
my narrow shoulders thrown back, my hands on my
hips, feet splayed, one knee locked, one bent. He seemed
to be in love with the spirit of me. And I was thinking
that I knew what I was doing, how much I'd give him,
just how far I could allow him, and myself, to go. I*

ducked my chin, I glared at him, I turned, and, thinking I might be able, finally, to avoid him, I reared away. When I peeked back over my shoulder to see whether he was still watching, whether he might have been inclined to follow, I could see that, to my warm satisfaction, he was, he would.

I stretched my fingertips out toward him, but then when he reached to touch me, I pulled back, giggling, and skipped off.

His hands were small, his fingers long and slender, his wrists narrow; he was a gentleman, with delicate bones. He trimmed his fingernails with a sharp scissors, straight across. Dark hairs curled on the backs of his knuckles. The shadow of his beard rasped when he rubbed his cheek against mine; a deep, satisfying sound, it soothed. I allowed myself to be lulled by him, to be made stupid, and blind. He liked to smile, he couldn't help it—his lips spread, opened, his white teeth gleamed.

I loved him, in my girlish way.

His pointed fingertip was pressed against the soft inside white surface of my arm. He pulled at my elbow and drew me toward him, closer. His breath was damp, humid, fermented, like the aura of a ripe, sun-warmed fruit. His fingers squeezed, pressed, and bruised. He threw his head back, he showed me the bare sinew of his throat, and he was laughing, pleased, when I wrenched away from him and managed, somehow, to twist myself free.

3

I twirled by, and his hand brushed me, and his fingers skimmed, briefly, softly, up high in the shadows underneath the silky folds inside the sheer flowered fabric of my lifted skirt.

An oven's cold, flameless hiss.

Or carbon monoxide, indiscernible gas.

A big-finned black car, turned into traffic, off a cliff, into a tree.

Or the sly sharp glint of a razor's open blade.

Cut lengthwise, up the smooth forearm, gentle flesh, pale, blue-veined, cut up and not across, from inner wrist to inner elbow, there would be no gush, no sudden spurt of blood, but only a soft and smooth outpouring, a heavy seepage, into the warmish bath. Bright eyes would sparkle and then dim, jaw would sag, and dry lips part. A girl could swoon and fall, she could sink toward the sweet, bright, ever ecstasy of Death.

And in that deep sleep her face would be exquisite; her skin would be as clear and smooth and perfect as a china doll's. Her dampened hair would drift in the tepid water; it would swirl and float across her breasts.

Her legs would be bent, and, softened, her knees would part.

The curtains at the window stir. The tap drips and leaves an imprint on the pinkish-tinted water, a slow ripple of waves that lap and roll, an outward billowing, silent and black and deep and, finally, cold.

Chapter One

HERE'S THE IMAGE THAT I HAD, THIS IS ALL that I was able to suppose: there was Frankie's big old black Lincoln Continental parked near a caved-in chain link fence at the shadowed end of a cul-de-sac, a back alley someplace lost and out of the way in downtown Des Moines. The front left fender ruined; both headlights shattered. The hubcaps were missing. The wheel rims were gone. Inside, the radio had been extracted, and the empty space that had been left behind in the center of the dashboard gaped. The glove box had been pried open; its lock was broken and bent, its papers and pamphlets strewn.

The luxury automobile had been turned into a husk, a shell, cast off and left behind, abandoned like the firm case of a chrysalis on the underside of a branch of a tree. And there was not one trace left behind inside it of anything that had ever belonged to that girl, Frankie

Crane. Not even a crushed-out cigarette with lipstick kisses on its filtered tip. She might as well have never been.

She'd met with foul play, was what the policemen said that they feared. For years, hers would remain an open case. A young girl, missing. Find Creighton Temple, the detectives said, and then you'd find Frankie Crane. But he was just as gone as she was. He seemed to have vanished into thin air, too.

What did I know about it? they wanted to know. I told them, solemnly, nothing. Or at least, I said, nothing much.

A car in an empty alley. An empty car in an empty alley, parked there too long, long enough for bits and pieces of it to have been scavenged, picked at and stripped away, night after night, carried off part by part. Somebody finally took notice of it, and they called the police, who took a look at it and did some checking and cross-checking and then found out that it had belonged to a man in Kentucky, Elgin Crane, whose niece turned out to be that girl named Frankie Crane who had been reported missing out of Linwood for going on three weeks already by then.

Afterward, my mind kept coming back around to that same image, again and again. It haunted me, the picture of that left-behind car. Cars and trees and shoes, that's what it was. Whenever I'd think about my friend Frankie, that's what I'd ponder: cars and trees and shoes.

The news reporters were all over the story in the beginning. For a while they swarmed the Linwood, Iowa, police station, and every day one of them called or came by our house. It was because of the fire at first, a gas explosion that had destroyed our furniture store downtown, and because of the fact that they'd found what was left of Paul Gerald's body in the ashes, and also because of Frankie's disappearance, and finally it was because they'd found her car. Everybody was wanting to know what we thought might have happened. They were asking us to tell their listeners and viewers and readers what we thought we were going to do. They were looking for a definitive statement of some kind from us. They wanted to see the pain in our faces, after all our suffering and loss. They were searching for a squint of regret in my mother's eyes. They were looking for guilt, and for a while they thought they'd found it in the way that my father kept clenching and unclenching his fists. They even came to me. They asked me, What kind of a girl was this Frankie Crane? Had she been a troublemaker? Was she the type of girl who might have run away? And had I any knowledge of this young man, Creighton Temple, who had been following her? Did I think he was involved? Had I ever met him? Could I imagine that anything bad had happened to Frankie? Did I have any idea where the girl might be?

Most of what I told them was the truth, and it was a fact that I didn't know where Frankie had gone. All I did know and all I ever could be completely sure of was why. But nobody had asked me to explain about just exactly that.

I simply said the things that I thought that they thought they would want to hear from someone like me. I said that Frankie had been my friend. That Frankie had been my sister, sort of. That I'd loved her, in a way. And the truth was, I had. I owed a lot to Frankie Crane. My whole life, maybe. My whole self, surely. Because if it hadn't been for Frankie Crane, I knew, I might have turned out to be altogether different than the person I would become. Nobody ever exactly understood that part of it; when I tried to do my best to explain it, they all just thought that I was raving, distraught, maybe, with grief and loss. But I knew what I meant, and what I meant was this: without that brief flame of Frankie's friendship, maybe I would have died young. Or, worse, I might have grown up to be nothing more than what I'd ever been—an ordinary girl and an unexceptional woman, unremarkable and unchanged. It's likely that I'd have hardly even been remembered, much less, even momentarily, renowned. I'd have been forgotten by my classmates, the children of my childhood, those kids who'd grown up with me and who, most of them, had known me, and as a whole, ignored me, all my life.

But the fact of it was, there had been Frankie. That was what changed everything, completely, and nothing that came later was ever going to turn it back again to what it had been before. There had been Frankie's belief in me, and there had been my infatuation with Frankie. All Frankie'd had to do was to recognize me for what I already happened to know myself to be—someone who was special, drawn to the outstanding and destined for something great. To me, Frankie Crane had been both a gift and a surprise.

Up until then, not even my mother had been aware of the fact that there might have been another side to her daughter that she had never seen. Not because she didn't love me enough to notice, just because I'd always been so secretive, and I'd found a way to hide myself from my mother so well, and besides that, my mother had never really looked at me, not closely, not clearly, and so she couldn't have known, not really. The fact was that my mother had had more than just Frankie Crane and me to think about that summer. She'd had her hands full, in fact, with her mother so sick and her father gone off fishing with her husband, and her brother Brodie to look after all the time, as always, and then there was the business at the store to run from day to day, besides. Anyway, I was sixteen years old by then, hardly even a girl anymore, and I was starting to be old enough to look out for myself, wasn't I? Old enough, anyway, to want to be left alone.

And besides that, Frankie wasn't even one of us. She wasn't a Haden or a Caldwell; she wasn't a part of our family, not really. She was an outsider. We hardly even knew her. She'd only become my mother's responsibility by a sort of long-term, long-distance default, just because we were all that was left, and there wasn't anybody else who was around to take on the management of the girl's welfare. Frankie Crane had landed in my mother's lap, and the truth was that we'd been more than generous, straight from the start. My mother did the very best she knew how to do with Frankie, and if that wasn't good enough, well, this was not her fault. Or mine either, for that matter. Nobody should ever have put the blame for what happened to me and to Frankie Crane on anything that my mother did or didn't do for us. That just wasn't fair. I have to continue to insist upon this.

Before Frankie came to live in Linwood, I had already tried

to kill myself three times. That's how bad it was. I hadn't done it very well, probably, or even very seriously either, and the truth of it is that no one even knew that I'd ever tried. But I had, and I knew it, and that was all that mattered. Even though I'd survived all three of those most feeble attempts, or maybe because I had, I was beginning to wonder, to have some serious doubts about the reality of my own existence. I'd started to suppose that maybe I was dead already and didn't even know it and that was why I hadn't been able to kill myself.

Maybe I was just a ghost, I thought. A chimera, like that girl spirit who was supposed to haunt a remote stretch of Old Highway 18 on prom nights after dark, standing on the shoulder of the road wearing the shimmer of a formal party dress, with pink silk pumps on her feet and a dead corsage pinned to her breast, and her hair done up into a fancy French twist. They said that she faded away like a mist if anybody ever stopped to offer her a ride, and that she left behind her a distinctive scent of lilacs and wood smoke and blood.

When Frankie came to Linwood, I was just beginning to come around to a belief in the merits and the magic of what I was starting to consider to be my own special brand of invisibility. I could do anything I wanted to, just about, and nobody ever seemed to notice me and nobody ever much cared. I'd become a girl of such an unremarkable appearance that even when people did take the time to have a look at me, they hardly ever seemed to really see. This wasn't their fault exactly. I never thought that other people ignored me out of any kind of malice, or even for any reasons they could have named. It was just that this was what my place among my classmates had always been. It was just that I was that kind of a girl. I didn't stand out; I faded into the background; I sank into the crowd, and I allowed myself to be buried by it, like a weighted stone.

I wasn't ugly enough to be made fun of and not pretty enough to draw a second look. I had no bad habits, but no real talents either. I was just a girl, just that, just plain. I could suppose that there must have been millions of others, just like me, all over the world. Not short, not tall. Not fat—if anything, too thin.

I didn't have breasts that billowed like Tanna Wilson's. My face wasn't splattered with Britt Jameson's coppery freckles or framed by Alice Manley's unsettling cloud of kinked red hair. I didn't have Angela Rodder's perfect fingernails or Janet Pine's seven brothers or Sally Dean's long slim legs.

My voice was too soft to draw attention. My face was even-featured, my brow smooth, my gaze unfocused, and my look bland.

Maybe there were some times when that vanishing act of mine happened to serve me, in a way. Maybe I did it on purpose. I might have admitted to that. And maybe, sometimes, it was something that I had begun to consciously strive to achieve. Sometimes. When I needed to rely upon my nameless facelessness, it could protect me. I knew how to be good, how to follow the rules, to stay out of trouble, to keep my nose clean. I turned in my homework on time; I wasn't sick much, and never late; I was friendly with my classmates, I pleased my teachers well enough, I passed through school with reasonable comments, and I earned average grades. I was good enough, but not too good, smart enough, but not too smart. I made myself easy to miss, easy to overlook. I'd found it to be just simpler that way.

I LIVED WITH MY PARENTS, CALVIN AND VIVIENNE CALDWELL, ON TYLER DRIVE, in a large two-story house in a serene, well-kept neighborhood on the good side of Linwood.

Our house was white, with black shutters and a wood shingle roof. Our front lawn was on a long slope, with a circular drive-way and a plain limestone walk that ran straight up over the grass from the sidewalk to the front door. There were flowers and bushes that my mother kept planted and trimmed, a lime-stone wall that encircled the back yard, a single maple tree on one side, and oaks and evergreens on the other. Inside, the rooms were crowded and warm: we had three bedrooms up-stairs, with a sleeping porch off the side, a den and a living room downstairs, a dining room and kitchen at the back. My mother had made the flowered drapes in the front room herself, and she'd covered the downstairs floors in a thick sea-green carpet-ing, and all the furniture was old and used, battered and worn, antique, because my father wouldn't allow us to have anything that was new.

He worked in a furniture store, he argued. "Have you seen how that stuff's made?" he wanted to know.

But all of that was really nothing very special. We were just like other people, and that was how almost everyone in our part of Linwood lived.

If it hadn't been for Frankie, I could have shown up at a class reunion twenty years after my high school graduation and been the one who stood to the side, alone and unrecognized, not the ugly duckling transformed into a striking swan and not the teen-age beauty worn down to homeliness by a weariness of years. I would have been the one among the others who would have seemed to have hardly changed, and my classmates—the balding men with their easy smiles, the women with their knowing eyes and widened hips—might have looked at me and then looked again, they'd have had to peer at my nametag, trying to recall whether I was somebody's wife, or was I an old friend that they should have been expected to know? I might have seemed faintly familiar, maybe, but who was I? My mother's family had owned the big furniture store on the corner of First Street down-town, hadn't they? By the river? Haden's? And that would have been it, then, all that any one of them could come up with about who that girl, their friend and acquaintance, May Cald-well, had been.

If not for the fact of Frankie Crane. If not for knowing her, for loving her, for making myself into Frankie's best friend. I would come to consider myself blessed. I would be the lucky one after all; because of Frances Crane, I would be transformed.

I HAD JUST TURNED SIXTEEN THAT WINTER, AND ALL ALONG I'D BEEN GROWING UP and holding myself in as if I were my own best-kept secret. I was a hidden picture, sitting perfectly still, mild and distracted, a girl gazing harmlessly at nothing, staring off into space.

I was smallish, thinnish, girlish—with dainty hands that I held folded, ladylike, frantic birds at rest, in my lap. I wore my light

13

brown hair pulled back, with a wisp of short bangs that feathered my high smooth brow. My fingernails were chewed. I wore on one finger a simple pearl ring that my parents had given me for my birthday that year.

But I'd drawn a deep red heart, outlined in black, high up on the inside of my thigh, with two felt-tipped permanent marker pens, and that was something else about me that I alone was aware of and no one else could see it, and only I knew for a fact that it was there.

CARS AND SHOES AND TREES. THAT SPRING, NEAR THE END OF APRIL, LINWOOD suffered some heavy storms, and one of the big oak trees at the edge of the front yard out at Grand Haden's house fell. That was the first sign. If I'd known to, I might have taken it as an indication of what was about to come.

There had been too much rain, and the ground had been too wet, Grand Haden said. Saturated, the tree's roots had shifted. A clenched fist, they'd opened, loosened, and lost their hold. I had a feeling, and it nagged at me; my intuition was that the tree might have been saved. If only somebody had cared to do it, if anyone had been paying attention, if they'd happened to be looking at it just at the right time, if they'd noticed that it might be about to go. The earth around its base must have moved, humping and writhing with the struggle of its great tangled roots; there would have been a soft creaking sound, like the stealth of a footstep on a loose floorboard, and then the louder strained screech of wrenched wood, and then the slow sideways slant of the tree's broad trunk.

Maybe they could have saved it, I thought, if they'd known what to look for before it happened, if they could have read and understood the signs. Grand Haden said that he'd heard the noise of it first, and that it had sounded like a plane passing over too low, or some distant thunder, the promise of another storm. There'd come that deep, steady rumble, and just at that moment he and Meems had both looked up, and then the oak went down. He'd watched the desperate shudder of its huge branches and the frantic waving of its few new leaves.

It fell away from the house, across the yard and over the front walk, and it crashed, bounced, seemed to shiver, before it settled, finally, on the grass. We'd been lucky, my father said, but Grand Haden had disputed that. If the tree had fallen on the house, he'd argued, then at least the insurance would have paid. What was lucky, my mother pointed out, was that it had been raining and cold, and so there hadn't been anybody out in the yard just then. No Brodie cutting the grass with his tractor mower; no Meems on the walk in her wheelchair; no old yellow dog panting in the tree's circle of shade.

At its broadest, the trunk was at least five feet across, if not more. Its dislodged roots had taken up a huge clot of turf, webbed with wet, black dirt. The walkway was cracked in half; there was a deep trench dug down into the earth, and the topmost tips of the branches had reached all the way across the grass to finger the rosebushes that bounded the yard on its far side. Grand Haden hired a crew of workers who came by the next day with chain saws and hatchets, and they fed the branches into a shredder, cut the trunk up into logs, cranked the stump the rest of the way out of the ground, and then loaded it all up into their truck and carried it away.

Looking at that toppled tree that afternoon, my first thought had been of Grand Haden. I'd pictured my grandfather fallen, sprawled across the lawn with his own face pressed against the dirt. Maybe this was a memory; maybe it was something that I'd actually seen for myself one time and then forgotten about later. I'd tried to imagine my father instead, because he was the larger man, and younger, still solid and strong. I'd pictured him with his back to the tree, his legs spread and his knees locked, his heels digging stubbornly into the earth, his broad face red and swollen, wet with the strain of trying to hold that huge tree upright, his body braced against it, until somebody else brought help. A truck with a rope maybe. Something sturdy and enduring to buttress the falling tree.

When she saw how upset I was about it, my mother thought she understood why. She guessed that I must have been reminded of something, some lost pleasure from the past, maybe. But I wasn't associating any of my old childhood memories with that tree. There was nothing in it to take me back and place me just there, a little girl, playing with my dolls on a blanket in its shade. Other trees maybe, but not that one. There'd been no rope swing tied to its lower branches. In fact, until it fell I really hadn't even much noticed that tree; I hadn't singled it out as anything that was dear to me in any way. I'd taken it for granted, complaining when I'd had to help Brodie rake its leaves or if I'd happened to step on one of its acorns with my bare foot. The only specific image of that tree that I'd had in my mind was of my grandmother, of Meems, as a younger woman, long before she'd been silenced and stilled by her stroke. It was sometime in the summertime, and Meems had ducked out of the rain and was standing under the spread of the oak's leaves, hoping to preserve the carefully contrived shape and form of her new hairdo.

I was not upset because the tree had been lost. I was only angry because I saw that it hadn't been saved. It wasn't up to me to figure out how, but I was certain that they could have done it. I continued to insist upon this, the same as, later, on my mother's innocence. If they'd wanted to. If there had been anybody out there at all who had cared.

My mother liked to tell people that she believed in the sure rewards of an honest generosity. What goes around comes around, was how my father put it. You get what you ask for, in other words. People get what they deserve, sooner or later. And at first, my mother liked to say that Frankie and I were between us the living proof of it: that whatever a person gives away, good or bad, she will get back again someday, and maybe even double at that.

I pictured it this way: my parents are lying in bed. It's nighttime. And it's springtime, early in May. And early in their marriage, too, when their being together is still something interesting and new.

My mother has been trying to explain to my father about this idea she has of how the world works. The TV is on, he's watching it; he's trying hard to follow the plot of an old war movie on the late show, and he's only half listening to what she's telling him.

"See, that's why it's better," she says, "to be more generous with what you want than with any of the things that you already have."

She runs a fingertip along the curve of his jaw.

"For instance, if you have a lot of money," she goes on, "but you don't have any time, then you just have to give more freely of your time and in some magic way you'll find that you've ended up with more."

He frowns. He's skeptical. He squints at her, then turns his attention back to the goings-on on the TV. She touches the stretch of his throat.

"Or," she continues, "if you have too much jealousy and not enough compassion, then give away the compassion."

He nods at this. He's beginning to see what she's getting at, at least. She's probing the dip of his collarbone, where his skin is especially soft.

"Too much hatred and not enough love?" she asks him.

He looks at her again. He's smiling now. "Then give away the love," he says.

She nods and palms the swell of his chest.

Now a commercial has come on the television screen—shots of young children with smudged faces, wide-eyed, solemn, clinging to a porch rail, or standing barefoot in a dusty yard with their grimy fists clenched helplessly at their sides.

"Won't you become a sponsor for this girl?" a voice is asking. My mother looks up at the TV, and my father sees the change that comes over her face, and right away, he understands what it is that she is about to do. That's how close they were to each other. What she's thinking, he already knows.

Only fifteen dollars a month, fifty cents a day—for the cost of a cup of coffee, a child's life can be saved.

What Calvin and Vivienne Caldwell had back then when they were first married was just each other. But what they'd wanted and been working for was a child, particularly a daughter, the baby girl that would fulfill my mother's life, the living doll that she could hold and feed and dress up in pretty clothes. Someone who would climb my father like a tree, who would sit on his lap, who would pull his hair and tweak at his nose and tell him he was the handsomest, wisest, strongest, bravest, best daddy in the whole world. What they'd been longing for was me.

So, they made the phone call, gave their pledge, and then turned to each other, their bodies bathed in the blue TV sheen. And the proof of my mother's theory about giving and needing was that it was just almost exactly nine months later that I was born.

MY MOTHER HAD ASKED THE FEDERATION TO SIGN HER UP WITH AN APPALA-chian child, because her idea was that it might be better if she could keep her charity close to home. If it didn't have so far to go, she reasoned, then maybe it would come back to her again more easily and more quickly that way. In two weeks, before she even suspected that she was already pregnant, she received a picture of her foster girl.

It was a three-by-five color snapshot, with a name stamped in black letters on the back. Frances Anne Crane. Frankie was almost two years old, with dark curly hair held back by a pink plastic headband, thick-lashed round blue eyes, rosy pink cheeks that might have been glowing with health or maybe they were wind-burned and chapped, and a perfect little pale button of a nose. She was wearing a white blouse with a round collar and brown corduroy pants with an elastic waistband and blue tennis shoes with rubber over the toes.

The form letter that came with the photograph explained that Frances Anne Crane and her older sister, Holly, were living in Jackson County, Kentucky, in a four-room, wood-frame, oil-heated house with their father, Frank, and their grandmother, Grace Crane. That the girls' mother had died of an illness a year before. That Frances was in good health. That she liked to play outside. That she preferred blue jeans to dresses, and, if Vivienne wanted to send clothes, Frances wore a little girl's size three.

Those form letters continued to come to us from the Federation just before Christmas every year, along with updates on the family's living conditions and a new photograph of Frances. My mother could spread the color snapshots of Frankie out on the table, in chronological order, side by side, to see how, over those years, she'd changed and grown. Her hair was cut short for a while, and then she let it come back out long and curly again. Her arms and legs got longer and paler and thinner. When she was fourteen, she began to bloom, growing breasts and curves, and when she was fifteen, she was wearing earrings and dresses and low-heeled shoes. For most of that time we didn't send

Frankie any presents, only the card that the Federation asked us to sign for her birthday and, at Christmas, an extra fifteen dollars cash.

When Frankie was almost ten, that was when her own handwritten letters first began to arrive. Frankie wrote them out on lined notebook paper; her penmanship was sloppy, and she had no punctuation, but she did know how to spell.

> *Mr. and Mrs. Calvin Caldwell*
> *I.D. #15460792396*
> *Jan 15*
> *Dear Sponsor,*
>
> *I will write you a few lines to say hello how are you both by now fine I hope this leaves us all ok I thank you for the birthday card and thank you for the gifts you have sent me in the past you are the best sponsors and are so nice and so thoughtful and I love you for that how is the weather where you are it is cold out here but it is sunny.*
>
> *So I had better close for now. My grandmother says I should add May God bless you all real good.*
>
> *Bye bye now.*
> *Yours truly,*
> *Frances Anne Crane*

FRANKIE WAS ACKNOWLEDGING A BENEVOLENCE THAT MY PARENTS HAD hardly shown. Maybe someone had told her she should write this way, figuring that if she could show the right amount of gratitude, her sponsors might turn generous. It was something like the flip side of my mother's belief—the hope that if you could thank somebody enough for what it was you wanted, then maybe they'd decide to go ahead and give it to you after all.

And it had worked, too, because, after a while, that was just exactly what my mother began to do.

Frankie sent these letters off and on for almost eight years. The last one that came had been written sometime in the early winter, when she was seventeen. It was followed a few months later by a notice from the Federation informing us that our sponsored child—Frances Anne Crane—would no longer be able to participate in the project. Even though it wasn't for the benefit of Frankie anymore, still my mother kept on sending her checks off at the first of every month. Because, she said, she was superstitious. She was afraid that something unfortunate might happen to me or to my father—or maybe even Grand Haden or Brodie or Meems—if she decided to quit. That whatever goodness had come to her through her generosity to Frankie Crane over the years might all of a sudden turn off and become something else instead. That I might be taken away from her, for instance, like a promise that had been reneged.

And then Frankie showed up on our front porch in Linwood on one wet evening in late spring. Already there had been weeks of weather that had been filled with rain, when it was sunless and dim every day for what had begun to seem like forever to all of us who lived there and were starting to think about the summertime that should be coming around our way again soon. The ground was drenched; the landscape had been relentlessly glacial and gray; the sky had looked leaden and bruised.

And then Frances Anne Crane was there—a bit of color and warmth, standing out against that background of dark and dank.

My mother was in the kitchen just at dinnertime when the front doorbell rang. She crossed through the house in a hurry, drying her hands on a dishtowel, smoothing her wild hair, tucking it back behind her ear, and she was annoyed by the interruption because she hadn't been expecting anybody, and the pork chops were cooking and the spaetzle to go with them, and she always had to worry about the spaetzle. If it stayed too long in the water, then it would be ruined, and my father would have had something to say about that. Which didn't mean he'd bother enough to get up and answer the front doorbell himself when it rang.

He was in the den watching the news on the TV, and I was upstairs in my room with the door closed, and that was why it was left to my mother to go and see who was out there and what they wanted from us.

She turned the bolt and unhooked the chain and opened the door to find a girl in green stockings and a purple coat and a red hat and orange gloves, and she was rosy-faced and smiling in a way that seemed to be an expression of her shyness and her boldness both at the same time. She was pretty, bright with the colors of her clothes—she was a blossom in the twilight gloom. And that was Frances Crane.

There was no reason that my mother should have known right away who Frankie was. The face might have reminded her of something, someone, that was all. It was a face she knew she'd seen before but just at that moment and out of context couldn't find a way to place.

And for her part, when Frankie saw all that puzzlement and confusion working in my mother's eyes, it may have made her smile broaden some. Frankie loved surprises and secrets and knowing more about what was really going on than anybody else.

I had come out of my room, and I was standing at the top of the stairs, in my school P.E. T-shirt and sweatpants and bare feet. Curious, I'd come partway down, leaning sideways, but all that I could see of Frankie at first were just her legs in the green stockings, her feet in the black boots, and the wind that was blowing around outside, sniffing up her skirt, wet and cold.

"Mrs. Caldwell?" Frankie said.

ON A SATURDAY ABOUT A WEEK BEFORE THIS THERE HAD BEEN A STRANGE OLDER boy who'd come begging through the neighborhood, going along from door to door. He wasn't looking for a handout, he said. He only wanted some honest work. He had a bike that he'd picked up somewhere, probably stolen, my father said. The boy would ride up to a house, drop the bike on the grass, stride up to the front door, and knock on it with his fist. He had on a ragged old blue and green striped sweater and baggy trousers. He was a young man with dark hair and blue eyes, a baby face that was beginning to show a shadow of darkish whiskers.

Just wanted some work, he said.

Like what?

My mother had been cautious. She didn't much trust strangers. She stood there inside the screen door, which was latched shut and locked, and she wasn't about to open it to anybody she didn't know, not even in the middle of the day.

Anything at all, he said. Whatever chore she needed done, he was able-bodied and willing to get to work and do. Gardening, hauling, lifting, carrying, sweeping. He didn't have a place to stay, he told her. He'd been sleeping under somebody's porch for a couple of days, but now it looked like a storm was maybe coming and if it was going to rain that night, he didn't want to be caught outside, in mud turned to muck, so he thought he'd try and find some odd job, to earn enough money to get himself a room at the Y downtown or maybe in a motel.

My mother had listened to his story, but then she'd had to harden her heart and tell him no, she was sorry, but she didn't have any work for him to do. She sent him away, shut the door and latched it and locked it, too, and then she went back into the kitchen to get a glass of water and put in a call to my father down at the store.

He was with a customer, and she had to wait on hold for a good five minutes before he finally picked up, and then I could see by her face that she could tell by his voice that he was already annoyed even though he didn't yet know the reason that she'd called. So he must have been just that much more impatient with her when she told him.

"What is it that you want me to do, Vivienne?"

My father held on to his anger with his teeth, clenching them hard around it. He was always careful not to ever let it go.

My mother told him that there was this young man who'd

come to the door looking needy, but that she hadn't given him anything and then she asked, did he think it looked like there might be a storm coming tonight?

"Go find him, Viv," he'd said. "Give him some money or some food. If it makes you feel better."

By the time she got off the phone, the boy had moved far enough down the street that he was out of sight, so we had to get into the car and drive around the neighborhood a little bit before we were able to find him again. He'd made his way into the next block, and he was standing outside on the front stoop of old Mrs. Abernathy's house, looking at a bottle of milk, seeming to consider whether it would be worth his while to steal it or not. My mother honked the horn to get his attention, and he came off the steps and down the walk looking puzzled. Wary. Not sure what we wanted from him, not too much different than she must have looked to him herself, when he was standing there on the other side of our screen door waiting to see what she would say.

One thing I knew for sure was that Mrs. Abernathy wasn't ever going to answer her bell, even though she would have heard it ring, and I thought I saw a movement in the curtain at an upstairs window. The boy smiled and then came around to the driver's side of the car. He stood there for a moment, looking at my mother, studying her face.

"Do I know you?" he asked finally.

"You were at my house," she told him. "A while ago?"

She had a ten-dollar bill in her hand, but he couldn't see that from where he was standing outside the car.

His smile broadened, and he nodded his head. "Sure," he said. "The one with the shutters? Red geranium in a pot inside the front door, on a table next to a wicker chair?"

She didn't like it very much that he seemed to know so much about just exactly which house was hers and what she had inside it. But she gave him the ten dollars anyway.

"Here," she told him, without admitting to the shutters or the geranium or the wicker chair, "take this if it helps. Go find a place to stay. Before it starts to storm."

"But can't I do some work for you?" he asked.

"No," she answered. She rolled up her window and turned the car around and drove home. When I looked back at him, I could see that he was still standing there in the middle of the street, watching us go and holding that ten dollars in his hand, with the rain starting to splatter down on his bare head.

My father said later that we'd probably insulted the boy's dignity because we'd made him into a beggar, when all he'd asked for was the opportunity to put in an honest day's work. But my mother hadn't wanted him around, that was the problem. Even if he didn't rob or rape or murder us, if she'd given him the job that he'd been asking for, some small chore to do around the house, then he'd probably get to talking and then we'd find out what his name was and where he came from and how he'd got to be here, riding up and down our street on a bicycle, knocking on strangers' doors, begging them to give him a job. My mother had just not wanted that connection. She hadn't wanted to be his friend. She'd only wanted him to be cared for, and that was all. To be in out of the rain and the cold when it came. But at the same time, she hadn't cared to commit herself too far to making sure that he was.

And that was just about how it had been with Frances Anne Crane at first, too. My mother had sent her those checks and she'd written her those letters because maybe she did care about Frankie, but that was really only in an abstract way. Maybe she even loved her a little bit, at least the idea of her, a sponsored child, a bargain that she'd made in exchange for me, a real live, living, breathing, in-the-flesh daughter of her own. But that didn't mean that she wanted Frankie to care back about her, too. And it sure didn't mean that she wanted to get to know the girl. Or to meet her. Or to have her come and live there with us in Linwood in our house.

It was the Kentucky license plate on the dirty black Lincoln Continental that had been parked out in the curve of the driveway that finally brought my mother around to figuring out who Frankie was. She looked at her again, and she put two and two together, and then the realization dawned on her and she said quietly, "Frances?," using just about the same questioning unsure tone that she herself had heard speaking out her own name not half a minute before. And Frankie was nodding and grinning, and her eyes were watering, but maybe she wasn't really crying, it might only have been the wind that had picked up outside just then and begun to bother her eyes.

Her cheeks were flushed, and her dark hair was loose in an array of curls across her brow. She was a pretty girl.

By that time my father wanted to know what was what, and he had got himself up out of his chair and was standing in the doorway to the den, holding his cigarette in one hand and his glass of whiskey and water in the other. He was looking first at Frankie and then at my mother, with his eyebrows raised and asking, What?

My mother shrugged and shook her head, as if she wanted to clear it, and then she told him who the girl was. She did it by way of an introduction, with one hand reaching this way toward Frankie and the other one that way toward him, saying to them both, "Cal, this is Frances Crane. Frances, this is Cal."

He took a step toward them, put his cigarette in his mouth and, squinting through the smoke, said, "Frances. Well, hi." And then he looked at my mother again, with his eyebrows still raised, asking, So?

And she smiled, and repeated herself. "Frances Crane," she said, more loudly, as if she thought that it might have been likely that maybe he'd gone deaf.

He spoke the name out then, too, rolling it around in his mouth as if he were tasting it, and he studied Frankie for a minute, frowning, picking up something that seemed familiar about her, and, seeing that, she grinned, watching him back, patiently, waiting until he got it. When it did finally come to him it was like a light of recognition that rose up shining in his eyes.

"Frances? You're Frances?" Looking at my mother and then turning back to study Frankie's face again. "Well, hell," he said, shaking his head, as if he didn't believe it.

My mother remembered her manners then. "Come on in, Frances, come in." She took Frankie's arm, and she pulled her inside, out of the wet and cold.

"I sure am sorry to barge in like this on you all," Frankie said.

And my mother looked at her and said, "Well, don't be sorry, Frances. We're happy you're here. Aren't we, Cal?"

It was awkward, with my father not knowing what he was supposed to say, and my mother herself not exactly sure how she felt about having Frankie there. Because there was a part of her that was genuinely happy to see the girl and to have her there in front of her—she had missed the letters and she had wondered what might have become of Frankie and she also didn't at all mind having been given the chance to have a look at her foster daughter face to face. But there would also have been some other part of her, a darker part that would be sinking her stomach with a leery feeling about just what the implications of Frankie's visit might turn out to be. About what kind of expectations the girl might have in her mind. About whether maybe she wanted something more personal from us now and if she did, what would it be and did we have it to give away?

"Well, I'm on a trip across the country," Frankie said, finally, even though nobody had asked. "My uncle Elgin let me have that car out there, and he told me I could do whatever I wanted to with it, so one day I just got fed up and I climbed inside it and I took off. And when I got this far and I realized where I was, well, I thought I'd just stop by, you know, say hey, and, I don't know, maybe a little bit of thank you, too. After all you did for me, Mrs. Caldwell, I . . ."

30

Her words trailed off. I had come downstairs.

"May," my mother said, "this is Frances."

Frankie smiled at me. "Hi," she said.

I nodded and smiled back. "Hi yourself," I said, and blushed, feeling stupid and dull in my dingy T-shirt and gray sweatpants compared to Frankie's bright coat and orange gloves and colored tights.

"Would you like something, Frances?" my mother asked. "A soda maybe? Something to eat?"

"Oh no." Frankie's words seemed to come out in a singsong, a gentle Kentucky drawl that pulled on the vowels and then left them to linger in my ears. "I don't want to put you out or anything. Really, I just came by for a minute. I just wanted to have a look at you all. I guess I shouldn't stay."

"Well, you can't just go," my mother said. Her words seemed flat and short by comparison. "At least you can have some dinner, can't you, Frankie?" And she turned to my father, and she asked him, "Wouldn't that be okay, Cal?"

And he answered, because what else could he say, "Well, I guess so, sure. Of course. I mean, I don't know why not."

So, then the next thing there we were, all four of us sitting at the table, with my mother at one end and my father at the other and us two girls across from each other, like sisters, in between. And Frankie had her head bowed, and her hands were folded under her chin, and she was saying the grace.

Chapter Two

Mr. and Mrs. Calvin Caldwell
I.D. #15460792396
12/19
Dear Sponsor,

Hi there and how are you this Christmas season? Is there any snow at your house? We have some but not much yet We are all set for our holiday celebrations already The tree is up anyway My sister Holly is asking for a puppy this year and I'd sure like to see her get it but our dad says it's just one more mouth to feed I think he's pulling Holly's leg I know he likes dogs I want to thank you for the card and for the gift too It will come in handy as I'm sure you must already know I didn't know that I had such a sponsor who is as nice as you are

Have yourselves a Merry Old Christmas and a happy new year too
From your good friend and foster girl
Frances Anne Crane

THERE WAS ONE TIME THAT I COULD REMEMBER AND IT WAS SOMETIME in the dead cold of winter, sometime before I was even five years old, and we were out at my grandparents' house. The grownups were in the living room playing cards, and they'd put me to bed in my grandmother's room at the back of the house. They left the light on in the hall. And the radio, playing music, softly.

Meems had her own bedroom in that house, she said, because Grand snored and paced and had a tendency to wake up in the middle of the night and not be able to get back to sleep. He disturbed her beauty rest, Meems said. He kept her from it and then complained if she didn't look pretty enough for him. Saying this, she'd turn to him and smile, show him her delicate face and frail features. And he'd look back at her and frown. I could imagine how his gruffness might have damaged her, over time.

I lay on Meems's bed, and I held my breath and listened—to the radio playing softly, and then my father's voice, and then Grand's, drifting through the house toward me, from the living room where they sat talking and laughing and slapping down their cards. Outside, it had stopped snowing. I fell asleep for a while, and then my father came in and got me, ready to take me home. He bundled me up in my coat and in a blanket; I lolled in his large arms, groggy and half asleep. He carried me out to the car. He covered my face with his gloved hand. Darkness. My breath making the wool moist and hot. A gust of wind blew at his hat, and he lifted his hand, and the cold snapped at me. My mother was outside already, waiting for us in the car, with the motor running, warming up.

Then there was the wobble of headlights, at the end of the driveway, coming toward us too fast.

My mother called out to my dad. He stopped and turned and stepped back, sinking into the snow. The car swerved sideways, slid past us, and then hit the bank of snow that the plow had piled up at the far side of the drive.

My father was holding his breath, holding me. The car door opened, and my uncle Brodie tumbled out. He lay sprawled in the snow on his back, with his arms and legs outflung. His nose was bleeding.

"He's drunk," my father said, stepping out of the snow and opening the car door and setting me down on the back seat. My mother had climbed out and was standing over Brodie.

"He's hurt," she said.

I got up on my knees and watched the three of them out the back window, rubbing a clear circle on the glass with my fist. My father was standing next to my mother. Brodie's car sat sideways in the driveway, its taillights splashing red over the snow. And then the front door of the house opened, and a shadow was looming there. It was Grand, swaying from side to side like a bear. He strode down the walk and across the drive. He reached down and hauled Brodie up to his feet.

Brodie came back to life again then. My mother was yelling at Grand. My father was trying to get my mother to get into our car. Grand shook Brodie. Brodie put his hand up to his face, brought it away to look at it, was stunned to see blood. Meems was in the doorway with a blanket thrown over her shoulders, peering out, looking small and frail and inconsequential, like someone who'd survived a disaster in which everyone else had been killed.

Grand let go then, and Brodie wobbled, staggered, found his balance, steadied himself. And then he was laughing, hooting, howling. He put his arms out and threw his head back, and he turned around and around in the snow, with his face bloodied and his coat open and his hair wild.

There was the open door, with Meems standing in it, haloed by the yellow light that spilled from behind her out onto the snow. There was me, forgotten, in the car. There was the thrum of the car's motor, running. There was the warmth of the heater, blowing against the backs of my legs. There was Grand's voice and my father's, deep and muffled and far away. There was my father pulling my mother to the car. My mother was silent. My father was angry. Our car fishtailed as he backed it out of the drive, and I could still see Brodie there in the front yard, in the light, turning around and around, like a maniac.

"He's crazy," my mother said softly.

"He's an idiot," said my dad.

His words froze into a white cloud that flowed out and fogged the windshield. He spun the steering wheel with the pressed palm of one hand, and he shifted into drive with the other. And I was thrown back into the seat again as we skidded and veered away.

AFTER DINNER WHEN WE WERE IN THE KITCHEN CLEANING UP THE DISHES, Frankie mentioned that she was going to try to find a motel room if she could, but my mother waved her hand and said, "Nonsense, you can stay right here with us tonight." And then she turned to my father and asked him, "Can't she?" And, again, what was he going to say?

Frankie looked at all three of us, one after the other, and she smiled. "You're very kind. But I really couldn't impose upon your hospitality any more than I already have. You've done too much as it is."

My mother had that same persuasive expression on her face that she would get when she was trying to talk a customer into buying the walnut dining room table he'd been admiring, as well as all eight of its matching cane-bottomed chairs. As far as she was concerned, it was over and done with already, and all that was left was to take care of the paperwork.

"Frankie, don't you think twice about it," she said. "We're not going to turn you out into the street. Are we, Cal?"

She made up the bed in the extra room, and then she ran a warm bath with bubbles in the tub, and I watched while Frankie took both my mother's hands into her own, and she said, "Thank you. I mean it, Mrs. Caldwell. For everything you've done. It means a whole lot to me. More than you can possibly know."

FRANKIE WAS UPSTAIRS IN THE BATHTUB, HUMMING, AND I WAS STANDING IN THE hallway downstairs, outside the den, and I heard my father say, "You'll have to call her family."

And my mother answered him, "And tell them what?"

"That she's here."

"Why?"

"What if they're looking for her?"

"What if she doesn't want to be found?"

"That's not our problem."

"Whose problem is it?"

"Frankie's. Theirs."

"If she ran away, then she probably had a reason."

"And that's not our problem either."

"She's here, Cal. That makes her problem ours."

"Well, she's not going to stay here long, is she?"

And my mother said, "I don't know. Where else do you think she has to go?"

MY MOTHER SENT ME OUT TO THE CAR TO GET FRANKIE'S THINGS AND BRING them into the house for her, and I was happy to have been given that job to do. If I couldn't get a closer look at Frankie because she was in the bathtub, then the next best thing would be to take a closer look at her car. I bounded down the porch steps and slopped in my socks over the wet grass to the drive where the Lincoln sat, like a large animal, hunched, dark, mysterious, and still. I pulled on the handle, and the heavy door groaned open. I looked up at the house to take in the comfort of the warm lights glowing in its windows, and then I made up my mind and slid in behind the wheel and shut the door behind me.

The air inside the car was dark and cold and stale, and it

made me shiver. I reached out and poked a finger at the flow-ered silk sachet that had been tied by a bit of ribbon to the rearview mirror, and I watched it slowly turn and swing. The car's leather upholstery was burgundy, creased in places, shiny, dark as blood. The ashtray was full of crushed cigarette butts and crumpled cellophane. The full-across seat had been pushed back, and my legs were that much shorter than Frankie's that my own feet didn't quite reach the pedals, but I gripped the steering wheel in both my hands anyway and I pretended that they did, thinking about what it might feel like if maybe I were Frankie, if I could be someone else other than my own small self, a strange girl who was setting off someplace alone, driving along in this big car, sailing down the straight line of the interstate highway, lost and lonesome and wholly on my own. I may have already been in love with Frankie by then, or maybe only with the idea of her. I leaned my head back, and I closed my eyes. I breathed in the cool scent of pine from the stirred sachet, and I thought that must be just how it had smelled out in the woods where Frankie had grown up in Kentucky.

There was a rumble of thunder, slow and deep and far away. The wind was restless in the high branches of the trees.

I leaned across the seat and opened the glove box to pop the trunk. I pulled out a maintenance book and a thick car manual and a pink registration slip in a plastic case. So, it wasn't Frankie's car, after all. It was registered to an Elgin Crane on Route 6 in Kentucky. There was a tube of lipstick, red, a pack of cigarettes, filtered, a hairbrush whose bristles were webbed with a snarl of Frankie's fine dark hair, and a pint of bourbon that I held up to the light and could see was already half gone. I unscrewed the top and sniffed at it; I touched the tip of my tongue to its lip, wincing at the sweet, numbing, burnt wood taste. And then when I set the bottle back down into the glove box again, I heard the glass clink against metal, and I reached in and folded my fingers around something flat and hard and cold, and I lifted it up and pulled it out and saw that it was a gun. I turned it over, savoring the seriousness of its weight. I had never seen a real gun before, much less held one in my own bare hands. It was so black against my palm that it seemed to create a space there, an emptiness, a hole, as if a part of me had somehow been removed.

Upstairs in my parents' bedroom, a light came on. Rain spattered the windshield for a moment, and then it settled to a fine drizzly spray.

I could feel the awkward, scared tumble of my heartbeat in my throat. I could see my father's shadow, bearlike, misshapen and large, moving in the window upstairs. Carefully, I settled the gun back down into its safe place at the bottom of Frankie's glove box, and then I rearranged the rest of the things on top of it. I punched the release button and felt the trunk sigh open behind me.

A fine mist of rain licked at my face. There were two suitcases in the trunk. I reached in and pulled out one and then the other, staggering with their weight as I hauled them across the yard and up the porch steps.

My mother was waiting for me.

"What were you doing out there?" she asked.

I blinked at the rain and licked it from my lips, wondering whether she was going to be able to smell that taste of bourbon still lingering on my breath.

"Nothing," I said. "Trying to figure out how to get the trunk to open, that's all."

"Your feet are all wet. Don't track that mess inside."

I sat down on the bottom step and pulled off my wet socks. My mother took one of the bags and began to carry it up the stairs.

I hoisted up the other one and followed her. If I were all alone and on my own, driving across the country to I didn't even know where, I might want to have a gun in my glove box, too, I thought. It made sense, didn't it? For protection? For security? For just in case?

We put both the bags down on the bed, and Frankie came in, wrapped in my mother's old blue terry cloth bathrobe. She was pink-skinned and barefoot, steaming after her hot bath. Her toenails were polished red. She looked at the bags and then at us, and then she laughed.

"You sure didn't have to bring that old thing inside," she said. She reached over and flipped the latches and opened it. Inside was a typewriter, an electric Smith-Corona with a cartridge ribbon and a white-out correction key.

"Your mama bought me this, May," she said. "Did you know that? Do you remember it, Vivienne?"

My mother nodded. "Yes, Frankie," she said. "I do."

"Well, I'll bet you thought I went and sold that thing, now didn't you?"

"No, of course not." She reached out and fiddled her fingertips across the molded keys. "I knew you wouldn't do something like that."

Frankie was peering into the mirror on the back of the closet door. She mopped at her damp hair with a towel.

"I have a plan," she said. Her eyes were wide with it, and bright, as if she was just as surprised as anybody that she was there. "I'm thinking maybe I can get a job somewhere. Get so I'll be able to support myself now. I'm old enough. And I have a skill. Thanks to you, I can type real well. I got all A's. My spelling's perfect and all. No mistakes, seventy-five words a minute, which is more than average, better than Holly ever could do. And I practice it whenever I can, besides. So I'm just getting better and better at it every single day."

My father was hovering in the shadows outside in the hallway.

"Vivienne?" he called.

She looked over her shoulder, then smiled at Frankie. "Shouldn't we call your grandmother, Frankie? Just to let her know you're here?"

Frankie winced. "Well, you can call her if you want to, Vivienne," she said. "But it's not likely she'll answer you."

"Why not?" my mother asked.

"Well," Frankie said, "because she's dead, that's why. We buried her two weeks ago." She turned to me. "Pneumonia," she said. Tears sparkled in her eyes.

My mother had folded her hands together, and she was squeezing them into one fist against her chest.

"I'm sorry, Frankie," she said. "And we're glad you decided to come here and see us," she went on. "Really we are."

Frankie was across the room in two steps. She didn't walk, she flew, she floated, she glided into my mother's arms. She was reaching for her and putting her arms around her and hugging her, squeezing hard and rocking her from side to side. Her damp hair covered her face and hid her eyes, so I couldn't judge what Frankie was really thinking, but her words came out soft and snagged with feeling.

"Thank you," she said. And then, "I'm glad, too."

My mother pulled away. She picked at her own hair with her fingertips and swiped at her eyes with the back of one wrist and then she turned away, quickly, toward the door. Over her shoulder, she said, "School tomorrow, May. Don't you stay up too late, all right?"

And I answered her, dutifully, obediently, "No, Mom, don't worry. I won't."

FRANKIE'S OTHER SUITCASE WAS AN OLD LEATHER THING, RAGGED AT THE CORners, with broken latches and a man's black leather belt cinched around to keep it shut. Frankie opened it and began unfolding her clothes—blouses and sweaters and skirts and jeans, shaking the wrinkles out. I pulled a handful of hangers out of the closet for her. Frankie's clothes smelled like spice—cinnamon and cloves and, faintly, pine.

She set a framed picture out on the table beside the bed. It was a three-by-five color snapshot of a man in a baseball hat. His face was half in shadow, and he was leaning back against the high fender of a rust-red pickup truck with his arms folded over his chest.

She saw that I was looking at it. "My daddy," Frankie explained.

She'd brought out a small, brocade-covered jewelry box. She sat down on the edge of the bed next to me, and she opened it. Inside there were mirrors and drawers and a row of padded creases for holding rings.

"My finery," Frankie told me, smiling.

She pulled out a long string of pink and blue plastic beads and held it up for me to see. A bright glossy earring that was shaped like a wedge of watermelon. A turquoise cuff link. And a gold link chain with a sparkling stone that might have been a diamond in a delicate heart-shaped setting swinging from its loop.

"Is that real?" I asked her.

Frankie winked at me. "Maybe," she said. "Maybe not."

I leaned in closer to her, peering into the jewelry box, wanting to see some more. There was a string of yellowy pearls, a silver ring with a purple stone, and a gold link bracelet set with a dazzle of red and blue and green gems. Frankie fished out the bracelet.

"This one's pretty, isn't it?" she asked. She held it out and I took it and turned it over in my palm, studying the colors of the stones against my skin.

"My uncle Elgin Crane gave me that one for my high school graduation. You can have it if you want it."

"Oh," I said, surprised, handing the bracelet back as if it had burned my hand. "No, I couldn't."

"Well, why not?"

"Because it's yours, Frankie."

Frankie was smiling. She pulled my wrist toward her, looped the bracelet around it, and snapped the clasp. "Looks pretty on you, don't you think?"

And it did. She held my hand up, turning it to let the stones catch the light. She nudged me with her elbow. "You could use some brightening up, you know." And I knew that that was true, too.

I unclasped the bracelet and cradled it in my palm. "I sure don't want this, Frankie," I said, but we both knew that was a lie. I might have liked it if Frankie had insisted, tried to talk me into keeping it. I couldn't accept it from her too easily, that would have been greedy and selfish and wrong. She'd have to wheedle me about it for a while first, make it seem like I was the one who was doing her the favor by agreeing to take it off her hands.

But Frankie only smiled. "Well, if you did want it, I'd give it to you. That's all."

I looked at Frankie, keeping my eyes steady, gray and quiet and calm. "Why?" I asked.

"Because," Frankie said, "I owe it to you. Or, I guess more precisely I owe it to your mom. For what she did for me." She laughed. "Maybe to you it seems like it was nothing, May," she said, "but for me, it was a lot. When things got bad for me at home, I'd think, it's okay, Frankie, you've always got Vivienne. That was a lot more than my sister ever had. I'd say, Frankie, Vivienne Caldwell doesn't even know you and that's just fine, because she loves you anyway. Every month, like clockwork, that check of hers would come. And every birthday, every Christmas, a card and fifteen dollars sent on just especially to me. It was like having a fairy godmother out there. It was like there was this one secret guardian angel I had, somebody who knew who I was, and knew where to find me and who understood what I needed and who would keep on looking out after only me, Frances Anne Crane, for just as long as I was in need. How am I ever going to be able to find a way to thank your mother for that?"

I slipped the bracelet back into the box on Frankie's lap. "I don't know," I told Frankie. "Maybe she doesn't want any thanks."

"That won't keep me from still owing her some, though, will it?"

I looked over at the closet, full now, with Frankie's hanging clothes. "No, I guess not."

Frankie closed the jewelry box and latched it and put it aside. "My sister Holly used to braid my hair for me at night," she said.

"You miss her?"

Frankie stood up and walked over to the mirror. She frowned at her reflection. "Some. Not too much. I'm glad I got out of there, if that's what you mean." She turned back to face me. "Would you do it for me tonight?"

I gathered the glossy dark fall of Frankie's damp hair up into my hands. My fingers moved quickly, plaiting the hair over and under itself. She handed a rubber band over her shoulder, and I looped it around and around the braid's thick end. Our eyes met in the mirror. Frankie was smiling.

"Thanks," she said.

I shrugged. I brushed my palms together and tried to make it seem as if I did this sort of thing every day, when the honest truth was that I didn't. That I didn't have any friends. That I hardly ever even talked to anyone besides my family. I had been an only child and a lonely girl, and now I had a foster sister living in my house, offering me jewelry, and asking me to help her braid her hair.

"Well. I'll see you in the morning, I guess," I said.

Frankie grinned. "I'll be here."

FROM WHERE I WAS STANDING IN THE HALLWAY, I COULD HEAR MY PARENTS arguing behind their closed bedroom door. My mother had turned up the volume on the TV, thinking she was going to be able to cover up some of the noise of their voices and keep us from hearing their fight, but it didn't work, because it only made my father have to shout over it which made him sound even madder than he was. I stepped forward and knocked on the door and heard the sudden silence that welled up behind the racket of the TV, and then my mother's voice was calling out to me sweetly, "Come in." Two syllables on the word "in."

My father was red-faced and tight-jawed, standing there in the middle of the bedroom in his boxer shorts, with his hairy chest and his big gut and his hard fists clenched into knots at his sides. He avoided my eyes. He went into the adjoining bathroom and shut the door after himself. My mother sighed and shrugged and asked me if I was going to bed.

I nodded.

"Well, good night, then," she said.

"Night," I answered.

She frowned. "You okay?"

I nodded again. "Sure," I said. "I'm great. I'm fine. I'm okay. Is Dad mad?" I wanted to hear what my mother was going to say.

"He'll get over it."

And I nodded again. Of course he would.

She smiled. "So, what do you think?"

"About what?"

"About Frankie, of course. How do you like her?"

"She's nice, I guess." She has a gun in her glove box and she smokes cigarettes and drinks bourbon and that car doesn't belong to her. This was what I didn't say.

"Pretty, don't you think?"

"Mm-hmm."

She put her arm around my shoulders and pulled me close and hugged me. Her own dear girl. "This is an adventure, isn't it?" she asked. "I mean, I just can hardly believe it, can you? That she's actually here?" She shook her head. "It had to take a lot of nerve on her part. She must have been pretty unhappy where she was if the only thing she could do was to run off and take the chance of coming to us here."

I knew what she was thinking. That she was making up a picture of Frankie's life, imagining a little girl growing up without enough to eat in a cramped and dilapidated shack with a dirt floor and no electricity and an outhouse in the back. She was seeing all the pitiful images of neglected and forgotten children that they'd shown in the commercials that the Federation put on the TV.

But people like that didn't drive Lincoln Continentals, did

they? Or have boxes of gold and silver jewelry with diamonds that looked like maybe they might be real?

"I mean," my mother went on, "that was a big chance Frankie took, wasn't it? How could she have known that we're the kind of people who might be willing to take her in?"

My father came out of the bathroom. He padded barefoot over to the bed. He flopped down on his back, and he stared at the ceiling with his hands folded behind his head. His body was furry all over, on his stomach and his chest, his knuckles and toes, and under his arms.

"She didn't," he said.

My mother glanced over her shoulder at him.

"What's that supposed to mean?"

"Nothing. Just that she didn't know. Or she should have known better. Nobody in their right mind would take a stranger into their house, Viv. Nobody but us."

"She's not a stranger."

"Might as well be."

My mother shook her head. "We're doing the right thing, Cal. I know it."

"We don't even know her."

"We do a little."

"Not enough."

"She's just a child." She stood at the foot of the bed with her hands on her hips. Her hair was wild around her head, curls like a swarm of golden bees. "She's sweet. And so grateful. I can't believe she has it in her to do us any harm."

"Maybe not," he said. "But she's out of here tomorrow."

"We'll see," she answered.

"I mean it."

"We'll see."

He shook his head. "I don't like it," he said. "Tomorrow I want her gone."

"You are not going to kick her out into the street, Cal," she said.

"I'll kick her anyplace I want to. This is my goddamned house."

"No, it is our house. We all live here together, remember?"

I opened the door and slipped out and pulled it shut behind me.

THE NEXT MORNING IT WAS RAINING AGAIN. MY MOTHER WAS UP EARLY AND HAD made the coffee already and a plate of toast. She was just putting a lunch together for me, and there was Frankie Crane. She came into the kitchen looking disheveled, sleepy and warm, wearing red long underwear faded to almost pink and an oversized man's black and green buffalo plaid flannel shirt. Her braided hair had been slept on and was coming undone, tangled in what I thought was a pretty way.

I had come downstairs early that morning, and I was sitting at the table, chewing on toast with jelly, washing it down with milk, when it was more my usual way to be sleeping in too long and then having to rush because I was running late. I liked lying in bed in the mornings, caught in between sleeping and waking, dream-world and thought-world, and it was hard for me to tear myself away from it, to step out into the harder, sharper edges of daylight and schoolwork and whether I should raise my hand in class or why didn't so-and-so ever talk to me or look at me and would I be sitting all by myself again today at lunch? Most mornings I wouldn't even take the time to eat any breakfast at all, but just grabbed a can of Coke out of the refrigerator and then was out the door. But on that morning after Frankie came, I'd somehow managed to get up all on my own, without my alarm going off, and without my mother having to call upstairs to me twice or more. That morning I was showered and dressed and down even before my dad.

He was a man of habit and routine, and he came into the kitchen the same as always, quietly, smelling clean. His face was shining, his hair was damp and combed, there was a fleck of shaving cream in the curl of his ear that my mother annoyed him by trying to swipe away. She knew he didn't like to have to talk to anybody until after he'd had his first cigarette.

He helped himself to his own coffee, not wanting to have to use the words that it would take for him to ask us for it, and I went ahead and poured a mug for Frankie, too, and set it out in front of her, with milk and sugar and a spoon, in case she wanted them, which she was polite enough to say thank you for. She reached out then and helped herself to a cigarette from the pack that my father had put down on the table, and he held out his lighter for her, then caught my mother looking at him and shrugged. Frankie saw that, too, and she smiled at all three of us.

"I'm just not worth a thing in the morning before I've had my coffee," she said, blowing smoke.

She reached for the milk and poured a good splash of it into her mug. She heaped in three big teaspoons of sugar, too, stirring them in with some distracted concentration, until she realized that we were all watching her, and then she looked up at us, and she grinned.

I WAS REMEMBERING ONE TIME WHEN I WAS A LITTLE GIRL AND MY GRAND-mother had taken in a stray cat. It turned out to be a purebred Siamese, with a sandy belly and a gray face, dark brown ears and paws, and a disconcerting startle of deep blue eyes. That beautiful cat came into Grand Haden's house one day, and he made himself right at home there.

Somebody must have left a door open. We found the cat lying on the back of Grand's chair in the study, stretched out in a shaft of sunlight that was coming in through the opened shades. We never could come up with a name that suited him, even though we tried out several. Meems had ended up just calling him Baby.

To Meems, Baby had seemed like something of a wonder. He surprised her by how beautiful he was, and she couldn't understand how it had happened that a valuable creature like that one had found itself abandoned and left behind as a stray.

Baby wasn't an affectionate cat. And he didn't like Meems nearly as much as she liked him. He wouldn't tolerate the confinement of being held by anybody, not even Brodie, who after his accident everybody said had a way with animals. But she couldn't keep her hands off the cat, anyway. When she picked him up, he made a miserable growling sound that came from deep down in his throat, and he struggled and twisted and wiggled himself away. But then the next minute, there he'd be, rubbing against Meems's legs, purring out loud like she was the best friend he had in the world. It was as if the cat just couldn't make up his mind about whether he wanted her to love him very much or not. He was temperamental that way, the way that my mother told me that purebred cats can be.

Baby did like the sunshine, though. He'd find a bright puddle of it on the floor, and then he'd sit right in it, moving along with it as it moved, following it across the furniture and the floor from one end of the room to the other.

One morning he was sleeping on the rug the way he always did, and I saw Baby curled there and I decided that the cat looked like something soft that I'd like to bury my face in and run my hands over and hold. I knew that Meems couldn't hold that cat, but I thought that maybe I was different, and that maybe for some reason Baby was going to like me more. I'd tried to sneak up on him. I'd come around behind the sofa and I'd lunged for Baby, but the cat was smarter than me, and faster, too, and he leaped away so that I fell and knocked my forehead against the sharp edge of the coffee table.

There was blood, warm and dark and streaming into my eyes so I could hardly see. It wasn't Baby's fault, and Meems knew that. It wasn't anybody's fault. It was an accident, that was all. But when she got back home again from taking me to the hospital, Meems found Baby and she picked the cat up and tossed him right out the back door, and even though Baby stayed around for a while, crying and crying to be let back inside the house again, Meems would not allow it. Finally Grand made Brodie tie the cat in a pillowcase and throw it into the creek.

———

My mother had poured herself a cup of coffee, and she was sitting down at the table across from Frances Crane.

"You shouldn't smoke, you know," she told Frankie. "It's a bad habit. Hard one to break." Mothering her, just like she thought she had the right to do—she was her daughter in a way, after all.

"Oh, I know that. I know," Frankie answered. She tapped ashes and took a sip of coffee. "I don't do it so often, though, and I never buy any of my own. Just borrow."

She smiled and blinked and waited for what she must have known was going to come next. I was thinking about that pack of cigarettes in the glove box of the Lincoln, knowing Frankie was lying and thinking I could understand well enough the reason why.

"Where will you go now?" Dad asked.

My mother coughed, annoyed and embarrassed that he'd just come out like that and asked Frankie straight about what her plans for the future were. He had no subtlety, no tact, she said.

But Frankie wasn't offended. She only shrugged. "Well, I guess I don't know where I'm going to go, Mr. Caldwell," she said. "Or what I'm going to do when I get there, either."

She said that she just wanted to see something of the world, that was all. She was young. She had no obligations. She didn't mind the idea of letting herself wander for a while, aimless, drifting, loose.

When my father was angry his eyes tightened up and turned dark, and they could be mean and hard as the sharp black stones at the bottom of the creek sometimes. He could scare you into doing just about whatever he told you to do, and he didn't even have to raise his voice to do it. Just then he had Frankie fixed with his coldest look, as if he was trying to stare her down, to shrivel her up, but she only sipped at her coffee and smoked her cigarette and didn't even seem to notice. Or if she did notice, she didn't seem to mind.

It bothered me all right, though. I shifted in my chair, and it creaked. I tipped it back, and when my mother tapped my knee to get me to sit straight, I lost my balance, flailed, and let the front legs thunk back down. The noise of it startled Frankie. She looked at me first, and then she turned to my mother, who was avoiding everybody's eyes. She didn't want to have to look at Frankie, I guess. She dabbed at the corner of her mouth with her napkin.

Frankie had been holding her mug of coffee in both hands, and the steam from it was rising up into her face, giving her a dewy, damp look. Her fingernails were manicured and polished red to match her toes. The silence in the room felt like it was a cold shadow, dimming us.

"Oh, God." Frankie squeezed her eyes shut and shook her head, wagging it from side to side. "I'm so sorry," she said. "How could I be so stupid? You all have to go to work this morning, don't you?" She looked at me. "And school?"

She stood up and carried her mug over to the sink. "And here I am, lolling around in my peejays, acting like I'm some kind of a special princess or something."

"It's all right, Frankie," my mother said.

"God, what you must think of me."

She turned and crossed the kitchen toward the doorway. She stopped and looked at my father. "I'm sorry," she said. "I'll just go get some clothes on. Won't take me but a minute, then I'll be gone and out of your way."

My mother had begun to clear the table, carrying the coffee mugs and the dirty ashtray over to the sink and dumping them there. She turned and leaned back, crooking her elbows against the edge of the counter behind her. She was wearing a bright yellow blouse, with pads that squared her shoulders and a stand-up collar that flattered her face and at the same time made her look businesslike, I thought, and strong.

"It's okay, Frankie," she said, avoiding my father's hard eyes. "You don't have to go."

Frankie was stopped in the doorway, straddling the threshold, teetering there, not sure still whether she was supposed to go or maybe she was going to be able to stay.

She turned to my father. "I know what you're thinking," she said.

He frowned. He didn't like to be told that. His idea was that the workings of his mind were so complicated that they must be a surprise to everybody, sometimes even himself. "Oh yeah?" he said. "And what's that, Frankie?"

"Well, you're too polite to say it, and I appreciate that, but I guess you're not really sure whether you feel quite right about letting some strange girl hang around in your house all day when you're not here."

"Frankie . . ." my mother began. But Frankie put up her hand to stop her.

"No, it's okay. I mean, I understand. You hardly even know me, except for a few letters back and forth over the years. And you're not sure that you can trust me. Isn't that right?"

My father stood up. "Well," he said.

I looked at Frankie, framed in the doorway, tall and slim, with her small hands and her dainty feet and her open face and her tousled hair.

"Mrs. Alt will be here this morning," my mother said, and that stopped my father dead in his tracks. Mrs. Alt was our cleaning lady. She came in once a week to do the heavier housework for my mother, who would have thought of this already and would have known that Frankie wasn't going to be left in our house all day long alone.

"Listen. Why don't you do this, Frankie," she went on, "get yourself dressed and then come downtown and meet me and Cal for lunch? We'll talk. We'll get to know each other better."

Frankie grinned. "Okay. That'd be fine. Thank you," she said.

My mother drew Frankie a map to show her where our store was downtown. And then she left a note out for Mrs. Alt, explaining as simply as she could who Frankie was. A houseguest. An old friend who was here to visit with us for a little while. A daughter, of a sort.

"Now don't you worry about a thing," Frankie said.

My dad took his coat down off its hook by the back door, and my mother picked up her purse. Frankie had turned to me.

"Bye now," she said. She took my hand and shook it, surprising me with the intimacy and the formality of it both at the same time. "Sure was nice to get to meet you for once, May."

And I smiled back at her, saying how I was glad to have met her, too, and maybe I'd see her later or something. All in my most awkward, red-faced, mumbling, invisible girl way.

"And you, too, Mr. Caldwell," Frankie said. "Thank you for your trust in me and for all your kind hospitality."

We left the house then, because there was nothing else that we could think to do. We filed out, one after the other, and Frankie stood in the doorway, waggling her fingers, and calling out after us, "Bye now. Bye."

She held the door open and watched us go. Dad backed the car down the driveway, maneuvering around Frankie's mud-spattered black Lincoln. A cloud of white exhaust was billowing out from the tailpipe, Frankie was reaching out and bringing the door back shut again, and then we'd turned the corner and behind us our house and then our street and after that our neighborhood were gone.

Chapter Three

ON THE WAY TO SCHOOL THAT MORNING
after Frankie came, I was sitting in the back seat of my
father's car, and I was gazing out the window, silently,
and there he was, that boy again, the one who'd come
to our door looking for a job. He still had his bicycle,
just the same as before, but he was on it, and he was
riding, pedaling away, moving in a big hurry down the
middle of our street, flying by fast with his hair blown
back and his face pinched against the cold and his eyes
squinted tight, just about shut. What crossed my mind
at first was I wondered what the trouble was that he
might have been trying to get himself away from. What
had he done? As he went by he got a glimpse of my
face at the back window, too, and he could see that I
was seeing him, and when he looked over his shoulder,
he took one hand off the handle bars to wave, and he
wobbled, almost losing his balance and just missing the
front bumper of a black panel truck that was at that

moment rounding the corner of Forest Street where it crossed Tyler Drive and turned into the dead end of Lincoln Place. I closed my eyes, fully expecting to hear the screech and thunk of a collision, but there was nothing but the whoosh of car tires treading pavement and the revving of the truck's engine as it shifted gears, and when I opened my eyes to look again, the boy was gone.

My book bag was heavy in my lap, and I could feel the silence between my parents growing, booming, filling me up with its swelling emptiness. My father's jaw was working. He rubbed his lower lip with his thumb. He braked, signaled, and turned.

Their struggle was an old one. They'd been waging the same battle with each other for as long as I could remember. Sometimes one won the fight, sometimes the other one did. One gave in on one thing and the other gave in on another. It was like a game they played, as pointless as a scoreless game of football—they pushed each other back and forth over the field without ever getting anywhere or accomplishing anything at all.

I was looking at my father's big hands, and I was trying to picture them on my mother's body, moving over her skin. His palms on her hips, fingers closing, crushing her. She would have given in to that, I knew; she had, again and again, and gladly, too.

OUR HOUSE ON TYLER DRIVE SAT UP HIGH OFF THE STREET, ON A GENTLE RISE OF land that gave us a generous sweep of front yard and a good, clear view of whoever might be coming or going, passing down the sidewalk or along in the street below. Ours was a neighborhood of big houses without fences, broad lawns and tall trees, brick walkways and circular driveways and limestone walls. We were situated just close enough to the local school that I could walk there and back every day. A group of the mothers had held a breakfast meeting about the safety of that, and they'd decided to tape red construction paper hearts up in their streetside windows to let everybody know that they were there, watching their children on their way to school first thing in the morning and then back home again later in the afternoon. That way, they thought, any child who had a problem of any kind could feel comfortable about coming to any one of them for help. Or if there was somebody who had a mind to do harm, maybe he'd think twice about it, knowing there were mothers there at the windows, watching, within arm's reach of the phone.

Mornings before she went to work my mother would stand at the window in our dining room, and she'd watch me go off out the front door and down the driveway to the street, where I joined in the stream of other kids who were passing by on their own way to school. We children all walked along through that corridor of red construction paper hearts, and we could believe that we were protected and that we would never come to any harm.

THE WIPERS WERE MOVING BACK AND FORTH OVER THE WINDSHIELD, LIKE AN argument, swiping at the rain.

"Do you think she'll be all right, Cal?" my mother asked. She had her hands in her hair.

"It's a little late to be wondering about that now," he said.

I'd turned away, and I was looking out my window at the rain and the trees. They were waving their leaves at me, gesturing, a warning of some kind, but I couldn't quite get what it was that they were trying to tell me I should do. My hand was at my mouth, my teeth were nibbling at my fingertips, worrying the ragged edge of the nail on my thumb.

Mrs. Alt trundled past in her car, but she didn't see us, she was so intent on maneuvering safely over the wet streets. My mother pointed her out and immediately felt better. "See?" she said. "There, I told you. Everything is going to be just fine."

We stopped at the curb outside my school. And then I was out of the car, and they were pulling away, and they were arguing with each other about what to do with Frankie again, so they didn't even look back to see that I was standing there, waving goodbye.

MRS. ALT WOULD HAVE PARKED HER DENTED RUSTED BROWN CORVAIR BEHIND Frankie's Lincoln. She'd be walking up the driveway to our back door. She'd tiptoe, careful to avoid the puddles, because she wouldn't want to get her shoes wet. She would hold her big black purse over her head in an effort to keep the bristle of her gray hair dry. She'd find my mother's note on the kitchen table, and she would read it, and then she'd hear a voice coming from the den. Curious, she'd peek in and see Frankie there—a teenage girl lolling in my dad's big chair, wearing pinkish long under-wear, baggy at the knees, and a big green and black plaid shirt with the sleeves rolled up.

Frankie would be talking on the phone. She'd be looking up, and smiling and waggling her fingers to say hey. Mrs. Alt would turn away. She'd suck on her teeth, an expression of her disapproval. She'd lumber out into the front hall to hang up her coat. She'd run water in the kitchen sink, then think twice about how smart that was and turn it off again, craning, straining, trying to pick up the gist of whatever Frankie might be discussing on the phone.

Mrs. Alt would be suspicious. She'd hear Frankie, creaking around in our house, looking at our things, running a hand over the arm of the velvet loveseat in the living room, wiggling her bare toes into the deep pile of the green rug, squinting at the watercolor landscape that hung over the fireplace, plunking at the piano, skimming fingertips across the shining polished surface of the sideboard in the dining room, pulling back the drapes to peek outside and scowl at the dismal rain, sniffing at the blossoms on the gardenia that my mother had spent all winter coaxing into bloom in its pot on a table by the window in the hall. And Mrs. Alt wouldn't like it, not one bit.

AND ME, I WAS AT SCHOOL. MAY CALDWELL, SITTING IN MY FIRST-PERIOD CLASS—in my usual place, in the corner by the window at the back—and I was thinking about this girl who had dropped into my life, this somebody named Frankie Crane. I was remembering something about the warmth of her hand when it was shaking mine.

I took a look across the room at pretty little Alicia Bell, a girl with straight black hair and even bangs, blue eyes and white skin, and not one freckle or a single blemish that I had ever seen, and a waist so small that Barry Kern, who was two years older, could put his hands around it and almost touch them, thumb to thumb, something that he liked to demonstrate again and again, just for the pleasure of touching her and holding her in his hands. She was leaning across the aisle, whispering something to Jessica Landon, who was laughing and whispering something else back.

The classroom windows were streaked with rain. Mr. Matthews was calling out the roll. Outside the sky was still dark with clouds. Thunder was rumbling, softly, gently, safely far away. The whole school smelled like wet wool and rubber boots and mud. And I was thinking how surprised everyone would be if they knew that I was friends with a girl like Frankie Crane. Older. A runaway. With her own car. A girl who smoked cigarettes and drank bourbon by herself. A girl who carried a gun.

BY AFTERNOON THE RAIN HAD STOPPED AND THE SKY WAS, FOR THE MOMENT, clear again. I swung my locker shut, hoisted my book bag up onto my back, and head bowed, eyes down, gaze focused on the careless shuffle of my own two feet in their worn white canvas Keds, I shouldered my way through the crush of students toward the heavy double doors that opened out onto the parking lot at the north side of the school. Cars were glittering in the new sunlight, a sparkle of water and glass and chrome. A girl in a hurry pushed past, jostling me. Someone slammed a car door.

Horns were honking. Tires squealed as a pickup truck left the lot, in a hurry, showing off. A boy was standing on the sidewalk, waving his arms and shouting at his friends—his voice was strained, a deep, harsh, angry bark.

I stopped at the corner kiosk and sat down on the warped boards of the public bus stop bench, cradling my book bag in my lap. The sun reflecting off the puddles in the streets and on the glass and the grass was too bright, and it burned my eyes, made me squint.

"Don't frown like that," my mother would say. "Your face will freeze."

Crabby Appleton, she called me. "What's got into you?"

I had my head ducked down, and I was making a study of my shoes. The laces had snapped—I'd knotted them back together and tied them in sloppy bows.

An elderly woman in a thin flowered cotton dress with big buttons down the front came and sat down on the bench next to me, sighing heavily and fanning at her neck with her hand. Her mouth was a painted pink bow pressed against the crinkled tissue paper of her skin. I squinted up into the sky and scootched away to the other end of the bench. I hugged my book bag. The bony fingers of the woman's hands were bruised and bent like broken sticks, folded into fists against her brown plastic purse, protecting it. She looked over at me and smiled, deciding that I must be somebody who was safe. But I could easily have reached out and snatched that purse from her, if I'd wanted to, and then, that quick, before the old woman had even had time to register what I'd done, I would have slipped off down the block and disappeared around the corner, gone. But for what? Some crumpled dollar bills that she had tucked into her wallet, folded back behind the creased and faded snapshots of her smiling grandsons and their new babies and their optimistic wives.

I could imagine the time-lapse photograph, the slow-motion film, of my own methodical transformation, from girl to young woman to matron to crone, seated just there, in just that way, on just that bus bench, in just that same spot—it could have been me, my whole life condensed and blown by, in one long, uneventful tumble of time. Then there I'd be, that many years later, the one whose fingers clutched at my worthless brown vinyl handbag, instead of a bulky satchel of school books, the one who stared at the cracked brown leather of my shoes, instead of the graying fabric of old sneakers, who was smiling stupidly up at the cleared sky, whose face was flushed with heat and fear, whose lipstick was too bright, who fanned at the hanging wattle of my throat with my hand.

Maybe I'd rather die young.

I stood up quickly and began to walk briskly away, toward the next bus stop, my sneakers slopping through the muddy puddles on the sidewalk.

A horn honked, startling me. A car's engine roared; the heavy thrum of its bass speakers throbbed and shook me. A hand was out the window, waving, kneading the air. I was only halfway down the block when the bus bellowed by. I tried to catch it, running after it, my feet slapping at the pavement, but I could see that it was hopeless, and I gave it up, finally, and I stopped. It would be forty-five minutes, at least, until the next bus came. A long, dull wait with me slumped on the bench again, sunk down into my own blank self through three silent quarters of an hour, empty time. I couldn't have borne it. I wanted to get downtown. I wanted to go into our store and see whether Frankie Crane was still with us or whether my father had managed to make her go away.

I slung the book bag over my shoulder and, chin up, with purpose, arms swinging, I strode off, counting my steps, rolling with the sturdy rhythm of my own gait, enjoying the exertion of it and the steadiness that it brought me, the sense of accomplishment, of something getting done, as the sidewalk rolled off under my feet.

Sunshine was gleaming in the windows of the houses on both sides of the street. The inky heart high up inside my thigh felt damp with sweat, red outlined in black. I imagined the colors spreading, a secret stain, a bruise bleeding out over my bare skin.

AROUND NINETEENTH STREET LINWOOD'S NEIGHBORHOODS ABRUPTLY CHANGED. As if hemmed in by an invisible boundary, the houses there were bigger and older and less well kept, aging Victorians with fancy gabled windows and sharply sloped slate roofs, wide wraparound verandas and splintered gingerbread trim. Those houses had once been the grand showcase homes of the wealthiest Linwood families, who over the years had fled farther and farther out toward the outskirts, and they hovered there on the fringes of the city's ruined hub, hobbled hulks bought up by absent landlords, divided into smaller apartments, upstairs and downstairs, front, middle, and back.

The paint was peeling from the boards of their broad flanks. Plastic sheeting flapped in their wide windows. Puddles festered in the yards. Men were hunched on their front porch stoops, smoking cigarettes, squinting at the sky. Ragged children roamed the weeds between and behind the houses, past rusted wire fences, beneath windows framed by iron bars, under sagging porches, their railings snapped and broken like brittle bones.

At the corner there was a boy who leaned against the dented fender of a dark blue car. His arms were crossed over his chest, his knuckled fists clutched at his own elbows, and I could tell that he was watching me as I passed by, walking, with my chin still tucked, my eyes hooded, giving nothing away, my face averted, and my head ducked down. When I stepped off the curb to cross the street, I looked toward him, slightly sideways, just to check again and make sure, just to see whether he was maybe still looking at me, and my heart leaped, choking me, in a kind of fear it seemed, or surprise, or maybe it was a thrill, to see that, yes, he had seen me, he saw me, he was looking right at me, and he was smiling, too. I thought I might have heard him call out after me, but by then I'd turned my head away again, and gone on.

Eighteenth Street, next. Then Seventeenth. I was counting the distance backward, toward our First Street furniture store. HADEN'S, the big sign read, my grandfather's name spelled out in black and gold gothic letters on the glowing white marquee above the tall double front door. It was less than two miles away by then, I figured. Only sixteen more full city blocks to go.

A dog was barking; it threw its body at the solid mesh of a

chain link fence. A woman was sprawled on a cement porch step; a cigarette burned between her fingers. Her mouth was pursed, lips painted, rounded, blowing smoke. She had on blazing purple Bermuda shorts; her shins were flat blades, bruised, her feet were blue-veined, high-arched, and bare.

I didn't see the dark blue car at first, I only felt its engine rumbling as it pulled up behind me and slowed down a little, hanging back, coyly hovering just past my shoulder, just out of sight. When I picked up my pace and walked faster, the car kept up for a half a block before, finally, it pulled forward and then stopped, suddenly enough to rock the chassis, just far enough ahead. The boy rolled down the window; then he was leaning over toward me, across the seat. The passenger door swung open —it was an offer, an opening, an invitation in. Blushing, heart hammering, I ignored him at first. I pretended that I was stupid and that I hadn't seen that he was there. I turned my face away and kept walking. Shoe soles scuffing, fists clenched, arms swinging, determined, purposeful, step after step. A girl on her way somewhere. I could feel his car's brakes release; they sighed like a held breath suddenly expelled, and then the car jerked forward again. He pulled ahead just like before, and he stopped.

"Hey," he said. "Don't I know you?"

So, I stopped walking. I turned and bent to look at him. I peered into the interior shadows of his car. And he was there, smiling. He was waving his hand at me.

"I don't think so," I said.

"You want a ride?" he asked.

I shook my head. "No, thanks." My voice felt full of air. "I'm walking," I told him.

His mouth was wide, his smile broad, his teeth were white and thick and straight. He wasn't much older than me. "Aw, come on," he said, eyes creased, "I'm not gonna hurt you." I could see the pale flash of his opened palm. "Just let me give you a lift, okay?"

So, I looked around, both ways, first back from where I'd come and then off toward downtown, and, gasping, I climbed into his car. As if I were Frankie instead of me.

That thrill, that first rising fear—it gave me an aching in the pit of my stomach that seemed almost sweet, hungry-feeling in a way. It came from the not knowing what was going to happen next, whether it might be something good or something bad, or anything at all. The anticipation was almost all of it. Like climbing toward the top of the steepest slope on a roller coaster ride, waiting for the crest, and then off you go. I had my hands squeezed into fists against myself to stop the fluttering, and even though I was sitting with my shoulder pressed up against the door, still I could smell him and feel him, and I was sure that I could hear the whisper of him breathing in and out through his nose, too. That's how quiet it was.

It was like standing on a window ledge, several stories up, in the open air, looking down, dizzy, breathless, not knowing whether you were going to lose your balance this time and fall. Or maybe what you would decide to do was jump. Be careful, May, my mother had told me. Look out and watch what you do and pay attention to who you talk to and be cautious about where you go. Don't even look at a stranger, she'd said. Girls as pretty as you are kidnapped every day. Don't make eye contact, don't talk to him, don't sit down next to him. And, for heaven's sake, don't ever get into his car. But I wasn't pretty, and I knew that. I was ordinary; if not downright homely, then at least just plain.

The boy was driving with only one hand on the wheel; his other elbow was crooked out the open window, and now and then he'd let his hand drop down and he'd slap it flat against the outside of the door.

His hair was brownish yellowish blond, thin and ragged, damp-looking, like dried grass after the snow's thawed. His hands were dirty, and his fingernails were torn. He looked slightly stupid, maybe, with a thick lower lip and a loose jaw. But his smile, when he turned to me, was friendly, and there was a glint of mischief in his eyes that excited me. I took a deep breath and held it until it hurt, and then I let it go.

I was guessing that if his intentions were bad, he might be going to drive me out beyond the business district downtown. He could take me across the river and then some, not slowing, not stopping when I asked him to, when I insisted, only laughing at me when I started to plead with him to let me go. But it would be too late by then, and before I could do anything about it we'd be speeding off along the highway—traveling too fast for me to safely jump—with the bigger buildings of Linwood's business district diminishing into toys behind us, the yards around us widening, the houses thinning out, the wind of our passage blowing in through the open windows and tossing in my hair. And then he wasn't going to be able to stop, not even when I begged him to, not until we'd gone far enough out of the way and were all alone. Maybe he'd have found a place to pull over, some remote spot that nobody else knew anything about but him. A field somewhere. At the dead end of the dip and turn on a deserted dirt road. He'd slow down finally, and he'd glide the car to a smooth, sneaky stop. He'd turn off the engine so everything was quiet, and then I'd be able to hear him breathing again, and when he looked over at me and reached for me, his lips would be curling up into a smile.

I held my breath. I fiddled with the cracked black upholstery of the car seat, poking a fingertip at a wad of fluff that was spilling out of it, working to tuck it back in.

"So, what's your name anyway?" the boy was asking me. He drummed on the steering wheel with the edge of his thumb.

I told him. "May," I said.

He stopped thumping at the wheel and cocked his head toward me some.

"What?" he asked. "May?"

I nodded, and he smiled and slapped the car door with his flattened palm. "May-be," he said. "Or then again, May-be not."

He was laughing, but at his joke, not at me. His features were sloppy and clownish—his nose was too wide and flat, his cheeks were fleshy, his chin was dimpled and round.

"Well," he went on, "I certainly am pleased to make your acquaintance today, Miss May."

A scrolled letter J. had been embroidered in red thread above the breast pocket of his shirt. A mysterious initial, shorthand for something longer maybe, something sturdy and old-fashioned, like Jeremiah or Jacob or Joshua or James.

He'd pulled his car up behind a delivery truck that was stopped at the red light at the corner of Fourteenth Street. When the light changed and the other driver hesitated for a few seconds, J. was banging on the horn with his fist.

"Come on," he shouted. "Ain't getting any greener, pal!" He turned and winked at me.

I put my elbow on the door, and I held my hand out the window, and I kneaded my fingers against the pressure of the passing air. I thought about Frankie's gun, in the glove box of her car. I had a pocket knife in the outside pouch of my book bag, and if I had to I could pull it out, open it, use it to scare him off or even hurt him, if it ever actually came to that.

"So, anyway, how old are you, May?" he was asking.

"Eighteen," I lied.

He shook his head. He didn't believe me, I guess. Maybe he wasn't as stupid as I'd at first thought.

He braked and turned a sudden corner at Tenth Street, and I could feel my heart fly.

I thought that that was it. That I hadn't been imagining anything, that he was going to do it, after all. There would be an empty meadow out on the outskirts somewhere, and it would be lying in wait for me. Or an abandoned trailer, run-down, a shambles in the trees, off to the side of a forgotten back road. An unexpected clearing in the woods. Or maybe even an empty house. I put my hand on my book bag, and I fingered the smooth outline of my knife.

But then he braked and slowed and turned again. The car bounced up into the parking lot of a convenience store and bucked to a hard stop.

"You don't mind, do you, May?" he asked. "I'm back in a flash." And then he was gone.

I sat back and caught my breath. Still safe and sound. There was a guy on the phone, a salesman of some kind, with a briefcase and sunglasses, a white shirt with the sleeves rolled up, a gold watch, and a red and black striped tie. There was a kid in cutoff blue jeans eating a yellow banana juice bar. Three boys were huddled head to head over a pinball machine.

When J. came back out again he had a brown paper sack cradled in his arms. He dumped it out on the seat between us. Cigarettes and a six-pack of beer and a bag of peanut butter cups which he tore open first and then tossed one to me, but I didn't eat it, I held it in my hand and felt it soften there and begin to melt. He stretched his arm out across the back of the seat and looked over his shoulder as he pulled away. He opened a beer with one hand and then cradled it between his legs.

"You want some?" he asked.

He was squinting at me. Closed, his mouth narrowed and had a nice way of curling up at the corners into a natural kind of small smile, like maybe he couldn't help himself, he was just friendly, that was all. We were moving through traffic again, and he was holding the can of beer out toward me, so I took it from him. It was cold; I rolled it between my palms. I took a drink and then another. The beer was fizzy and sour. It burned at the back of my throat when I swallowed it down. I dabbed at my mouth with the back of my wrist, fighting an urge to burp.

He was laughing, but not because he thought it was funny, I didn't think, only just because he thought it was fun.

And then, just like that, before it had even started, it was over. We were there. At Third Street, we were pretty much in the middle of downtown, and that was where I'd told him I was heading, so there wasn't anyplace else for us to go. J. pulled the car into a parking spot against the curb and stopped.

Beyond the windshield I could see the park, and it was green and wet with spring.

"All right, then, May," J. said, "here we are. All safe and sound."

I took another sip of the beer and then handed the can over to him. His arm was still stretched out across the back of the seat behind me. He turned on the radio and fiddled with the dial and tuned in a song. Some man singing in a low, slow voice. J. had turned, and he was looking at me. The sun was shining in through the window, onto my face, like somebody's warm touch. His fingers were in my hair.

"You're a pretty girl," he said. His voice had thickened, deepened, softened. His thumb brushed against the curve of my ear.

I started to pull back, to turn away, but he was leaning forward toward me, in an expectant sort of way, and I moved to him, and I kissed him. His tongue slipped into my mouth and squirmed there. His breath smelled like peanut butter and chocolate and beer. His fingers were stroking my throat; they slipped down into my blouse, cradled my breast and squeezed it. His thumb hooked the hem of my skirt, lifting it.

I was scrabbling at the door handle, clawing at it, pulling at it until finally there was movement and the door opened, and I spilled out.

"Hey!" he called. "May! Wait!"

But I was gone. I stumbled on the sidewalk, juggling my book bag, and the song on his radio kept on playing in my head, low and slow, for blocks before I could calm down and get it finally to stop.

MAYBE IT WAS THE BEER. I WAS OFF IN A FOG, WANDERING AROUND DOWNTOWN Linwood in a stunned stupid daze, feeling like I must be somebody who'd survived a natural disaster—one of those people on the news, wrapped in a wool blanket, face wet with a spill of tears, watching through the black smoke while their house is burned down to a rubble on the ground. Or sitting by the roadside, hunched and shivering, comforted by a stranger near the complete twisted wreckage of a crashed car. I was following my own shadow, and trying to see whether I could catch the blur of my face reflected in store windows, car windows, dressing room mirrors, other people's glasses, other people's eyes, checking to be sure that I was still there and had not finally turned into the ghost that it already felt sometimes as if I had become.

I walked into Altman's department store, and I floated up and down its wide aisles, helping myself to what was there, sampling the perfumes and the makeup, spritzing myself with toilet water and cologne, dipping into lipsticks and powders and blush, running fingers through a display of crepe scarfs, poking at a rack of costume jewelry. I stopped at a round tabletop mirror on a stand in the hat department, and I saw my face there, and I was surprised to find that there was completely absolutely nothing special about it. It was still just me, May Caldwell—same eyes, nose, mouth, cheeks, ears, hair. And so what?

So what if I'd been in that store a hundred times and more and had seen everything in it, and it was all still just the same as it had always been—the racks of dresses, the piles of purses, the glass-topped counters, the chrome trim, the cold marble floor, round wooden pillars—not one thing was any different than it had ever been, and yet that was not true, because it was. It was changed. It was not the same. The glass was sparklier. The floor was more polished. The fabrics were splashed with bolder colors and wilder prints. Everything was prettier, or shinier, or something. There was just a certain gleam to things, it was a special kind of brightness—like in a cartoon, when they draw in that little shimmer, that little starlike glimmering thing to indicate a freshness and a glory and a shine—that was exactly the look that Altman's had taken on in my eye on that day.

I stood in the shoe department on the second floor, slipping my old sneakers off my feet and stepping into a pair of black tasseled leather loafers that I'd found poised on a clear plastic display stand, heels together, just so, toes pointed out. When I couldn't find a mirror to admire them in, I wandered off into the dress department to pose. There was a black skirt with a trim of pinkish roses circling its hem. A red-striped dress with a low scooped neck. A green silk shift. I held up one outfit and admired it, then another and another, and I wouldn't have been able to say just exactly how it happened, but after a while it came to me that I'd pretty much walked all through the whole of Altman's store, and I was still wearing those black leather loafers with the tassels on the toes, and not one person seemed to have noticed me, nobody looked like they very much cared, so that was when I decided that I'd just keep them.

I rode the escalator down to the first floor. I could tell that I'd become a ghost again; I was innocence, the picture of nonchalance. I strolled back through the jewelry department. I spoke to one of the clerks there, a young woman in spiked high heels, with reddened lips and eyelashes thick with black mascara. I even went so far as to try on a pair of earrings, blue glass teardrops dangling from a strand of delicate gold chain. Too plain, I told the clerk. I was looking for something a little more exciting, I said, something just slightly more wild. I needed some brightening up.

It was just then that I saw Frankie. Her pale, thin face was reflected there behind me, like a shadow, in the countertop mirror. She was smiling at me, watching me, and in the mirror our gazes met for a moment and held. But then when I turned around toward her, my mouth open and about to speak, Frankie was gone. She'd ducked away and disappeared, and then I couldn't be completely sure whether I had really seen her or did I only imagine that she'd been there?

It was time to move on, I realized, and then some. The loafers were pinching at my heels. I could feel a blister beginning to bubble there inside my sock. My heart was juddering again, and that felt good to me in its own way, as if it just could be the strength that I was going to need, a ragged inside sound to buoy me up and carry me off, send me safely out of the store and on my way. I left those loafers right where they were, snug on my own two innocent, or at least unnoticed, feet, and I kept my eyes cast down and I made myself invisible, the way I was aware that I could. I concentrated hard on just the progress of my feet, the leather tassels' jaunty bounce, a girl's light step, clever skip, up one aisle, down another, around a corner, through the door, and out of Altman's store.

I hadn't even gone a block before I reeled against the feeling that I'd been followed. And when I glanced back over my shoulder, I had only the barest glimpse of Frankie's face again, and I caught just the vaguest blur of her features, before I ducked past the black and gold letters of the Haden's marquee, up the steps, and through the front door, to lose myself in the labyrinth of sofas and breakfronts and dining tables and bedroom sets, the clutter and the chaos, what I was hoping was still going to be the old familiar sanctuary of my family's furniture store. I heard the doors close behind me, they were sucked shut with a whoosh of air that sounded in my ears like it could have come from me, as if it just might have been my own wild sigh.

HADEN'S WAS THE FURNITURE STORE THAT MY GRANDFATHER HAD FOUNDED AND my parents had taken over from him when he retired. The Haden Building sat on the corner of First Street and Second Avenue in the middle of downtown Linwood. The ground floor street sides were all show windows that my mother kept decorated with sample room settings. Walking by them could be like driving down the highway at night and peering through open curtains into lit rooms, where the people inside their houses lived their lives, moving through doorways, passing from room to room. Every window in Haden's was lit and decorated in a different style.

Behind the store the river rushed, noisy and dangerous and dark. On Saturday mornings in the summertime there might be some boys in shorts and no shirts fishing from the railings, casting their lines down off the edges of the Second Avenue Bridge. And maybe they'd look down to see me standing there alone on the loading dock, and maybe they'd whistle or wave.

Haden's had three stories of showrooms, and my parents kept all of them stocked to overflowing with moderately priced furniture. Plaid davenports and flowered loveseats, leather easy chairs and tapestry ottomans were laid out on the first floor. The second was for dining room sets, coffee tables, breakfronts and bookshelves and desks. On the top floor were the beds and cribs and roll-out sleepers. A cage elevator slipped between the floors at the back of the building, but it was faster to take the stairs, to trip up the marble staircase, its steps worn like a salt lick, to grasp at its polished brass railing and bound over the risers two at a time.

I DASHED THROUGH THE OUTER ROOM OF THE LADIES' LOUNGE AT THE TOP OF the first flight of stairs and into the bathroom and into a stall. I closed the door and sat on the pot, panting and afraid. I heard the outer door squeak open, a shuffle of footsteps, water running in the sink and then turned off. I sat there for a while, holding myself still, squeezing my fists into my stomach, wishing myself invisible again, listening for a sound, but there was nothing. Silence. Maybe, I thought, she's gone.

But Frankie was leaning against the sink, waiting for me, when I came out. She was smiling, hugging herself, with her arms folded over her chest and her elbows cupped in her hands.

I tried to look surprised.

"Oh, hi," I said.

Frankie pulled a pack of cigarettes from her purse, took one out, and lit it.

"Hi," she said, blowing smoke, dropping the spent match on the floor.

I crossed over to the sink, turned on the water, and began to lather my hands with the pink liquid soap.

"What are you doing here?" I asked Frankie, talking to her reflection in the mirror, avoiding my own face by looking into hers.

Frankie turned her wrist, peered at her watch, and smiled.

"You're late," she said.

I turned off the tap. "I missed my bus." I shook the water off my hands. Frankie yanked a paper towel out of the dispenser that was hanging on the wall beside her, and she handed it to me.

"Your parents have already gone home," she said. "Your mother asked me if I'd give you a lift."

I smiled. "Well, great," I said, nodding. I pressed the towel against my throat.

I was thinking that maybe Frankie hadn't seen me take the

shoes. And reasoning that if that was so, then how could she know that they didn't belong to me?

"Were you following me?" I asked.

Frankie didn't answer. She just looked at me, waiting, with her arms folded over her chest again, and she smiled through the smoke cloud that was floating up from the end of her burning cigarette. I waved it away with my hand, and I was turning toward the door when I looked down and it was only then that I noticed Frankie's feet. Wearing my wet canvas sneakers. And they looked like they were a perfect fit.

Frankie put the cigarette into her mouth, and she held it between her teeth, squinting as she retied the laces on one of the shoes. She put her foot out, wiggled it, admired the fit.

"This is lucky, isn't it?" she said. "I think we must wear the same size."

I looked at her foxy pinched face. "Will you tell?" I asked.

She shrugged. "Why should I?" She smiled, because she had me. "Your mother's going to know those aren't your shoes, May," she said.

And of course, she was right. I leaned against the wall. I dropped my book bag on the floor. I sagged and sank down next to it, cringing there, like something hateful and disgusting and despised, friendly with the filthy tiles on the bathroom wall, the scum-slick grout, a curl of black hair on the baseboard, the sick damp of the cold cement floor. The room smelled like bodies—waste, sweat and urine and tobacco smoke, disinfectant and bug spray and old ladies' rose water perfume. My hand, scrabbling at the floor, was small and delicate, my girl's frail fingers seemed almost transparent, nails gnawed clear down to the tender pink nub. And at the far end of my thin legs—blond-fuzzed, shin-bruised, purplish-skinned—my anklets, gray-white and lace-trimmed. And then, finally, on my dainty feet, those shoes, huge and hard and conspicuous, dark and shiny with a beetlelike sheen.

A wave of hot tears caught in my throat, and I did what I could to try and swallow them back down. But it wasn't any good and then I was crying, all tears and slobber and snot and slime, trying to explain that what Frankie had seen that afternoon in Altman's wasn't me, it was someone else, a different girl, made visible for a moment by the fact of having kissed that boy. It wasn't May Caldwell who'd walked off in that pair of stolen shoes, I said.

"It wasn't me," I wailed.

Frankie flicked her cigarette into the sink, where it hissed and died. She stooped down close to me and reached out and brushed my hair out of my face.

"Who was it then, May honey?" she asked.

I shrugged, shook, trembled. I didn't know. "Not me," I said, insisting, gasping for a clean breath. "Just not me."

I was sitting cross-legged on the floor. She straightened my legs and slid the leather shoes off my feet. She turned one over and looked at the price sticker still stuck to its sole.

"Seventy-five dollars," she read. "Not bad."

I saw that she was smiling. My skirt had got all bunched up; it was gathered in my lap, and my leg was bared, and so then Frankie saw the heart that I had drawn there. It was all smudged by then, and smeared, but you still could tell that it was a heart. I tried to cover it, but she brushed my hand away. She touched my leg with her fingertip, and she looked at me with her eyebrows raised.

"Oh, well. And I suppose this isn't you either, May, is it?" she asked.

Frankie stood up. She kicked off my sneakers and slipped her feet into the tasseled loafers instead.

"I like these," she said. She was grinning and bowing, shuffling her feet against the floor in a twirly dance. "Thank you, May, for your kind generosity."

She bent then and took hold of my hand, and she pulled me to my feet, hauling me up as if I'd been about to drown and she was dragging me out onto some hard safe shore. I was left gasping for breath, sopped and soaked. I put my sneakers back on again, and with trembling fingers tied them, and then Frankie had opened the door and I was following after her, down the stairs, out the back door, across the parking lot and into her car.

Chapter Four

MAYBE IT WOULD HAVE BEEN EASIER, MY mother said, if we'd found Frankie dead, if we'd been called downtown to identify her body, if we'd held a funeral service for her, if we could have stood by her grave somewhere and thrown clods of dirt and bouquets of flowers down onto her coffin's lid. That would have had some kind of a finality to it, at least. It would have put an end to things which might have felt better to us than the question mark that was there sitting at the end of the time that she had spent with us, a question without any answer. Where was she? Was she all right? What had happened to her? Where had she gone? My mother minded the incompleteness and the uncertainty of it. The unfinished feeling that it gave her, a puzzle left unsolved, words left unsaid, things left undone.

It wasn't very long before I began to have trouble remembering something specific about Frankie: how she'd stood, how she'd walked, what her voice had sounded like. And then all I could do to help myself was dig out some old picture from the ones my mother had kept throughout all those years when she'd been Frankie's sponsor and study it, and sometimes that would help to bring her back to me again, in a distant way. My mother told me that I would change, that I would be able to forget about Frankie, after a while. That my life was going to move on, that it had to, that even if I didn't want it to, in spite of me, it would. I was going to grow up and become a woman, a wife, maybe a mother. And Frankie would only be one among many of the memories I might decide to hang on to, an image that I could keep inside me; a girl forever, and never any more than just that.

My mother believed that Frankie was dead. Maybe I wasn't ever going to see her again in my lifetime, but I never could have brought myself to thinking of her as somebody who was dead. She would be growing up, too, I knew, aging in her own way just as I would do in mine. She'd change and become something, someone else, somebody that I wasn't going to be able anymore to recognize, a person whom I had never met, a stranger whom I would never know. We'd both be only memories to each other then, the leftover smoke and shadows of our own girlish selves. I don't know that I minded the idea of this so very much. Maybe that was how it was supposed to be. Maybe that would be fine.

LINWOOD WAS A MODEST MIDSIZE CITY THAT PRODDED A FOLD OF PLUMP IOWA farmland just the same as my father might have pressed his big fingertip into a roll of my mother's soft flesh. Its outline stabbed at the broadest bend of the Grundee River, which cut a short diagonal gash into the southeast corner of the state—like the thin white scar that halved the low arc of my left eyebrow— before, fed by scores of capillary small runoff streams and pretty creeks, it took its drastic dip south and spilled out finally, and headed for the breadth of the Mississippi farther south. Linwood was famous for nothing but the fact that, just like Paris, its government buildings were perched on an island in the middle of the Grundee, which split the city in two. Our courthouse and city jail faced each other across the breadth of First Avenue, and the river's water swirled around them on both sides. Linwood's businesses—stores and restaurants and offices and banks— flanked the river on both banks and then they started to circle out and out, into a spiral of residential neighborhoods, a whorl of streets that cut into the flattened landscape of the fertile flood plain, like a fingerprint smudged against glass.

Frankie used to say that Linwood was the most confusing place she'd ever been in. She was always getting lost there. She could never tell which way was which, because the streets seemed to curve back in on each other, they met themselves coming and going, and their circularity bewildered her. She preferred the straightforward lines of a grid, she said. She wanted roads that went someplace, not streets that bent in on themselves and then left you right back where you'd started all over again.

But it was just that curviness that was one of the things we all liked best about Linwood. It was what made it so pretty there. Linwood was like a pretend metropolis. A place that was too picture perfect, in a way. It could have been a model, a miniature or a movie set, and when I was downtown in it sometimes, I expected to walk into a building and find that it was only a front, empty inside, a mere facade.

"I've lived here all my life, you know," I told Frankie, when she was driving us home from the store that first day. I was looking to see if I couldn't pick up some more courage for myself from the fact of my own familiarity with the landscape of Linwood as we passed through it. "My mother has, too. And my dad. My grandfather and my grandmother and my uncle. Not one of us has ever had any desire to move away to anyplace else." I belonged there, was what I was trying to say. Even though I had already begun to doubt that belonging was exactly what I wanted for myself or for Frankie either, just then.

Outside the car windows scrolled the sprawl of Linwood's residential neighborhoods—the houses were spacious-looking, with wide lawns, brick walkways, wrought iron fences, brass lamp posts, shutters and awnings and wraparound porches. And as if just by knowing where I was, I could also be more sure about who I was, I started pointing out to Frankie some of the landmarks as we passed by them, those ordinary places that I'd looked at just about every day and didn't have to think about much anymore, naming them off one by one, like an incantation that might give me back my self again. If I even wanted it, that is.

There was the Mannings' big house, which had almost burned down to the ground ten years ago when a coffee maker was left on in the kitchen one Sunday morning while the family was away in church. So much for believing in the goodness of

God, my dad had said. Mrs. Anderson's magnolia tree that brought out the small fists of pink and white blossoms that my mother envied every spring. Duff Heller's cottage, where he'd been found in his bed, dead drunk with a pile of garbage and empty liquor bottles growing up around him. The sledding hill at the top of Hillside Drive. The wedge of rose garden where Park Street and Second Avenue crossed.

I pointed out the way, and Frankie did what I said, following Brand Boulevard all the way to its end, then swinging around through the maze of streets in Vernon Heights. The car swooped up the hill at Broadview Avenue, and just past the flare of the new shopping mall, we turned off onto the crested curve of Tyler Drive, its asphalt hump still blackened by the wet of all the rain.

FRANKIE HAD LIVED IN A FOUR-ROOM, WOOD-FRAME, OIL-HEATED HOME IN JACK-son County, Kentucky. The way the Federation described it made us picture a house nestled down in the deep crease of a glen, placed at the end of a long dirt drive that would be snowpacked in winter, thick with mud in the spring, soft with dust in summer when the days turned hot. There was a little bit of a runoff stream that rolled along through the trees out back, Frankie said, and it was likely to flood when the heavy rains came, rising up onto the flat swath of the back yard and spilling over into the cement basement of the house.

Frank Crane had been a road worker off and on before he was killed. He'd join on with the county crew whenever the weather was good. When it snowed he drove the town's plow.

Frankie said she didn't miss her mother, because she'd hardly even known her, she'd died when Frankie was so young, and it was her grandmother who had raised her, her father's mother, Grace Crane.

It was an out-of-the-way and isolated kind of a life, Frankie said. Cut off by geography and by habit both. Growing up, her view of the world beyond what she could see outside her own bedroom window came to her through the glass of a television screen, and even Frankie knew that was not how things really were—all beauty and death and trouble and jokes designed to keep an audience awake and entertained.

When her uncle Elgin got his arms shredded in a farm accident, he told Frankie that she could have his fancy car, maybe with the idea that it was something that his niece could use to carry her off out of there, into some other, better place. He'd told Frankie to get into that car and just drive, it didn't matter where to. Frankie had been putting aside some money for herself—most of it, she said, smiling, had come to her from my mother, at Christmas and on her birthday every year.

Frankie looked over at me. She slapped at the steering wheel with the palm of her hand.

"This car came into my life like a miracle, May. Because there I was one day, trapped in Jackson County, and then the next day I had this Lincoln, and here I am now, free."

She laughed, shook her head.

Frankie had followed the highway away from home without any clear destination in her mind. She was running away, and she didn't much care where to. She'd dropped down out of the mountains onto a rolling, snowy plain, and then crossed into the stubbled cornfields of Illinois. She'd seen cows gazing at her as she passed. A horse raising its head to watch. She'd looked over at other drivers, families, school buses filled with children, trucks with loads of groceries or gas, and she felt like she'd really become a part of the body of the country, like blood pulsing through a person's veins. That was how Frankie had felt, she said. Just like a corpuscle in a capillary.

At night, she'd slept in the car, wrapped up in a blanket to keep warm. So maybe no wonder she'd felt she needed to have that gun. She would pull into a rest area off the interstate, run the heater so hot that the windows fogged over, then turn the car off and curl up and sleep in comfort for an hour or two at a time. She'd used the gas station bathrooms to clean herself up. There she saw mothers with small children, scrubbing their faces, holding their hands under the cold water taps in the rust-stained sinks. The babies crying, getting their diapers changed. A little boy with coal black eyes watching her. She ate food that she bought in vending machines—packages of crackers and cans of juice, apples and chocolate candy bars.

"I just want to find some place that feels right to me," she said. A place where it looked like she might be able to live, and then she'd go hunting for a job, settle down and stay. At first she'd had her mind set on Chicago, even though everybody always talked about how it was such a cold city, people and weather both, and then when she passed through, she found out for herself that sure enough it was, with the wind blowing in wild off the lake and people in such a big hurry to get wherever they were going and all the buildings so tall that they blocked out any sunshine and left the streets and sidewalks looking gray and dim and mean. If she'd been smart right off, she mused, maybe she would have headed south in the first place, moved down there to where it was warm.

"Oh well," she said. She shrugged. "Live and learn, right?" She winked at me.

Now Frankie was thinking that maybe what she should do was to just keep following the interstate west. Go where it went. Follow it out to its end. She wanted to see the Rocky Mountains, she said. Old Faithful. Mount Rushmore. The Grand Canyon. Maybe she could drop down south out of the mountains and into the desert, then stop when she came to a place that was warm. She could live with some Indians, sleep outside on a mesa under the stars. Or maybe she could go all the way to California, wouldn't that be something? She might turn out to be an actress, maybe get discovered in a drugstore, be a star, wouldn't that be a big surprise to everybody back home? Frankie laughed and fished a cigarette butt out of the ashtray. She punched the lighter in with her thumb.

"Well, you'll have to stop somewhere, won't you?" I asked. "I mean, you can't just go and go and not end up someplace, can you?"

Frankie smiled. She pressed the lighter to the cigarette, inhaled, and blew out a full stream of smoke.

"Well, May," she said, nodding, "now sure that's true. And I know that. And I plan to get a job, that's what."

"Doing what?" My hands were folded in my lap, clutching at each other to keep them still.

"I can type," Frankie said. She was grinning when she turned to me. "And I like it here all right, I guess."

Here?

Frankie took one hand off the wheel and she put it out toward me. She fumbled in my lap, took hold of my hand, and pulled it toward her, squeezing it, with a firmness and strength that I didn't know how to resist.

"We're sisters, May, you and me," Frankie said. "You know that?" I gaped at her, as my fingers were rubbed against each other inside the smooth envelope of Frankie's palm. Frankie was still grinning. "This is going to be some fun, believe you me," she said. "I promise you that much. Fun and then some. You just wait and see."

I took my hand back. I rested it in my lap and felt it tingling with the surprising warmth of having just been touched and squeezed and held. Frankie stubbed her cigarette out in the ashtray. She frowned then and squirmed in the seat.

"I think these loafers might be too small for me after all, you know?" she said. "Feels just like they're alive and nibbling at my toes."

"I don't want them back, Frankie," I told her. And I didn't. I wouldn't have worn them even if she'd given them to me. I would have taken them outside and thrown them in the trash. I would have put them in Grand Haden's fireplace and set them on fire.

March 9
Dear Ms. Vivienne Caldwell,

    Hi! So what have you been up to lately? I have just been sitting around the house doing nothing as usual. How have you been doing since the last time I heard from you?

*I've been doing fine so far except for having the flu that
kept me out of school for a week.*

*I am very very sorry I haven't wrote you for a while.
But the good news is that I am passing in school. I made
one D (math) two C's (history and science) and two A's
(typing and English). That's not so bad I don't think.*

*I told my grandmother that since I made that one A in
typing I'd like to get myself a typewriter of my own,
because it's a skill that could maybe lead to a job someday.
She didn't say anything right away but I know she's
feeling bad for me these days since my dad died, and I'm
hoping she'll break down and get one for me if she can.
I'm up to 64 words a minute and I don't think that's so
bad do you? It's more than any of my class made so far
anyway. And I don't have very many mistakes. Some
sure. Who doesn't?*

*Well gotta go! Maybe winter will be over pretty soon.
It's been a long one that's true. Tell everybody back there
that I say hi to them and take care. Hoping to hear from
you soon.*

Yours,

Frankie C.

YOU'D THINK MY PARENTS WOULD HAVE BEEN GLAD TO SEE US, BACK
home again safe and sound, but mostly they were just angry
because we were late and everybody was hungry for a dinner
that was going to be soggy and overcooked because of that. My
father was waiting for us outside, pacing back and forth across
the front porch, looking from the street to the sky and back to

the street again, keeping one eye out for Frankie's car and the other one on the darkish clouds that had begun to mass and swirl and the wind that was picking up and tossing in the trees.

Frankie and I were hardly out of the car and right away Dad was down the steps and standing in the wet grass, throwing out his twenty questions, not even waiting for us to answer them one at a time. Where have you been? he wanted to know. Why are you late? What were you doing? Where did you go? It was maybe one thing to entrust his house to Frankie Crane, I guess, but it was something else entirely to give over the well-being of his daughter to a strange girl that he'd only met in person the day before.

My mother came out and stood in the bright circle that the porch light cast. She was wringing her hands, too, and she'd probably been worried herself, maybe as much about what might have happened to me as what would happen to her if anything had happened to me, which isn't exactly the same thing. She didn't like being the object of my father's temper any more than I did, especially when she could be pretty sure that she was the one who was in the wrong.

Her hair was blond and normally thick and wavy, but it curled like wild whenever the weather was humid or it rained. Her face was round, tending toward fat under the chin; her arms were thick, her waist was full, her breasts heavy. She carried them as if maybe she thought of them as a burden to her; she threw her shoulders back as a balance against their weight. When she saw me she came right down the steps in her bare feet and she didn't look twice at my shoes or at Frankie's either. She hugged me; she wrapped her arms around me, and she engulfed me there in the bog of her humid embrace, drawing me down like quicksand, sucking me in so I felt safe again, making me think that maybe everything was going to be back to normal after all, back the way that it had been before. Like when you wake up from some confusing muddle of a dream in the middle of the night and you've forgotten for the moment where you are, you're staring and staring around the room, and then your eyes become adjusted to the light and the furniture settles back down and it all makes sense suddenly, your room is in its place and you are in your place inside it, and your house is in its place, and Linwood is what it has always been and nothing more and nothing less and I am who I've always been and nothing has changed and everything is still comfortably and dependably the same.

Except it wasn't, and we all should have realized that.

Cars and trees and shoes.

It started with cars, I think; looking back on it now, it seems like cars came up even before the trees and the shoes, in the middle of February, on my birthday, in the winter before Frankie came, before we knew that she was coming, before we had even an inkling of what was going to happen to us next. I was sixteen, and I had been expecting that when I came downstairs that morning I was going to find that the kitchen table had been transformed, decorated with the usual display of streamers and banners and balloons. Because that was how it had always been before, and how was I to know that things were beginning to change? It was a clear routine, a sure tradition, a ritual that my mother had kept constant ever since I'd been a toddler, made wide-eyed by it all, and amazed. I'd seen the evidence of this on film, and it was in our photo albums, too—a shower of bright crepe paper streamers, bobbing balloons, and a silver banner that read HAPPY BIRTHDAY in colored letters that must have been at least a half a foot high. Why should anything be any different now, even though I had crossed the next threshold—moved one more step away from my girlhood and that much closer toward my womanliness—even though that day I had turned a supposedly older and wiser sixteen?

The table would be all set up for breakfast, with my mother's best china—passed on to her from Meems—a silver place setting, a cut crystal goblet, a folded linen napkin and a lace doily mat. My father would offer to cook up some eggs and bacon and toast, a full meal that I knew I wouldn't be able to swallow. I'd demur, graciously, smiling. I'd sip at the coffee that he poured me anyway, swallowing it too fast and scalding my mouth so that I'd have to carry its coarse sting like a foolish impulse on the tip of my tongue for all the rest of the day.

And I'd only just then notice that at my place there was a pile of presents, packages wrapped in childish paper, with clowns and flowers, cartoon characters, ribbons and intricate bows.

I rolled out of bed. My bare feet looked white and bony against the pile of the rug. I made my bed quickly, as an excitement, a hot knot of anticipation tightened in my belly—I pulled up the sheets and blanket, tucked the nubbled spread over the pillow's soft mound. My room was at the back of our house, and my window looked out on the back yard. If I craned sideways so far I could just see the hunch of our garage sitting there at the end of our drive.

My parents were waiting for me in the kitchen, both of them showered and scrubbed and dressed for work. My father was wearing a brown wool suit and a yellow shirt and a blue striped tie. His hair was longish, it curled over his collar and lay thick and dark and damp against his head. He was standing at the counter, looking at the newspaper, frowning. She was at the window, in a flowered dress and heavy cardigan sweater, staring distractedly up at the winter white sky.

But there weren't any decorations at all—not one streamer, not one single bright balloon—and I was surprised to find that this turned out to be a relief and a disappointment for me, both at the same time. My mother said that she'd come to the conclusion that maybe I was just too old anymore for all that silly fuss, and I did want to find a way to appreciate what I could see might be the more honest generosity of that. A girl who was grown up enough to have her own car shouldn't have been expecting streamers and balloons and banners, too, should she?

"Happy Birthday, May."

She was smiling at me. She was holding a cup of coffee in one hand; the other one was bent against her hip. At the open collar of her dress the lace trim of her satin slip peeked out, a dazzling white.

My father's smile was more like a wince. "Happy Birthday, kiddo," he said. He winked at me, and then he turned back to his newspaper again.

My heart was a wild hammer, and I couldn't get the blood to stop banging in my head. I thought that maybe my mother was just trying to trick me. Maybe she was only pretending that this was nothing; maybe she was just acting like she didn't care about my birthday so that she could ambush me later with the proof of how much she really did care. I figured that probably she was only trying to hide her own excitement, to drag it out and keep the surprise from me for as long as she could.

I recognized the fact that there was not the pile of presents that I'd been expecting at my place at the table, and I tried to take that for a good sign. There was only one package—a small, square box wrapped in red paper, tied up in a white bow.

Car keys?

I know I was blushing, but I couldn't help it. I was a lucky girl, I thought, the luckiest, most blessed, most charmed. My parents were kind and caring, and they loved each other to distraction, and they loved me, too.

I was going to let myself be lost in my father's big hands, buried by his huge, rough, woolly embrace. I'd submit to the nuzzle of my mother's soft, petal-like skin and the tentative squeeze of her more fragile, more ladylike, hug.

I sat down; I spread my hands on the tabletop and smoothed out the edges of the place mat.

My mother was pouring orange juice. I heard the rustle of the newspaper as my father turned the page. Nobody said anything. And I think it was that silence between them that was what always kept threatening to engulf me, to wash over me like a huge black wave. I gazed at my father's big wingtip shoes, and I told myself again, I comforted myself with the singsong that he loved me. I could tell it was true just by the way that he held himself. By the drift of his eyes, by the purse of his lips, by the working of his jaw. He didn't have to say it if he didn't want to, because I understood. I knew what he was thinking. His very silence was an eloquence that said it all. He loved me, all right, they both of them did, they loved me very much.

My mother's hand was on my shoulder, clawing, spidery. She leaned over me, and I felt the softness of her lips press like a flower against my temple.

And then the package was in my hands. I untied the ribbon, pulled at the bow, and wrenched it free. I dug into the paper, ripping it. I held my breath and closed my eyes. I counted to three, commanding myself to calm down.

Inside the wrap was a black velvet box. I balanced it on my opened palms. I turned it and rubbed my fingertips into it, soothed by its silky soft nap. I looked up to see my mother's smile and my father's dark stare. I pried the box open, breathless.

Inside, in ghastly white relief against the deep black velvet, a pearl ring.

"Happy Birthday, May," my father said, his voice low.

"Meems wanted you to have it," my mother said. "It's something that you can keep all your life." Sentimental tears were glistening in her eyes. She stumbled forward, took my hand and squeezed it. This was a gift that Meems had given her on her sixteenth birthday, she said, one that I could pass on to my own daughter one day, when the time came. I put the ring on my finger and held my hand out for her to see, pretending that I liked it, that I understood what a special gift it was, how meaningful to everybody, supposedly even to me. My mother had started crying and then she had to go upstairs to fix her smudged mascara, so my father and I were left together in the kitchen alone.

I was sixteen years old. I was almost an adult. My father was bending over me, he was kissing me, he was pressing his huge face against my cheek. I closed my eyes, and I breathed in his rich smell, of shaving cream and alcohol and smoke.

I knew that I'd been stupid. I hadn't asked for what I'd wanted, I'd only wanted it, and so then when I didn't get it, when it wasn't mine, who was there to blame for that but my own slow self? How were they supposed to have known? Could they have been expected to read my mind? No. Of course not.

I didn't even have a driver's license. I didn't even know how to drive. Why would they have thought I'd wanted a car? I was going to have to tell him, in so many words, to make myself clear, that was all.

"Daddy," I said.

He was looking at me. He was waiting.

"I wanted a car." My face was in flames.

He tipped his head to one side. "What?" He ran his fingers over his hair, smoothing it.

"A car." My eyes stung. "I'm sixteen. I think I should have a car."

He shook his head, ducked his chin, then looked over at me again, as if checking to be sure that I was who he thought I was, his daughter, charming May, meek and mild.

"What is it, May?" he said. "You know something I don't

know? Somebody call last night while I was sleeping and tell you we're rich?"

"No," I said. I was trying to hold on to his face with my eyes, to keep him from turning his back on me, from laughing at me and walking away. "I don't know."

He coughed into his fist. He shook his big head.

I squared my shoulders. Took a deep breath.

"I don't like pearls," I said. My voice had lowered—it was little more than a murmur by then, a mumble, garbled, a soft moan. "I don't want Meems's ugly old ring."

He'd heard the words, all right. He'd understood. He was across the room and looming close. His hand had wrapped around my upper arm, his fingers were squeezing, his fist closing and pressing into me, steadily, strong and hard. His face eclipsed mine.

"Don't let your mother hear you say that, May," he growled. "Don't say it out loud again."

I groaned, and turned my head away from him. Just past his shoulder I could see my mother. She was standing in the doorway watching us.

"What is it?" she was asking, worry in her face. Her dress was shiny, silken. The fabric swam across her belly, slid with the shift of her hips, glided over the swell of her breasts.

He let go of my arm and turned away from me. He put his hands out, and he shrugged.

"She says she wants a car," he said. He snorted.

My mother's smile was small and pained; her polished fingernails played at her throat.

And I was deeply ashamed. I was embarrassed for having asked, for having ever wanted anything at all. I shouldn't have said that about Meems. I was ungrateful and hateful. I was the worst girl. I deserved it if they decided to abandon me. I'd earned their scorn. If they despised me, it wasn't as much as I despised myself.

Before I blew out the candles on my cake that night, I had closed my eyes and wished, again, that I was dead.

But then with Frankie there, standing in our kitchen, helping my mother with our dinner and talking about furniture with my dad, walking around in that pair of stolen shoes as if she had every right to wear them, it seemed to me that something important had happened, there'd been a drastic kind of change. There was Frankie Crane, she might as well have been my sister, as she'd said, and she had a car, didn't she? She could drive and come and go as she pleased. She was on her own, and she wasn't so much older than I was, was she? Why should I be any different from her? Why did I deserve less, especially after we'd supported her over all those years? The money my mother had sent to Frankie would have added up to more than enough to buy me a car, I thought. Maybe not a Lincoln Continental, but something with four wheels and an engine to take me wherever I wanted to go. I was the real daughter in the Caldwell family, after all, not this Frankie Crane.

And then it all came pouring out of me, as if the fact of Frankie's presence there with me that night was what was giving me the courage to stand up to my parents in a way that I had never been able to do before. If I had a car, I argued, then I could drive myself. And then I wouldn't have to ride the bus and miss it and have to walk and be late. I'd be where I was supposed to be, and nobody would have to be worried, and nobody would have to get all upset.

I could see my dad's anger, boiling in his face and storming through him.

If I wanted to go to work, he told me, if I wanted to save and shop and plunk down the cash that I'd need, then I could go out on my own and buy any kind of damned car that I wanted to. That was my choice, he said. He wouldn't stand in my way in that case.

And looking at him then, I was able to picture him—a large man stepping off the curb into the middle of a busy street, with his arms outstretched and waving, trying to flag me down, trying to stop me, trying to stand in my way, and then I was wondering, would I be inclined to step on the accelerator if he did that, or would I slam on the brakes? He wouldn't stand in my way, he'd said. Well, I guessed maybe he'd better not.

"A girl doesn't need wheels," is what my father said. He winked at my mother, who pursed her lips and frowned and looked away.

"What?" he wanted to know, eyes wide. "A girl should have a boy who'll drive her where she needs to go, that's all I'm trying to tell you. Why is that so bad?"

I looked over at Frankie, embarrassed.

"At least you have a father," she said. And my dad took that to mean that she was on his side, and that made him start to like her a little bit more, I think.

April 17
Dear Vivienne,

Hi! How is everyone doing? I am doing fine. Just have a cold that's all.

You are so nice but really and truly you don't have to get me that typewriter unless you want to do it. I asked my grandmother yesterday if it would be okay and she said "Whatever she wants to get you I don't care a bit." Those were her exact words. I would prefer an electric typewriter since you asked. It is nice for you to do this but you know I am very shy about expecting anything.

I never get too busy to hear from you. I wish someday I could get to see you.

Well I'll let you go for now with lots of love from me to you. (I'm not expecting anything so don't feel obligated about the typewriter if you've changed your mind or anything.)
As always,
Frankie

THIS IS A DREAM I HAD: I'M STANDING IN MY ROOM, AND I'M GAZING out at a colorless night that's settled in beyond the window above my bed. It's winter—I know that because there is snow. The trees are heavy with it, their blackened branches are groping at an overhead spray of dark clouds.

I've hung a mobile from the knob of the overhead light, and although there is no breeze, its bits of color turn anyway. They seem to hum through the air, like quick birds, moving all on their own, flashing and friendly. I'm watching those circling bits of paper, and I'm listening to the deep silence of the house around me. It seems to grow. And I've begun to wonder whether maybe I'm in it all alone. Maybe there is no one else here. Maybe something has happened, and my parents have left me. Maybe I've been abandoned. Or maybe my parents are dead.

My room is perched at the top of the stairs. The sea-green carpet slips under the door and out into the hall. It nudges up to the scroll of dark woodwork that trims the yellow walls, past the brilliance of the white-tiled bathroom.

My parents' bedroom is at the end of the narrow hallway, behind a paneled door with a polished brass knob. I'm leaning toward it to listen for some sounds of life inside, but I hear nothing. No rustle of sheets. No footsteps. No murmur of voices. Only the roar of that silence, growing. Only the whispered hiss of the snow outside. And then I've reached out and I'm turning the knob, I'm opening the door slowly, and my voice cracks as I call out to them, "Mom . . . Dad . . . ?"

I've stepped into the cramped space of their bedroom. His suit is thrown over the back of a chair, the tie loosened but not unknotted. His shoes have been placed neatly, side by side, on the floor nearby. There are hat boxes piled up one on top of the other in one corner of the room, a precarious tower, like a many-layered cake. Near the window is Meems's old dress form in its clinch of bones and stays and laces, bound up by the corrective influence of a yellowing old Victorian corset.

And then my eyes have adjusted to the dark. I can just see through the dim shadows; I can just make out the two dark mounds that are huddled side by side on the wide mattress of the bed, tucked in beneath the circle and loop of a blue and green and gold wedding ring quilt. I have crossed the room to be closer, and now I'm a shadow, too. I'm so quiet, no one can hear me. I move silently, deaf even to my own self, my feet gliding soundlessly, my body drifting weightlessly.

When I was younger, a little girl with a blanket, a thumb-sucker small and scared, I'd go to my parents' bedroom in the middle of the night. My mother would awaken slowly, lifting her head from the pillow, blinking, confused. She'd reach for me. She'd cup her hands around my body and pull me up into the bed. She'd brush my sweat-damp hair off my face, and she'd wrap a protective arm around me, holding me there, found, safe, and in the right place. And I'd snuggle into that dark space between my parents, feeling as if their mingled heat might drown me, that my father might roll against me and suffocate me, and I believed that that was just how I would have liked to die, to be smothered between the two of them, melted, like softened wax, squashed flat.

But in my dream, it's different. Then I'm standing there beside their bed, and I'm watching over them. I am my best invisible self, I am an angel, a ghost, a sylph; I am something that is dark and unrecognized and unseen. I breathe in the familiar spice of their mingled smells—hers soapy and sour, his a smoky blend of cigarettes and alcohol and shaving cream. I need to touch them. My mother is lying on her side, with her back turned; she's curled in on herself like a snail. Her hair is rolled up in bristled curlers; the thin strap of her nightgown is slipping down from her shoulder.

"Mom?"

Her familiar freckled skin is cool under the brush of my fingertips. Startled, I've moved too quickly, I've grasped and pulled, harder than I know I should have—and her arm flops toward me, her hand slaps against me and then hangs off the edge of the mattress, limp. My mother's eyes are open, gray and staring, blind; her pale lips, dry, cracked, are parted slightly. I'm missing the sound of my father's heavy breathing now. It's too quiet here, I realize. I can see that my father is on his back, that his dark eyes are closed, that his jaw has dropped, and his heavy jowls are sagging, slack.

I snap awake at the realization that I was right, and both of them are dead.

FRANKIE SLEPT IN THE EXTRA ROOM JUST DOWN THE HALL FROM MINE. THAT night, I prowled the house and found her, sprawled out over the guest bed double mattress in her red long johns, with the covers —Meems's blue and yellow patchwork quilt—kicked off. Her skin was clear and creamy. Her dark hair curled around her face. When I pulled the quilt up over her, she opened her eyes, looked at me, smiled, and closed them again. The smile stayed.

On the table by her bed was the photo of her father in its wooden frame. This was something else that she left behind later, and the fact of it was one more piece of evidence that my mother used when she argued that either something unspeakable had happened to Frankie or else she would be back. It wasn't anything that they would have expected her to intentionally leave behind, because she treasured it. And so they reasoned that maybe her abandonment hadn't been intentional, maybe it had been an accident. That maybe she had been in the kind of hurry that didn't give her a choice about what she could take with her when she went. And maybe, my mother consoled me, that kind of thinking would have to include me in it, too.

In the photograph, Frank Crane stands with his arms folded over his chest, a cigarette in his mouth, smoke wafting up into his eyes. He squints against it. His face is long, thin. His chin is dimpled. His hair is black, cut short, close to the scalp. He is wearing a plaid shirt with shiny snap buttons, open at the throat. A gold cross gleams in the grizzle of his dark chest hair.

I kept searching for Frankie in the features of Frank Crane's face, but it was rare that I ever could find her there.

I WENT INTO THE KITCHEN AND FIXED MYSELF SOME WARM MILK—BECAUSE THAT tasted good to me sometimes; it calmed me when I'd had a bad dream and I was excited by it and I couldn't get back to sleep— and I was standing in the dining room, cradling the mug in my hands, sipping at it and thinking about Frankie and her father and how he was dead and how my father and mother weren't. More than once I had dreamed they were; did that mean that I wished they were and if I did what did that mean about me? I was gazing down toward the street thinking I'd just go on back upstairs again and climb on back into my bed and think about something else, something nice, something harmless and sweet until I'd gone on back to sleep, and I was noticing how the barish branches of the trees seemed to be reaching their sticks and twiggy fingers upward and raking the skin of the sky, when a shadow shifted in the corner of my eye, down near one end of our round drive, next to the neighbor's boxwood hedge, and at first I thought it was an animal, a dog or a cat or an opossum maybe, but it turned out instead to be a person.

He came around the end of the hedge and stepped out into the circle of light that was cast down onto the sidewalk by the streetlamp. He was standing stock-still then, with his hands in his pockets, and he was staring up at the windows of our house. I saw his face, and I knew right away who he was. It was that boy again, the beggar, the guy on the pink bike, and he'd come back, like a thought that you have and you can't get rid of it, some idea that keeps nagging at you, no matter what you do.

I don't know if it was fear or surprise or apprehension that I felt then, or was it only the hot shame of exposure, the understanding that somebody might have been watching me, without me knowing it or for how long or why. I ducked away from the window. I wasn't sure whether he'd seen me or not. I ran upstairs and shook my dad out of his stone-deep sleep. When he came over to the window for a look he saw the guy, too, so I wasn't dreaming it after all, and that was a relief in one way and a letdown in another.

"I should never have given him any money," my mother said.

She was in her nylon nightie, rocking back and forth in her bare feet, hugging herself. My father didn't hesitate for a minute. He got right on the phone to the police, but by the time they got there, the guy had been sucked back into the shadows again, and he was long gone.

So there we were, and I at least was feeling foolish and stupid and vulnerable, looking at my parents standing there in our open doorway, with the porch light on, talking to the police—anybody who wanted to could have looked out their windows and seen us, the police car parked in our driveway, all the lights on downstairs, and they'd have been wondering what we'd done.

The commotion had awakened Frankie. She'd heard the doorbell ring, and she got up and came downstairs—her hair was tangled and tousled and her eyes were groggy with sleep. She was nervous when she saw that the police were there, and she kept asking me what had happened, she wanted me to tell her what was going on.

And there was my dad standing there in his bathrobe, the green and white pinstriped flannel one that we'd given him for Christmas the year before, barefoot, talking to a policewoman in a blue uniform that looked as stiff as cardboard, with unbecoming black shoes on her feet and straight-legged pants that didn't flatter her hips. Her dark hair was pulled back tight and tucked inside her hat so her face looked childish, too young to be doing that kind of an important life-and-death job. She told my father that she couldn't arrest somebody just for standing on the sidewalk.

"What about loitering?" my mother asked. Or what if he was a prowler? Or a peeping Tom, what if he was spying on us? What about harassment?

The policewoman took a pad out of her back pocket, and she wrote some notes in it, asking questions but not looking up to acknowledge our answers—what was the guy wearing, what did he look like, what color hair, eyes, skin, how tall was he, how heavy, how old? She said she'd file a report if we wanted her to, but the feeling that I had when we closed the door and turned off the lights was that she thought I had an overactive imagination and even though my father had seen him, too, she didn't really believe that there had ever been anybody out there in our yard at all.

I WAS BACK IN MY ROOM AGAIN, WITH THE LIGHT OFF, IN BED, TUCKED IN, TRYING to make myself drift toward sleep, and there was a sound in the hallway. The stealth of a footstep, and a movement, too. The knob turned; the hinges squeaked.

"May?"

Frankie's voice was low, deepened by the intricate chains of cigarettes that I found out later she smoked, sometimes two at a time, the one forgotten, the other a distraction, lit in the fervor of midsentence, put down again in the reverie of midthought.

"You still awake?" she asked.

She was a long thin shadow, standing in my doorway.

It had made her nervous, she said, all the commotion. It had been the same way when her father was killed. She and her sister and grandmother had been sound asleep, and then the doorbell rang, and there was a trooper out on the porch in the morning mist, giving them the bad news.

Had I seen the guy outside? Frankie asked. What did he look like? she wanted to know. What was he wearing? Did he have long hair or short hair? Was he thin? Was he tall?

We sat facing each other, cross-legged on my bed. She was holding her cigarette between her ring and her middle fingers, an affectation that seemed sophisticated to me. She blew the smoke away, out of the side of her mouth. I gave her an empty pop can to use for her ashtray. She offered me a cigarette of my own, but I turned it down.

"I couldn't sleep. I have bad dreams sometimes," I said.

Her eyes were dark, like shadowed green stones.

She'd brought the brocade-covered jewelry box into my room with her. We looked at the bracelets and necklaces and rings and earrings again. She showed me the dainty brass key that unlocked the latch; she slid open a tiny drawer that I hadn't noticed the first time. The pills that she poured out of it into my palm were violet and yellow and orange and green, their colors so vivid that at first I thought that what I was looking at were more jewels.

"Pick one," Frankie said.

But I didn't understand her. I didn't know what it was that Frankie was telling me to do.

"Any one. They're all good."

"What?" I asked, stupidly.

Frankie thought that I was just being shy.

"Open your mouth," she whispered. "Close your eyes."

There was a small bit of bitterness on my tongue; I rolled it, like a pearl, inside my cheek.

"Swallow it," Frankie said, so I did.

"Tell me about your father, Frankie," I said.

"Picture this," she told me.

There's Frank Crane, she says, and he's out on a Kentucky turnpike in the wee-est small hours of the morning. He's working, filling in potholes. That's his job. He has a helmet on his head, and he's wearing an orange safety vest with silvery reflector stripes. He's put cones out on the road, but no one's going anyplace at that dark hour of the night. Everybody else is still sleeping, home safe and sound in bed.

Except for one car, in the distance. It's a Cadillac. It's copper-colored, Frankie says, with one headlight gone so it looks like it's winking at the road. It slides along the pavement just like a snake. There's a fat man at the wheel. He's got the radio turned up on high because he hasn't slept and he's getting drowsy. He's been taking sips of whiskey from a green glass flask, and that's made him feel a little bleary, too.

Frank Crane is whistling through his teeth, Frankie says. He's told everybody in the family how grateful he is to have this job, how lucky he is to be working full time for once to support his mother and his girls. He's got a headache from last night, though, and it pounds. There's a sour growling in his stomach. He's looking forward to his breakfast, to the daylight that will be coming on soon, to a cup of hot coffee at the counter of the cafe by the railroad tracks downtown. His breath comes out smoke, but he doesn't mind the cold so much. Its bite is familiar to him; it keeps him moving; it eggs him on. He dumps a shovelful of warm asphalt steaming into a pothole, then packs it down, stomps on it with the thick soles of his heavy boots. He gathers his cones and swings up onto the back of the yellow road crew truck. He waves at the boy behind the wheel to move it on.

Now the copper-colored Cadillac has bounced up over a near rise. And Frank Crane's jumped down onto the roadbed again. He's placing the cones just so. The man in the Cadillac has taken his eyes off the road. He's glancing down at his dash,

113

poking at the radio buttons with his thick fingertip, jostling his green glass flask, sloshing whiskey. So, Frankie says, shrugging, he's not watching where he's going. And so, he doesn't see that yellow truck. Or those orange cones. Or Frankie's father stooping with the shovel in his hand. Too late, the man has looked up at the road again. Too late, he's wrenching at the steering wheel of his car but, too late, his front bumper swipes Frank Crane, it tosses him, pitches him up into the air, where he tumbles, flies, soars, and then falls. The shovel's blade clinks and sparks when it hits the hard flat surface of the road. The Cadillac's not stopped. It travels over the shoulder and across the drainage ditch. It crashes through the brush, then it flips and whoomps into the solid shudder of a tree.

A white sidewall tire circles, lazily turns. Frank Crane's arms are outspread, hands outflung, legs akimbo. His head is snapped back, jaw clenched, dimpled chin thrust out, as if in defiance, toward the brightening sky. The reflective stripes across his vest gleam. A pool of dark blood spreads like oil over the roadway's back. A dapple of Frank's gore is smeared on the asphalt. The fat man is kissing the star shatter of the Cadillac's windshield glass. And the sun is rising up a dreadful orange, the sky lightens, the trees rustle, the safety cones throw their shadows across the road, and a blanket of bright stillness has settled into the deep shadows of the trees in the huddled woods.

I sank back into the pillows and closed my eyes. There was something I had to do, someplace I needed to go, but I couldn't remember what it was, or where. I swung my legs around and hoisted myself up to my feet. I'd become a monster, a huge something not myself, staggering, clumsy and reckless and large.

I lurched forward, stumbled, turned, then was spilled back onto my bed. Frankie was laughing at me. She tucked me in under the covers, like a doll.

"Don't try to fight it, May," she said. "Let go. Let go."

> *June 21*
> *Dear Vivienne,*
>
> *Hi! What have you been doing lately? I haven't been doing anything so far. These hot days have just about got me down. I am sunburned into a crisp.*
>
> *I do want to thank you for that typewriter. My family just loves it. I really don't know how to thank you but I do. Now I know you are the best sponsor that I've ever had. If there is anything you want me to do just let me know. I'll be willing to help. I just love it that you are so generous and kind.*
>
> *Tell everyone in your family that I said a special hi to them from me.*
>
> *This is a promise to you. My next letter I will type. I think you'll be impressed to see just how good at it I really can be.*
> *Love,*
> *Frankie*

Chapter Five

IT TURNED OUT THAT WHEN WE GOT
Frankie into an office at the store and sat her down at a
desk there, she could hardly type anything at all. Not a
surprise to him, my father said, but my mother
shushed him.

"Give the girl a chance, Cal," she hissed. "Of
course, she's nervous, aren't you, Frankie? Put to the
test this way. All of us gaping at you. She's frozen up.
I'd be a wreck myself. Anybody would. Relax, why
don't you? It isn't a matter of life or death, after all."

My mother figured that her talking might somehow
take the pressure off the situation. She was going to try
and fill up all the uncomfortably empty spaces between
us with her words and the sound of her voice saying
them, without bothering very much about what they
meant. But my father was, as usual, unmoved. He
folded his arms and crossed one foot over the other
and leaned his large body in this relaxed way against

the doorjamb to wait, quietly and patiently, because he knew that he had all the time in the world to prove to my mother that she'd been wrong.

And anybody could see that Frankie Crane was not nervous. That just was not her style. She hadn't frozen over; she wasn't stunned by shyness or some sudden stab of self-conscious fear. Frankie didn't have many scruples, and she had no qualms at all. She sat there in that office as bold as ever, smiling and snapping her gum, stretching out her hands, fingers meshed, to crack her knuckles, and wiggling in her chair until she'd got it to feel comfortable enough to suit her.

She found the machine's power switch and, with some bravado, flicked it on. She looked at my father and gave him a pleased-with-herself smile. She studied the keyboard for a moment, then looked up at my mother, then down at the keyboard again, and finally, slowly and steadily, she plunked out the spelling of her own name—Frances Anne Crane—with one finger, one letter at a time, all lower case but other than that without a single mistake. My father snorted. Frankie looked at my mother and shrugged.

"Guess maybe I must have lost the knack," she said. "Haven't had much of a chance to practice at it in a while."

My father turned on his heel and walked out of the room. My mother, scowling, followed him. I could see that she was building herself up into a rage, rustling up a storm of anger that might be forceful enough to blow away the truth of the situation and make a mess of my dad's cool and deliberate reasonableness. I knew exactly how it was going to go. Like this:

"I hope you're happy now, Cal." Pulling his office door shut with a good firm glass-rattling bang, just to get his attention.

"Happy?" Sinking down into his padded leather chair, languishing there, smug and infuriatingly self-satisfied, with his arms up and bent and his hands clasped behind his head.

"You wanted her to fail." Pacing, the points of her heels nipping at the rug's thin pile.

"No I didn't, Vivienne."

"But you're glad she did."

"I'm only glad to see you finally finding out the truth."

"Oh?" Stopping, her body straight, shoulders thrown back, neck rigid. "The truth? And what exactly is the truth here, Cal?" Approaching the desk, because she thinks she has him now. Placing her fists on its top—beneath the beveled glass is an array of candid family snapshots, including my own face, my own mild smile. With her elbows locked, she leans forward toward him. "That she's not as well educated as we are? That she hasn't had certain advantages? That she's not a child of privilege like May? Like us? Or just that she needs us? Only that we just happen to be about all the girl has?"

Now he's pushed his chair back, and he's on his feet. He towers over her, and so she has to take a step back—lifting her hands and leaving behind a pair of clenched fog circles on the glass. She has to tip her chin and raise her eyes to keep hold of his, and this makes her look even more defiant than probably she feels.

"The girl's a liar." His voice, corded with conviction.

Her face flushes. She wobbles. "You don't know that."

He steps around the desk toward her. "She said she could type. She can't. She lied."

"What if Frankie forgot?" Aware that she's on thin ice now, she raises her voice.

"You don't forget how to type, Viv." He can speak softly—because he has right on his side now, he doesn't have to scream to make himself heard. "It's like riding a bicycle. Once you've learned how, you always remember, it will always come back."

She knows he's right, but that's not the point anymore. Her best tactic now is to try to make a quick shift and come at him from the side. She steps toward the door. "Well, so what if she can't type? Neither can you." She's opened the door, prepared to let this be the last word and to claim it as her own, but he stops her.

"But I never said I could, Vivienne. That's the difference, don't you see?"

She looks at his hand on her arm. She shrugs it off.

"Splitting hairs," she spits. And then she's out the door, and she's slammed it after her, harder this time, because in an argument with my mother, the one who can make the most noise at the end of it is the one who automatically wins.

IT WAS SUMMER, AND SCHOOL WAS OUT, AND WE'D COME UP AGAINST THAT endless loom of idle vacation days. My mother enrolled Frankie in a typing class at the community college—she went on Tuesday nights from seven to ten, although she often stayed out later than that. She'd found some friends among her classmates, she told us, and when they invited her to join them for a cup of coffee or a bite to eat after school, she went. She practiced her typing at home in the mornings before work, but she did it behind the closed door of her room. We could hear her clicking and clacking, and she seemed to be moving along steadily enough, with a triumphant ringing ding at the end of every line as the carriage was thrown back, but she was sneaky about getting rid of her finished pages, so it was hard to tell whether what she typed made any sense or if it was just gibberish meant to impress us and whether she was making an inordinate number of errors. My guess is that she never even went to the class at all, but that she practiced on her own and her typing was good enough to get by on when Dad put her to the test again by finding a job for her to do down at the store.

And anyway none of us much cared about it anymore by then. My mother had made her point and my father had made his, and I was just glad that Frankie was there in the house to make my life seem as if it might be something interesting enough that I'd actually begun to look forward to getting up to it day after day.

"Busy girls are happy girls," my mother liked to say. It was a line that she'd stolen from my high school principal, Mr. Langley, who'd actually said it about boys. But my mother, in her way, chose to take Mr. Langley's catchphrase literally, turning it into something that she could apply to herself first, and then to me, giving it a girlish definition, explaining that it is part of the feminine nature to want to nurture and create, to take care of the world and its parts. As in, not just making love and babies and beds, but also cooking dinners and cleaning houses and washing dishes and ironing blouses and laundering clothes; as in, balancing business accounts and buying and selling furniture and keeping a file cabinet alphabetized and up to date. As in, learning how to type.

Right from the start, all those years ago when Grand had first opened his store, Meems had begun to make a record of every buyer's purchasing history, and my mother had kept it up, too, in a kind of a card catalog, arranged alphabetically by last name, sort of like books in a library. There was the name and the address and the phone number of every single customer who had ever crossed the threshold of the store and what they'd bought from us and how they'd paid. You could pull out one of those cards and just about see a whole family's history on it—the living room set, the bedroom set, the baby's crib, the bunk beds, the bar stools, the patio table and chairs. People who died and families that moved away were pulled out of their alphabetical position and put away in a separate drawer that had been labeled Closed Accounts. And every time anybody bought a piece of furniture they were sent a personal thank-you note, handwritten, from Meems.

As long as Frankie was going to be staying with us, my mother reasoned, we might as well put her to work doing something that was going to be useful. And why couldn't I be there, too, helping Frankie, which would keep me busy over the summer vacation, and at the same time I could keep an eye on Frankie so that Dad would get his files done and Mom would see that he'd been generous in the way she'd expected him to be, too. One stone for a whole handful of birds, was what Grand's comment on the arrangement was.

"You do know the alphabet, don't you, Frankie?" my father had asked. And that was just the kind of wisecrack question that was liable to make my mother raise her voice and slam things around in the kitchen for a while, but it was in Frankie's interest to keep her own good nature around my dad, and so she didn't let him see her taking any offense from it herself. She only laughed and told him, sure, of course she knew the alphabet. Who didn't?

We worked in the basement, sitting face to face at two narrow desks placed back to back in the middle of a small square room at the back of the building, underneath the loading dock. We made ourselves as comfortable as possible there. The customers never saw us, so we didn't have to dress up even though Frankie sometimes did anyway. Mostly we just wore shorts and T-shirts and jeans and sleeveless sundresses. The walls of the room were the exposed limestone foundation of the building painted over white. Frankie tried to tape posters up to give the place a little character, but the room was too damp, and the walls were lumpy and irregular, and the tape wouldn't stick. The floor was green and blue and brown speckled linoleum—moist and warm and slick against the soles of our bare feet. After a week, Frankie brought along a radio so we'd have some music to listen to and keep us company and occupy our thoughts. There was a deep window well on one side of the room, with wire-meshed glass that let in the light from the street level above us. The old gas incinerator loomed in the far corner, made obsolete since they'd overhauled the furnace system to maintain the showrooms' temperatures with air conditioning and forced-air heat. There wasn't any air conditioning in the basement, though, but with the window cranked open and a fan blowing on us, combined with the natural chill of being underground, we were comfortable enough.

Our task was to go through all the old files, card by card, and copy them over and clean them up so that their information was accurate and up to date and legible, besides. This was not a simple job—at least it wasn't as easy and automatic as it may sound. Because, in the first place, there were about a million and a half index cards to go through. And in the second, ninety percent of them were just about impossible to read. Some had been around so long that they were yellowed and ragged and, often, torn, and many were blurry and smeared. Old names and addresses and phone numbers had been crossed out or erased and replaced with new ones. There was Meems's ragged handwriting, small and cramped. And Grand's heavier scrawl that was too extravagant and took up too much space so he often overflowed the card, spilling off onto the back or onto another card, stapled to the first. And there was my father's almost illegible scribble—he held a pencil forcefully enough to make it snap in two, and he pressed too hard. Only Frankie could consistently untangle the sense of what he'd written—she did it by squinting and screwing up her mouth and turning her head from one side to the other. Both of us could easily read my mother's tidy printing, but it only came up now and then, because over the years she'd hardly been involved with any of the actual selling that went on in the store. Her main job had been to travel to Chicago twice a year to do the buying or to stay at home and look after me.

When I wasn't deciphering the secret language of the cards, I copied over the thank-you notes that my mother, following Meems's example, sent out to all our current customers. It was good P.R., she said. And Frankie—after a lifetime of practice—had the best manners among us for seeming to sincerely say thank you to people, so she was chosen to do the composing of the notes, as a way for her to practice on her typewriter, and then it was my job to copy them over with my calligraphy pens —one of the only stolen things that we brought home that I ever actually used. On the nights when Frankie was supposed to be at her typing class, I'd taught myself the methods, copying the letters over and over, practicing until I had the swoop and dip of the loops and curves and curlicues just right.

Here's what I remember:

The damp heat. An odor of mud and moss and mildew overlaid by the spicy scent of Frankie's perfume. Frankie's polished fingernails poised over the rows of typewriter keys. My own handwriting, as beautiful and perfect as if it didn't belong to me. The wet scraping of my pen nib traveling on automatic across the gray pebbled grain of the heavy bond note paper that I'd been given to use—with HADEN'S FINE FURNITURE embossed in serious square letterhead across the top. Frankie's presence, Frankie sitting at her desk across from me like my own mirror image, with her own stack of file cards piled up next to her. Frankie trying her best to do the typing, pecking out the letters and numbers, names and addresses, phone numbers and past and present purchases, slowly and carefully, with one pointed finger, one single key at a time. Frankie frowning in concentration. Frankie chewing on her lip. A breeze from the fan stirring in her hair. A cigarette burning, balanced on the rim of the ashtray near her; another one burning in her hand. Frankie pausing to listen when a song that she liked came on the radio—leaning her head back, closing her eyes, humming along.

And this:

The pulse-quickening pleasure of me writing Frankie's words, of me reading them over, of me taking them into my mind first and then spilling them out again through the carefully measured movements of my hand as I transformed her halting faulty typing into the spread of my own calligraphic flow. Of me taking Frankie's own thoughts and words and phrases and smoothing them over and making them into mine.

WE TOOK OUR BREAKS AND ATE OUR LUNCHES UPSTAIRS IN WHAT WAS CALLED the kitchen, an alcove off the storeroom with a sink and a refrigerator and a coffee pot, and sometimes Paul Gerald would be there when we came up, or maybe he'd come in after we'd already sat down, and then I'd make a mess of things, and I wouldn't know what to do with my hands or my sandwich would fall apart or my salad would become impossible to pick up with a fork or I'd drop my napkin on the floor. I'd go from being my quiet and invisible self-possessed self to a clumsy and awkward and embarrassed and red-faced adolescent girl with a pimple on her chin and hair that wouldn't fall right and ankles that were too thick and legs that were too short and nothing to say or only the wrong thing to say and just the wrong words to say it with. Frankie was her same charming self and she just straight out flirted with Paul, because that was how she was and nothing embarrassed her and she was afraid of no one, especially not a man, because she knew that she could charm him like a snake without hardly even having to try.

We were standing at the open window sharing a smoke when he came in, and I was just passing the cigarette back to Frankie, so he saw me with it for that moment, but he didn't even blink.

"Back at it again this summer, May?" he asked, because I'd worked for my parents sometimes before, during vacations when there was nothing else for me to do.

"I guess I must be," I told him. He smiled and nodded, then turned his sleepy eyes on Frankie.

"Who's your friend?" he asked.

And Frankie laughed. "I'm Frankie Crane," she said.

"Frankie," he said. He blinked and smiled.

"This is Paul Gerald," I told her. "He works here."

"Well, it's nice to meet you then, Mr. Gerald."

He told her she should call him Paul.

"He's in sales," I said.

Frankie raised her eyebrows and pursed her lips, as if this fact impressed her. "Sales?" she said. "Me and May, we're only in files. Up to our elbows in them." She smiled and looked at me for confirmation, which I gave.

I nodded. "Up to our chins," I said.

"Up to our butts." Frankie laughed and blew out a billow of smoke.

"Just started?" he asked.

"Oh, well, I've been around for a couple of days already, I guess," she answered.

"Funny I haven't seen you," he said.

"I suppose that's only because the old man's got us tucked away safe and sound in that dungeon of a basement back room." She took one more puff of the cigarette and then she handed it back to me. "Sort of like virgins locked in a tower, except we're buried underground."

Frankie moved away from the window to position herself in front of a standing fan. She let her hair tumble in the moving air for a moment, then she lifted her chin and leaned forward so the breeze was blowing straight down into the front of her blouse, billowing it. Paul Gerald watched this for a moment, then he turned away to look at me. And I stared out the window, pretending to be absorbed by something interesting in the scenery, sensing the drift of his eyes as they skimmed me—seeing what? I wondered. A child? A young woman? The boss's daughter? I could feel the sweat beading up in the cleft between my breasts. It trickled down my back, too, and tickled into the crease of my buttocks at the base of my spine.

I looked at his hands, pale and long-fingered with flat manicured nails. I wondered if he buffed them. His gold wristwatch gleamed. He reached past Frankie into the refrigerator, and he left the door open so a blast of its cold air flowed out. He took out a plastic bottle of water, cracked it open, and drank it down all at once. The lump of his Adam's apple moved in his throat as he swallowed. His eyes were closed, so I could look him over openly and take in the faint shadow of his beard on his cheeks, the smooth white skin inside the opened collar of his shirt, the curve of his long fine ears. Until Frankie coughed, and I looked over at her and knew that she'd seen me watching him. She winked and licked her lips. She went over to the refrigerator herself and stood with her head stuck inside it, letting the cool air flow out over her back.

"Hot day," Paul Gerald said. But the truth is that he didn't look uncomfortable at all. His shirt was crisp and white and his pants were creased, not rumpled in the crotch and knees like my father's always got to be, and his skin looked powdery and cool.

Paul didn't mention the cigarette or the fact that he'd seen me smoking some of it. He acted like it wasn't even there, except he opened a drawer and pulled out a glass ashtray and set it down on the windowsill for us to use. And Frankie grinned and thanked him for it, and he said it was nothing and he'd probably see her later or something and then he went on about his business, and Frankie turned to me wide-eyed, and, taking the cigarette back for herself again, she asked me, who was that?

THE FIRST TIME I SAW PAUL GERALD IN A WAY THAT MADE ME UNDERSTAND THAT he was more than only someone who worked for my dad was one late afternoon, when the sun was casting a precise crisscross pattern of buttery rays over the linoleum in the aisles of a show-room in the store. There was a smell of burned coffee and the muffled sound of the traffic that was moving along on its way through the streets outside. Business as usual. A telephone was ringing behind the closed door to my dad's office downstairs. And a conversation of some kind was being carried on else-where; the faint mingle of voices came wafting upward through the old heat registers from a full two stories below.

And there was a middle-aged woman in a suntan-colored

corduroy coat. She was smallish, mouselike, with tiny hands and dainty feet and a round head of tightly curled dark hair. She'd come to Haden's to buy a new TV chair.

And there was Paul, tall and thin, surrounded by furniture, a dark tree standing in a garden of blooming chintz. He was wearing a bottle green shirt and perfectly pressed brown pants held up by a thin black leather belt. And soft narrow shoes, more refined than the huge, heavy, thick-soled Florsheims that my father preferred.

The woman was sampling a sunflower yellow velvet chaise. She told him that it was a piece that would have to be for her, not for her husband. Paul smiled. He understood, perfectly. He told her that a woman ought to be able to pamper herself once in a while; she should treat herself to some little bit of luxury sometimes, fixed income or not. In fact, he said, she looked something like a movie star just then, lounging there on those bright cushions that way. It brought out the color in her cheeks, he said, and that made her look ten years younger, at least. She was shaking her curled head and smiling and blinking her eyes.

Then she sat in a leather chair with a puckered cushion back. He reached past her, leaning close enough that she could smell him and feel the warmth of his breath against her face. She giggled, unsure at first of what he might have been going to do. He'd pulled the lever at the side of the chair, and she fell back. She giggled again, helpless, her coat thrown open and her feet raised up in the air. She tugged at the hem of her skirt and waggled her legs in their thick brown hose; she kicked out her two dainty feet in their rubber-soled black slip-on sensible shoes.

He stood away from her. A smile wafted over his face, and he folded his arms across his chest. He rubbed one hand over his hair. He took the woman's elbow, finally, and he helped her up. She was blushing back at him. She was fiddling with her hair. She'd take it, she said.

Later, he was sitting at his desk in the corner, back downstairs on the first floor again. He was filling out the paperwork. He looked up. His face was white, his mouth wide, his lips damp, and his eyes gray, like ash. When he saw that I was watching him, he tapped his pencil against his chin, shook off his thoughts, and smiled.

UNTIL THAT SUMMER WHEN FRANKIE WAS THERE, PAUL GERALD HAD BEEN A sort of a secret that I'd been keeping to myself. Not a big secret, only a small one. I hadn't ever expected that there would be anybody else who, like me, would recognize that he was a person who was something out of the ordinary and, in his way, special. Not that I'd dreamed about him every night. It wasn't like that. It was more like that tree in Grand's yard that toppled after the rains. No one noticed it, until it went down. Except me. The fact of it is, I'd always liked Paul Gerald, and maybe he knew that, maybe he was aware, maybe he had a sense of some things himself.

His face was long and his cheeks were hollowed out. His eyes were dark, but they had a gleam to them, too. And he carried in his body a sort of a weariness—there was a gentle slump to his shoulders that made you feel sorry for him, as if he were weighted down by a personal burden of some kind. My mother said it was all that business with Brodie and April Delaney.

I HAD ALWAYS BEEN A SMALL SPY, CROUCHED BEHIND A SOFA, CREEPING AROUND a breakfront, peeking over the rounded arm of an overstuffed chair. When I was five my father caught me making faces behind a customer's back, and he pulled me up and smacked my behind, just hard enough to let me know he meant it this time when he told me I'd better just scoot. The lady had laughed. She'd tipped my chin, brushed back my hair with her fingertips, and asked him, was I his? And wasn't I just the sweetest little thing?

My uncle Brodie was working out in back, loading tables and bed frames and chairs wrapped in plastic onto the back of a waiting truck. The other boys were sitting on the loading dock, swinging their legs, smoking cigarettes, tossing stones. All I had to do was smile at Brodie, and he'd dig into his pocket for a nickel for me. There was a rainbow of gumballs in a glass globe that stood at the front of the store. It had a chrome frame with a blurred black and white photograph of a crippled girl with braces and crutches and a wildly needful smile filling up her face. I slipped the nickel into the slot, turned the knob, caught three yellows, two greens, one blue. I rolled the gumballs in my palm; the blue one stained my skin, a soft smeary tattoo.

I looked up when the bell above the front door rang, and there was Brodie's girlfriend, April Delaney, bringing in with her a blast of cold air. She wore a green wool coat with its fur collar pulled up against her throat. I put the gumballs into my mouth all at once, and then I dropped behind a sofa before she saw me. I sneaked along between a row of recliners, ducking and bobbing, tracking her path toward Brodie in the back. I crouched in a corner and watched him pull her into the shadowy recess of an alcove in the far wall. She was laughing. She put her arms up over his shoulders and buried her face in his neck. He splayed his hand across the small of her back. They stood there, the two of them, holding each other and swaying, as if their feelings were a wind that was blowing against them so hard it might be about to knock them down. When I coughed, choking on the juices from my gum, Brodie heard me, and he pulled me up from my hiding place. He lifted me and swung me to his shoulders. April was holding a silver compact, dabbing on orange-ish lipstick, straightening the coppery waves of her hair. She was smiling. She waggled her fingers at me as Brodie swept me away, to deposit me at the feet of my dad.

HERE'S WHAT I CAME TO UNDERSTAND LATER, AFTER FRANKIE WAS GONE: IT wasn't Paul Gerald who changed over the days and weeks and months of that summer when Frankie was still here. He didn't go from being nobody to becoming somebody the way that I did—he stayed the same as he'd always been. It was only me who was the one who changed. Something had begun to happen inside of me—womanhood, Frankie said, squinting at my face.

"Look at that, May," she said. "You're actually beginning to grow yourself some respectable tits."

But about this Frankie wasn't as completely right as she had

been about some other things. Because there was more seriousness to what was happening to me than only that, the ratio
between the circumference of my chest against my waist against
my hips.

"It's not the size itself," Frankie explained, "it's more the
relationship of the proportions in between."

But what went on between me and Frankie and Paul Gerald
was not just a simple matter of biology—the stone surface of my
girlish longings rubbed against the hard flint of his desire. There
had to have been some bit of spirit involved in it, too, I believed. Something that was rare and beautiful, something that
didn't have anything at all to do with my physical self, or his. It
was almost as if a spark had been struck inside me, and by its
sudden light I was able to begin to see things for what they
really were.

When the policemen and the reporters all asked my dad
about it, he told them honestly that he'd considered Paul Gerald to be his best salesman. He was good because he knew just
how to cajole the customers. He could make people think that
they were happy and secure and feeling good. They trusted him,
because he was soft-spoken and shy-seeming, and when he said
things he always made it sound sincere, and not pushy, like
some of the salesmen who'd come and gone over the years. He
never made any judgments on what particular piece had caught
a person's fancy, either, no matter how extreme it might have
seemed to him. Our customers genuinely liked to buy their
furniture from Paul Gerald. Maybe, too, that was partly because
he was such a solemn man and so they felt like they were doing
him a favor, maybe they could cheer him up by purchasing the

things that he was supposed to sell. All of this came out sounding like some kind of an indictment of Paul when it appeared in print or when the reporters spoke it into their microphones, standing in front of spotlights outside the blasted ruins of what was left of the store.

They ran the same picture of Paul every time the story came up, which got to be less and less often as more and more time went by—it was a black and white snapshot of him standing in his kitchen, holding a cocktail glass. I don't know where they got that snapshot; it wasn't one that I'd ever seen before. They must have found it someplace in his apartment when they searched it, looking for who knows what incriminating evidence. Matches, maybe. Incendiary devices. Pieces of Frankie Crane's body hacked to pieces and stuffed inside a suitcase and hidden at the back of a closet. There had been nothing like that, though, nothing so blatant, only the suggestion of Frankie's presence. Her white canvas hat, for one thing. And a note that was analyzed and determined to have been written by her—it was in her handwriting and it had her fingerprints on it—and it told him that she loved him, on a piece of Haden's letterhead stationery with a lipstick kiss pressed in one corner.

They must have chosen that shot of Paul because it showed his face so well, straight on, looking right into the camera's lens, features clearly outlined by the flash. If you saw him on the street, after studying that picture of him, if he hadn't bleached his hair or grown a beard or put on weight, you'd have been able to recognize him right away.

They characterized him as a loner, the dangerous and unpredictable unmarried man. But, in fact, he wasn't a bachelor at all.

He was an ex-husband. His wife had walked out on him years ago, and moved away to Colorado where her parents lived. And the wife hadn't only taken her own self out of his life, but she'd made off with just about every single thing of any value that they'd had between them, too. One day Paul Gerald had had a nice house, a car, a dog, and a wife with whom he was living an average, decent sort of life, and then the next day he was all alone and riding the bus to work and living by himself in an apartment that didn't allow pets.

He told me that there was a part of him that was honestly glad when that happened. A part of him that had been relieved, he said. That, in a way, he'd come to like himself and his life better since then. Unencumbered, he called himself. Pared down to only the necessities, peeled back to the mere bare bone.

AFTER WORK, FRANKIE AND I SIGNED OURSELVES OUT ON THE WORKERS' LIST that hung on a clipboard by the back door and then walked across the softened tar of the driveway to Frankie's car. Below the bluff, the river ran past, sluggish and slow and dark like molasses. A boy was fishing from the railing of the bridge above us. The air hummed with gnats. The Lincoln's leather seats burned the backs of our legs and made us yelp and squirm when we sat on them. Frankie put the top down and then drove fast out of downtown so the wind could cool us off. The Lincoln swooped along the bends and curves of Linwood's streets, turned off onto Post Road, followed along the ragged line of Grand's split rail fence that hemmed the fields that rolled off like long skirts toward a central huddle of house and grounds and gray trees. Grand Haden's land was a straggle of woods and a flow of meadows and flat creekland that sprawled for more than twenty acres out alongside Post, just past the place where it crossed over Old Highway 18.

I told Frankie to slow down, and she turned the car where I pointed, off the road toward the driveway, and we bounced onto the macadam and rolled in past the open gate and stopped.

I guess I can pretty much imagine what we must have looked like back then on that day, Frankie and me, our two faces a pair of pale ovals bobbing side by side, as we sat peering out through the grimy windshield of the Lincoln at the generous spread of Grand's single-story house with its brick face and neat black shutters, the rugged stone chimney, the ripple of red tile roof.

As we pulled in, the side door of the house opened, and Brodie appeared, struggling with a full bag of trash that he was taking across the driveway to dump into the metal incinerator at the far edge of the yard. Coming back, brushing his hands against his pant legs, he stopped to study something that was there in the dirt at the side of the drive, and then he looked up to see Frankie's black car sitting there on the macadam, its engine turned off and ticking. He put his hand up to shade his eyes, and he peered at the Lincoln's broad windshield until the car doors opened, both sides at once, like a spread of black wings, and then we two girls got out.

We were walking toward him down the drive. A breeze had picked up and was blowing through our skirts, and it spun the leaves in the trees and turned them silver against the white-hot shimmer of the sky.

May. I could see Brodie's mouth shape the single syllable of my name. He was smiling then, I guess both at the fact of his knowing that it was me and his being able to say so, and also at the fact that it was me. He raised his arm up, and he waved. But there were two of me, it must have seemed to him, with Frankie there. There was me and then there was Frankie; she was some other version of me, a distorted reflection, a shadow stretched taller and thinner, a wavering figure, a smudge of color, and both of us were coming toward him down the drive. He lifted his hand again, and he waved again, and then that time I waved back.

FRANKIE CALLED HIM HUMPTY DUMPTY, BECAUSE OF THE LONG WHITE SCAR THAT split his forehead in a diagonal line, as if Brodie had been cracked into two perfect pieces and then glued back together into one again.

"It's like he's there and not there," was all that I could come up with to try and explain to Frankie about how Brodie was. There was a special kind of a stillness to my uncle. He was as placid as a pond. It was a literal absent-mindedness—some of his brain happened to be dead, so that part of his mind was gone, and it made him seem like he was distracted and elsewhere most of the time, like somebody who was listening to something privately, words and phrases that maybe no one else around him was able to quite hear.

Brodie is damaged, was how my mother explained it, if anybody asked, which just about nobody did anymore by that time because the story was already such an old one and everyone who knew us knew that when Brodie was twenty-two years old he'd had an accident that hadn't been an accident at all.

It was late in August when it happened, early in the morning. I was six years old, shivering in the air conditioning, in only my skirted stretchy striped bathing suit and pink rubber thongs. My mother had come in through the back door, calling out to Brodie in the gloom as she moved from room to room. There had been too much quiet. No music, no voices, and no lights on either, too much shadow, too much silence, too much dark. Grand and Meems were out of town on one of their trips; they'd gone to Michigan to stay with some friends there in a cabin on a lake.

She found him at the back of the house, in Meems's bedroom. He was sitting with his back straight and his legs crossed over at the knee, one long pale bare foot pressed against the dark green carpeting, and his hands folded, resting quietly in his lap, nails trim and clean. But he was naked, and he'd soiled the flowered chintz cushions of Meems's upholstered reading chair.

There had been no marks on the pale, boyish features of Brodie's face, so my mother hadn't been able to tell at first what exactly was wrong with her brother; she'd had no idea at all what it was that he might have done, that he'd opened his mouth to the long round barrel of a Ward's Western Field 22-caliber bolt action rifle, and he'd pressed its cold muzzle against the smooth pink dome of his palate. That he'd closed his eyes, and he'd pulled the trigger, and the sparks of bird shot, too small to kill him, had plowed into the flesh and bone behind his boyish face and scattered through the crumpled fist of his brain—like a night sky, strewn with a sudden radiance of serious stars.

The rifle had been kept in a locked closet in a corner of the cellar right there in Grand Haden's house. Brodie had taken the gun with him into the woods a few times, and he'd teased me with it, scaring me bad. He'd told me he was going to kill that old snake that we'd seen shimmy through the high grass at the far side of the front yard, where a hedge of wild roses rambled alongside the whitewashed fence that separated the lawn from its half circle of trees. Brodie had known that I was afraid of both snakes and guns and that the dilemma for me was deciding which was worse—the thought of a copperhead coiled up, sliding, lunging, striking, and sinking its fangs into the bare flesh of someone's leg or the vision of Brodie with that gun raised up to his shoulder, squinting down its barrel, squeezing its trigger and blowing that snake to smithereens.

Grand had hired a crew to come in and tear up the carpet and take down the drapes in Brodie's bedroom. They burned all his soiled clothes. They threw out the mattress on his bed. They polished the tiles on the bathroom walls and floor, and scoured the bloodstains out of the grouting with wire brushes and chlorine bleach. My mother had them take Meems's reading chair away, too, and, as if she would have removed all memory of how Brodie had shot himself, and why, when the chair came back, weeks later, the wild swirl of its flowers was gone, and the cushions had been covered over again instead in the pure bright empty dazzle of a clean white muslin slip.

Brodie had been unlucky in love, my mother explained. She

didn't talk about where they took him, afterward, or about how he'd been locked up in a hospital that was like a jail, until he'd recovered as much as he was ever going to, until they decided that he wasn't going to hurt anybody again and that it was safe to let him go. He'd had his heart broken by a girl named April Delaney, was all that my mother would say. He'd just gone off the deep end for a while, and that was it.

IN GRAND'S BACK YARD THERE WAS A SWIMMING POOL—A RARITY, AT ONE TIME IT had been one of the only privately owned outdoor pools in the whole state. At its deepest it was an ear-crushing twelve feet down, and it was twenty-five yards across from ramp to ramp, with four racing lanes marked by wavering black lines that had to be repainted on the bottom every other year. Before you could play in the deep end, Grand Haden said, you had to be strong enough to swim it, across and back, alone.

When I was a little girl, I liked to follow Brodie up the narrow ladder of the high dive, a gritty metal plank set up on top of a complicated web of struts and supports. I'd cling with white knuckles to the side rails, wet feet clambering, slippery, on the flat, grooved metal rungs, eyes set straight ahead—Brodie warned me, May, better not look down. When I got to the top, he put his pale hands on my shoulders, encouraging me to go on, and I'd venture out, one step at a time, one foot in front of the other, and then stand there, frozen with fear, high above the dark wavery surface of the water below.

From there I had a bird's-eye view of my grandparents' land— the smudge of the woods on one side, the rolling curves of the full trees that spread gracefully down toward the creek, the shimmer of the road in the distance, the roof of the house that loomed at the top of the hill.

I was six years old. I was a good swimmer, my uncle Brodie said. It was June, and Brodie was still okay.

I could see my mother, sprawled on a towel; her oiled skin glistened. My father was in the chaise, asleep, with one arm thrown across his face. Meems was engaged in a game of solitaire at the white wrought iron table, protected from the sun in the broad circle of shade that was cast over her by a bright yellow canvas umbrella that bloomed and nodded there like a fat flower over her bowed head. Grand Haden was in the water, swimming lap after lap, back and forth, arm over arm, as slow and determined as a water bug in his pace. And April Delaney and Paul Gerald were in the yard, playing a game of croquet.

Beneath my feet, the board dipped and bent. I swayed, arms flailing, so high above the water and the ground, even higher, it seemed, than the tallest trees that encircled the yard. Brodie was behind me, he was urging me on, nudging me forward, until there was nothing for me to do but hold my breath and step off, a plummeting dead weight. There was just enough time to pinch my nose as the water rushed to meet me, and then it hit me, hard, a stunning slap across the back of my legs.

Whoomp!

Brodie stood above me with his long arms loose at his sides, his bare legs long and straight, his blond hair darkened by the water, shining, flung back. He closed his eyes and tipped his face up to the sun, drinking it in before he moved, took one step forward, and then another, off the end of the board. He lifted his hands up over his head and slipped into the pool without a splash.

Out on the grass, Paul Gerald slammed his mallet against April Delaney's ball and sent it soaring off toward the trees.

FRANKIE AND I PUT ON OUR BATHING SUITS AND HEADED STRAIGHT FOR THE BACK yard and plunked our two hot bodies into the pool for some relief. Frankie went right into swimming laps—she had made up a plan for herself to swim ten laps every day to keep her legs trim and her belly flat—but I'd never been anything but too thin already so I just let myself sink, taking in a good strong deep breath and then drifting down to the bottom of the shallow end and holding myself there, sitting with my legs out, looking at my hands and my feet flowing away from me as if they weren't mine at all, clenching my own fists and flexing my own toes and in a dark way finding myself surprised to see them responding to my thoughts because they looked so distorted and felt so separate, so much not me.

I could see, off in the distance and the darkness and the dimness of the center of the bottom of the deep end of the pool, the black hole of the grate over the drain. I swam toward it.

Just exactly how deep was the deep end? I wondered. I didn't know exactly, but my mother had always warned me that if I went too far, if I swam too long, if I dove too close to the drain I might be sucked up, or was it down? It, something, a pull that was stronger than my own resistance to it could ever be, might snatch hold of my fingers and grab my wrists and then slurp me in and swallow me down, or was it up?, until I'd been devoured, whole and alive, until I was gone.

So, I always did it. It was a dare. Brodie and April Delaney and me—it was one of our best games. It was a test to find out who was brave and who was not. Who was the crybaby. Who had endurance and courage and nerve.

Frankie moved above me, her feet churning, her arms stroking, her face turned away to grab a mouthful of air and then spew it back out into the water again. And underwater, my feet fluttering, my blind hands groping, I brushed my fingertips across the whorled surface of the drain, then snapped them back into safe fists again. I folded my body into a muscled ball, rolling, swiftly turning, angling off, slithery as a fish, before the whirlpool could grab hold and tighten its grip and begin its slow determined steady deadly downward pull.

Frankie and I wrapped ourselves in towels and sat on the back porch, drinking lemonade. The sky overhead was white with heat. The grass in the yard was shiny, glistening wet from the sprinkler spray. Brodie was out in the garden, using a hoe to turn the dark soil between the rows of vegetables that he'd planted. All summer we'd be watching him pick peas and tomatoes and peppers and beans, and the day nurse would cook them for dinner for Brodie and Grand and Meems, and for us, too, if there was enough. Brodie's sweat had seeped darkish damp ovals into the thinned fabric of his blue work shirt, on his back and over his chest and under his arms. The dirt that was smudged on his face and into the palms of his hands made him look more childish and goofy than ever—he seemed to me to be as boyish as Frankie and I were girlish ourselves.

Meems was over on the other side of the yard, propped up in her wheelchair. The day nurse had wheeled her out there to get some fresh air, although the air was hardly fresh. It was hot and thick and wet. She'd rolled Meems down the walk and over the grass and into the shade. Gnats swarmed, but Meems was oblivious.

She was old and sick already by then, and I couldn't help it, even as much as I loved her, still sometimes her smell would remind me of the stink of stagnant water at the bottom of a vase of forgotten flowers. Her wheelchair's rubber tires whispered across the carpeting or squeaked on the hardwood floors as she prowled her house, gliding along like a ghost from one room to another, haunting the hallways, searching for something, but it was never exactly clear what. For one thing, her voice was gone. She had been quite a singer once, but by that summer she had no songs left in her—she'd forgotten both the melodies and the words, too. Sometimes she would cry out, in an unexplained agonizing way that made Brodie duck and cringe and brought Grand hurrying to be with her, to hold her, to cup his hand over the back of her head and press her face against him. Her old hands, grasping at the blanket in her lap, looked like a bird's clawed feet. Her hair that had once been dark and thick was by then not much more than an airy white fluff like a bird's down, and it feathered her skull, with an absurd bright flowery bow bobby-pinned on the top. Something to make her feel pretty, my mother said.

Meems had once been a real beauty, a party girl, raucous and fun, my mother told us. But that summer she was just frail. She couldn't talk. She was helpless and hopeless and pitiful. She couldn't do one thing for herself. She had to be brought into the bathroom and bathed and shampooed, dressed and brushed and fed. Grand read to her sometimes, and he tried to entertain her, to keep her from sinking so far down into herself that she disappeared, like a stone dropped into deep water. When Grand got tired of doing all the talking, he'd roll her wheelchair over in front of the television set and then she'd sit there and stare at it, and it was hard to tell how much she was able to understand.

Sometimes the nurse would give her cards and let her play her own crazy kind of solitaire at the kitchen table. Meems turned the cards over, painfully, one by one, with her only good hand, but the game she played didn't seem to have any relation to a real game of any kind. The plays she made didn't make any sense. Meems couldn't understand the suits and the numbers on the cards anymore, and she could barely tell the difference between the colors, either, so she just laid them out any which way, pretending to be deeply involved in the game, pondering moves as if they meant something to her. This made Grand go crazy trying to correct her, but the nurse would shoo him off and tell him to leave Meems alone. She liked the game she played, she was happy playing it, so what difference did it make if the rest of us couldn't follow the logic of it anymore?

After he was retired from the furniture business, my grandfather had become an artist. He didn't paint or draw, but he was a whittler and a carver, a sculptor who liked to sit for hours and hours working on a piece, finding a figure in a hunk of wood, drawing it out, with his lips pursed into a kiss and his eyes pink and shining wet. Most of the time he worked in a deep silence that was as thick as a wall around him. Sometimes he listened to the garble of a foreign language on his shortwave. Sometimes he whistled to himself, distractedly, under his breath.

He'd made an oak hand for holding a gold pocket watch, a bouquet of delicate mahogany flowers, a woman's bare torso, headless and legless, and a man's arched foot. Pine bookends carved in filigree patterns, teak eggs, a maple bud vase. An ashwood chess set. An ebony cane. All sorts of interesting and useful things.

Brodie saved Grand's scraps and leftovers, and he used them to make what my mother called his thinking burls. These were rounded knots of wood that had been cut and sanded, whittled down until they would fit perfectly into a person's palm. They were grooved on one side, for thoughtful thumb-rubbing. You could hold one of Brodie's thinking burls, you could touch it and turn it, you could weigh it in your hand, you could rub it like a magic lamp, and if you were patient, if you could wait for it, there might be some good thought that would come thrashing up through the surface of your dim unconscious, into the light of your mind.

Evenings when it was cool, Brodie and Frankie and I would sit outside in the yard for a while to look at his garden and to take some fresh air. We'd each hold a burl in one hand and we'd rub and rub it, working our smells and our sweat and our oils into the swirls of its grain. It looked like Brodie was trying to unravel something that way, Frankie said, or maybe he was working to find a way to dredge up his memory again, or to reconstruct the scattered bits and pieces of his shattered mind.

That summer, Grand had begun to do work in clay. There was a big soggy mound of it wrapped in a wet cloth and a layer of plastic wrap on the sculpting stand beside the table where Frankie was reading. He'd asked us to keep it moist by dampening the cloth down for him every now and then.

He was making a bust of Meems, but because he was using an old portrait photograph of her that he had tacked up on the wall, the face and head didn't look anything at all like her. No one had the heart to tell him this. I was sure that he knew it anyway—mentioning it out loud would have been unkind.

In clay, Meems's cheeks were full and fleshy and high, rounded like apples, and her throat was strong and smooth, and her shoulders were soft. In reality Meems's head was a shrunken, papery thing; her body was frail-looking and saggy and huddled in; her feet were bunioned out of shape; her hands were twisted up in knots, and her face was crazed with a million little tiny wrinkles, like the cracked glaze on an antique china plate. But Grand was quick to explain that he wasn't trying to capture the reality of how Meems was then; he only wanted to reconstruct her as she had been before. He said he was bringing her back from the past by remodeling her in clay. Maybe by some magic, he said, winking at Frankie, she could be miraculously restored. He thought he could make a golem out of his clay sculpture of Meems. But if that had been possible, why hadn't he tried to do the same thing with Brodie first?

I lifted my eyes and looked up across the yard, past the pool, at the woods that were so lush and beginning to be wild with summer. They were a desperate tangle of prickly nettles and high-grown, uninviting weeds. I had never cared for the woods that encircled Grand Haden's house. I didn't like how they felt to me, hovering there at the edges of things, like shadows, waiting, it seemed, for their chance to take me by surprise and close in. They were rooted things, conjoined and conspiring, and their branches seemed entangled; their shade seemed like a threat and a shelter both at the same time.

Even if I pulled my chair closer to Frankie's, still I could just see the shadows of the trees out of the corner of my eye. When I looked up and studied them face on, then it made me wonder if when I wasn't looking, maybe they had shifted? Had their half circle contracted some slight bit? Were they creeping in somehow closer to the house? I knew that this was not a possible thing—trees didn't move, they couldn't—and yet it felt to me as if anyway maybe they had, all the same. I thought I'd ask Grand if Brodie could take his tractor mower out and try to clear a path down through the trees, all the way to the creek. It would make me feel better, I thought, just knowing that I could get there, if I wanted to.

I studied the stillness of the swimming pool, so solid-seeming that it might have been ice. Except for the heat that rippled the air and appeared, instead, to be flames.

Chapter Six

OUT OF SIGHT, OUT OF MIND, FRANKIE said, about Meems in her bedroom at the end of the hallway at the back of Grand Haden's house. She meant, like dirt swept under a rug or junk piled up on a shelf behind a closed closet door. Frankie could be sharp sometimes, if that was what she wanted to be. She could cut right through you, if she wasn't careful. Or if you weren't. She was like a knife that way—mishandled, her blade could draw your blood. She was like sharp glass. And even if she would have been the first one to admit it that she maybe did have some jagged edges on her, she never did believe that it was up to her to try and smooth them down.

And besides, the fact was that about Grand and Meems, Frankie's opinion was most likely right. He did tend to tuck her off in her bed at night after dinner, sometimes as soon as he could. He did it because he needed to have her out of his way, Frankie said. He didn't like to have to see her all the time. His eyes would drift around her, his look would skim her surface, like a fly that was trying to find someplace to light. It wasn't that Grand didn't like Meems anymore. It wasn't that he didn't love her just as much as he ever had. More likely it was only that he didn't care for the memories or the thoughts that the sight of her conjured up for him. His retirement years had been ruined, after all, and the fact of that must have made the rest of his life, all of it that had come before, seem in some way tainted. The past kept getting stained by the present, because all that personal history of his— his hard work, his devotion to his family, his dedication to his business—all it had brought him, finally, was this: a big house in the country, a swimming pool, a station wagon and a fishing pole, one addled son, one old dog, one damaged, speechless wife, one resentful daughter, a silent, sulking granddaughter, and her sneaky friend. And by the end of that summer, even the store would be gone, too. So, what had it all been for, then, Grand's whole life? Only that? He didn't want to think about it. Who would?

He hardly ever seemed to sleep. He stayed up until all hours of the night, by himself, in his study, at the far other end of the house from Meems. We'd see his light on there; it streamed out like a sunrise through the crack that was at the bottom of the door. We'd hear the sound of his heavy shoes clumping a pathway back and forth across the carpet, his restless pacing in the middle of the night. He was studying a few things, he told us. Old people don't need so much sleep, he said. And Frankie said out loud what I was only thinking to myself, which was, what a waste. Because there was Grand, an old man all by himself, with nothing to do but drink his scotch and smoke his cigars and try his best to do whatever it took to smother once and for all the embers of his unexpressed rage. He was just biding his time in there, dreaming up a new sculpture to carve from wood or shape with clay.

We all felt sorry for him, to tell the truth.

And we felt sorry for Meems, too, because she was even worse. She was stuck there at the back of her own house, with only a nurse or me and Frankie for company now and then. My grandmother was sent away to her room, Frankie said, just like she was maybe a child who had annoyed the grownups with some bit of bad behavior, and I thought I could understand that. I knew what it felt like. I could remember it well enough, because I was pretty much still just a kid myself, and it hadn't been all that long ago when what Meems had become used to be me. Spanked and sent to bed. Enough's enough, my mother would say. You're out of here, May, I'm counting and by the time I'm finished you'd better be gone. And even though compared to somebody like Frankie I was mostly obedient and good, still when you're a kid all you really have to do is just be your own wild self at exactly the wrong time and that's enough to make the grownups who are in charge of you lose their patience and send you—hands on hips, fingers pointing, faces creased with disapproval—away by yourself into the dark and empty loneliness of your own little upstairs room.

Grand had bought Meems an aluminum-framed hospital bed, with cranks and rails and different positions. He'd paid cash for it, because he never did believe in credit, which had been a big bone of contention when my mother took over the books and decided to set up charge accounts so that her best customers could continue to buy whatever struck their fancy whenever their fancy struck, and with interest besides. Grand had also bought Meems her own color television set, and it was perched up on a sturdy metal stand at one side of her bed, so she could see it clearly, without having to peer. She couldn't change the channels, though. She didn't quite know how to do that. It was just one more task that was beyond her, and so she had to settle for whatever was on the screen at the moment, as if the TV were a window, and she was sitting there beside it, looking out through the curtains, a victim of circumstance and timing, subject to whatever might be about to happen out there within her range of vision next. Sometimes we watched old movies with her.

That fancy mechanical bed and the television set didn't exactly fit in with the rest of the old-fashioned decor in Meems's bedroom. They stood out there, and that was a good thing in a way, I thought, because it made it seem to me that maybe their presence was only something temporary, a minor inconvenience that was being kept around only for the time being, until she got better, and then she could have her old bed back again, to sleep in just like she had before. And yet at the same time that could be a kind of a discouragement, too, Frankie pointed out, because maybe she wasn't ever going to get any better, and meanwhile those things were an intrusion, clashing cruelly with the true serene nature of the place the way it had been before Meems had been brought down and knocked over and changed forever afterward by the unexpected event of her stroke.

When Meems had slept in her own full-size antique mahogany bed—because my grandparents had always had their own bedrooms in that house; they were old-fashioned that way, and they both liked to be able to have the choice of keeping their own privacy, my mother said—her sheets had been satin, shiny and slippery and cool, waves of soft pastel colors, pink and blue, or deep seaweed green or cool peach. But the nurses made up her bed with crisp white linens and a thin brown and yellow patterned cotton blanket, and I knew that Meems must have hated that, not just the bland brown-ness of it, but also the stiff sheets, rubbing raspy and harsh against her papery soft skin. Which she cared about like almost nothing else. She'd had a dressing table full of lotions and ointments and creams to prove it—an elaborate compilation of elixirs made and meant to keep a woman womanly, soft and young and unlined, a hopeless and pathetic ambition for somebody who was so old and who had had a stroke besides, like Meems.

The least I could do, I thought, was to cover her pillow with one of those old satin cases that she used to use, and she'd nestle her head into it, and maybe that was a comfort to her somehow. I think she was grateful for that kind of special attention that she sometimes got from me. I tried to keep myself alert to the glimmer of a smile from her, but there never was anything much that I could see, though Frankie found it there whenever she wanted, or needed, to. Which isn't to say that Meems didn't appreciate the things I did for her. It's only that her sweet face had been frozen into a smirk that was just not becoming to her in any way—which would also have bothered her, if she'd been aware of it, I think—and it wasn't even close to what she meant to communicate to any of us besides, I was sure.

Meems had never smirked at anybody. She'd always only been soft and supple both inside and out, just like her skin. Just like her pretty sheets. She was gentle and quiet and happy.

"Look on the bright side, May," she used to say to me. "See if you can't find a way to make the best of a bad situation."

She was still gentle, even if her face did look like it had been frozen stiff, and she was quieter than ever because she couldn't talk at all. But it was too hard for anyone to know whether she was happy still.

The drawers of her dressing table were the same, full of all her cosmetics and creams, none of which she used or needed anymore. Her skin looked like it was falling from her face, dripping off the framework of her bones like melted wax. One time Frankie and I tried making her up, just for the fun of it, but that was a mistake, because Meems looked something like a clown and when we showed him what we'd been up to, Grand was angry with us, although he was too polite to actually say so. He only tightened his lips in that hard, cold way that he had, and he turned away.

Frankie and I had snooped through their closets. Meems had veiled hats and heavy furs. Chiffon dresses and silk blouses and a bruise-blue cashmere sweater with pearlish white buttons that my mother told me if I liked it I could have. In fact, she'd said that we could take whatever of Meems's old clothes we wanted, and so that's exactly what Frankie and I did. They were all just rummage anyway, my mother said, and that made Grand wince. My mother didn't dare have anything taken away and donated to thrift, but she hated at the same time to see so many good things going to such waste. We found some dresses and skirts and blouses that we liked, and I helped myself to a dark blue wool coat, too. It was double-breasted, with two rows of bright brass buttons, but I had to save it for winter and by the time I got around to wearing it, Frankie had already been gone from our lives for what seemed like a long time.

Meems's shoes were mostly too big and too old-fashioned for us. She'd been drawn to spectator pumps and crippling pointy-toed rickety high heels. Frankie did turn up a spectacular pair of red and purple tooled suede cowboy boots that Meems must have bought to wear to a western-themed costume party once, and she kept those. And there were a few pairs of pretty sandals, white and gold and rainbow-colored. And some satin slippers that had old-fashioned-looking silk roses sewn onto the toes.

Even without the shoes, though, we two girls did manage between us to take quite a lot of my grandmother's old things. Only not her underwear. That might have been going too far, even for Frankie. We sifted through them, though, the panties and the girdles and the elaborately boned brassieres.

When either one of us happened to be wearing something of Meems's, Brodie and Grand both would give us funny looks. Grand would flinch and turn his head away. Brodie just blinked and smiled. I couldn't tell whether Meems herself ever noticed any of it or not.

FRANKIE LIKED TO SIT ON THE PINK CHAISE IN MEEMS'S ROOM, WATCHING HER. The wallpaper had an angel motif—chubby baby cherubs with pudgy legs and dimpled cheeks and thick, feathered wings, all of them giggling and snickering, whispering secrets and pressing their fat fannies against each other. There were a few books there, too, but mostly there were only Meems's stacks of old magazines, because that was what she'd always liked best to read. She'd liked to look at the pictures, once, so Frankie would hold them up and show them to her sometimes. There was an antique phonograph in the room, too, with some of the old albums that Meems had collected over the years. Frankie and I would play one for her every now and then, just for fun. Sometimes we danced, Frankie throwing her head back and waving her hands and swinging her hips. We found that mostly what Meems liked were the most simple-sounding jazz tunes, romantic melodies sung by men with deep voices and torch songs belted out by women that Frankie said sounded like they had the strep throat.

In a basket on the floor in Meems's room was her match collection—books and boxes of matches that she'd tucked into her purse or her pocket and then brought home with her from all the places around the country and even the world that she and Grand had visited during all those years of their marriage. She liked to look at these with us, and that was one of the best things that the three of us could do together, I thought. I'd start out by closing my eyes and fishing around and pulling one out and showing it to Meems. Then Frankie would read out loud what it said. Sometimes it might even be in another language, but she could pretty much sound out whatever it was and even if she got it wrong none of us knew the difference. It was hard to tell how much Meems understood about it anyway. She'd sit still, absorbed and intent. Only her eyes would move, as she watched Frankie. She'd see her hold up the matchbook—a bit of color that she didn't have a name for. Her tongue would start to move in her mouth; she'd lick her lips, as if she were going to say something, but nothing ever came. Or maybe it was that the place the matchbook came from was conjured up for her like a flower, a bloom of memory that brought back to her a sense of who she'd been, once, and of where she'd traveled to in her lifetime, with Grand.

I thought about the flame that must have been burning still, someplace deep down inside of the darkest depths of Meems. And what flared there inside of Brodie, too. It would have been an old warmth, a small glimmering that was always dimming inward, like a pond in winter, as it slowly freezes over, from its shallow outer edges on in toward its depths.

One of the matchbooks in Meems's basket had come from a hotel in Vienna. She'd brought my mother a set of finger puppets from there, too. She was always thoughtful, and she always brought back gifts for her children, even after they were grown. There'd been a wire boat that she'd picked up in Venice. A plastic Statue of Liberty from New York. The Eiffel Tower. But from Vienna it had been five finger puppets crammed into a painted wooden theater box—a girl in a red apron, an old woman in a flowered gown, a man with a gray beard, a boy with a green cap, and a sharp-featured devil, grinning from ear to ear.

His nose was a knife blade. His eyebrows were thin and dark. His mouth was open, and his blue eyes squinted with a gleeful sort of malevolence, happy to be bad. I'd never liked him very much. I'd always had the feeling that his nasty laughter was something that he was aiming straight for me.

Frankie lit one of the matches, and she held it out closer, for Meems to see, and Meems's eyes moved from the flame to Frankie's face then back to the flame again. She watched it burn, and it was hard to tell whether the look on her face was a reflection of her interest or of her fear. She seemed, beyond her smirk, to be frowning some. Maybe she was worried that Frankie might be going to somehow hurt herself. Or me. Or it could be that she was thinking that Frankie was considering burning her. That she might blow the match out and then hold its hot tip to the back of Meems's one paralyzed hand, just to test her, just to see how much she might still be able, in spite of everything else, to feel. She might have been able to gauge Meems's sensitivity by the strength of the reaction from her that she got. Would Meems have cried out? Or might she possibly have found a word somewhere there, bubbling up from the hard startle of her pain? It was difficult to say. No, not difficult. In fact, impossible.

But Frankie only lit a cigarette, anyway. She took it from the pack that she had tucked away in the pocket of the apron that she was wearing over her dress—which was one of Meems's, flowered and hanging, a drape of airy fabric, with a lace collar that it was possible Meems may even have made herself. The apron was custard yellow, and it had a spray of purple flowers that Meems had embroidered on the pockets.

I opened the window, even though outside it was so hot. My mother had told Frankie that she was forbidden to smoke in

Grand's house, especially not in Meems's bedroom, but of course Meems would never have told on us. Even if she'd wanted to, even if she'd be able to, she wouldn't have. We all knew that. When I pressed my cheek to the screen, I could see the light from the den that was cast across the grass. The windows of Meems's room looked out on the back yard and the swimming pool. The struts and structure of the high dive made it look like some kind of a long-legged insect that was crouched there, a grasshopper all set to spring.

Meems had turned to watch the TV. I watched the end of Frankie's cigarette as it burned down. She lit all the matches from Vienna. The heat from outside was pressing in through the open window, and it moved against me. Warm as a fire, building. Cherub wings, curling. Cabbage roses blackening behind billowy plumes of dark gray smoke.

IN THE KNOTTY PINE KITCHEN AT GRAND'S HOUSE WAS THE KNOTTY PINE TABLE that Grand had cut and carved and sanded and stained and put together by himself. Its surface was so soft that if you were sitting at it and if you were trying to write something down, the point of your pencil would press right through the paper and leave its mark on the wood itself. You could look at the squiggles that were snarled and twined over the wood's surface like a sample of Meems's most delicate lace or a tree's bare branches outlined against the sky—grocery lists and phone numbers, math problems and term papers, love letters and thank-you notes, gin rummy and bridge and Scrabble scores—and find there the trails and traces of Brodie's handwriting and my mother's, April Delaney's and Paul Gerald's and Meems's and Grand's, too, all of them intertwined with and, finally, indistinguishable from mine.

Grand was fixing an egg sandwich for his dinner because that was just about the only thing he knew how to make for himself to eat. He fried two eggs up into a solid mass with the yolks broken, and then he put them between two pieces of toast and smothered the whole thing with ketchup. He used to be the only one who would eat this, but when he offered to make one for Frankie she accepted and then told him that that was about the best thing in the world she'd ever eaten, which Grand said he already knew and it was about time somebody else realized it, too.

So he fixed Frankie and me each a fried egg sandwich first, and then he cooked another one for himself, and then he sat down at the table with it and while he ate he showed us the list that he'd been writing, two columns, on one side the pros and on the other side the cons of whether he should go off with my dad on a fishing trip up in Canada over the Fourth of July. On the pro side—he loved to fish. It would be good for him. It would make him stronger, and in the long run that would make him more relaxed and then he would have more patience and he'd be better about looking after and being kind to Meems. On the con, he'd be going off without her. And he'd have to hire three shifts of full-time nurses. And he'd have to ask my mother for her help.

He turned to me and Frankie, and shaking the ketchup bottle to get it to start to pour, he asked us straight out what we thought he should do. Should he go or shouldn't he? Taking off for the Quetico in Canada for a couple weeks of canoeing and camping and fishing was something that he'd used to do all the time, just about every year, but now, with Meems in her disabled condition, he was feeling a little guilty just for having had the idea of it, and he couldn't decide what was the right thing, what was fair. Was it mean and selfish of him to even want to go, or would it be more destructive for everyone involved if he sacrificed himself and his own desires and stayed at home and did nothing but look after her? Grand was as troubled by this as I'd ever seen him be. He wanted to do whatever was the right thing to do, not just for Meems, but for himself, too. These were hard questions that he was asking us. They were too hard for me, because what did I know? I was only sixteen.

It was Frankie who suggested to Grand, her mouth full of egg and bread, "Ask her, why don't you?" What she meant was, why not go on and consult with Meems? Find out what her feelings were. Try to determine what she would have wanted him to do, if she could talk, if she could tell him. Which would have been beside the point, of course, because if she could talk then she'd be well and there wouldn't be this problem in the first place, but Frankie was able to ignore that fact and still she said to Grand, go ahead and ask Meems. We all three of us looked over at my grandmother then. She'd been sitting there in her wheelchair, watching us, listening, and it was hard to tell how much of what we were discussing she was able to understand. Maybe that new permanent smirk of hers did seem just then to be some sort of an encouragement, if that was what you were looking for in it. Her hands were moving in her lap. Frankie jumped up and knelt down on the floor next to her and peered up into her face, looking to find the answer to Grand's dilemma there. She held Meems's hands in her own and squeezed them until they were still.

"Look," she said, finally. "See that?" She turned to Grand to check whether he was seeing the same thing that she was seeing there in the twist and grimace of Meems's withered old apple-doll face. "She's smiling at you. I swear it. And that must mean she's happy. And that has to be an indication of the fact that in her heart what she wants for you is what you want for yourself and what that means is that you definitely should go."

Frankie stood up. She brushed her hands together and nodded, sure of herself now, completely convinced.

"I'd say you've got your answer right there, sir," she told Grand. "Plain as day, it seems to me."

Grand stood in front of Meems with his hands in his pockets, and he bent toward her, stiffly, from the waist, with his head tilted to one side and his great broad forehead knotted by the frowning tangle of his doubt and his hope and his curiosity and his avid concentration all at the same time, as he peered into his wife's eyes for a look from her that he could begin to understand and interpret as approval for what he thought he'd like for her to like for him to do.

It wasn't any cooler in the evenings than it had been in the middle of the day, but the drive back home from Grand's to Tyler Drive always felt more comfortable anyway, with the wind blowing over our damp skin and through our wet hair.

I asked Frankie if she'd teach me how to drive.

"Maybe I will someday," she said. "When the time's right."

I took that to be a promise, and that made me begin to feel genuinely happy in a way that wasn't usual for me. It was a thrill of potential that filled me, a recognition of a future and a possibility that had something to do with working all day and then going swimming and something to do with riding in a convertible and something to do with having an older girl who was dangerous in one way and as safe and dependable-seeming as a flesh and blood big sister might have been in another, and it wasn't only the suspense of wondering what might be about to happen to me next but also the unfamiliar expectation that something would, in fact, happen.

For once in my life I wasn't longing to turn out the lights and close the door and crawl under the covers and go to sleep. For once in my life I didn't really believe anymore that what I wanted was to die. It was like the anticipation that comes to you at the beginning of a movie when the lights go down and you settle in and open your eyes up wide and let the images come at you one after the other so that someone else's story, dazzling and huge, can unfold right there on the screen, right there before your very eyes.

It seemed just then that my own life was a story, too, and that the music that was playing on Frankie's radio, which she'd reached forward and turned up louder because it was a country song about dancing in the rain with your boyfriend that we both liked to sing along with—it was as if that song were a background soundtrack to what had become the amazing adventure of May Caldwell, a story that I was only just beginning to be able to open my eyes to, that I was only just starting to grow into, that was only at that moment turning out to make some sense and seem entertaining even to me and even as it continued to evolve.

We rounded the corner and pulled up in front of our house just at the moment that Paul Gerald came out the front door and started walking down the driveway to his car, which was parked against the curb. He was digging in his pockets for his keys. He looked up and saw us, and he squinted and waved, and we waved back. Then he got into his car and he started it up and he pulled away.

"What's he doing here?" Frankie asked.

I shrugged. "I don't know. Business, I guess."

"Does he come here a lot?"

The fact was, I told her, no, he didn't. But sometimes he had some papers that he needed signed. Or an order that he'd been asked to drop off. Frankie pursed her lips thoughtfully and watched his taillights brighten as he braked and stopped at the corner and waited for another car to pass.

"What?" I asked her.

She put up her hand and shook her head to hush me. I thought she was still listening to that song on the radio and maybe she was going to wait to hear the end of it or something, so I started to get out of the car to go inside, but just as I opened the door Frankie took her foot off the brake and she let the car roll forward for a few feet, just long enough to give me a chance to pull myself back in and sit back down and close the door, and then she pulled away from the curb and as Paul Gerald's car turned the corner, Frankie picked up speed and took off after him.

"What are you doing?" I asked her, but I already knew.

She grinned. "What does it look like I'm doing?"

I looked at her, then at Paul's car disappearing over the top of the hill ahead of us. "You're following him?"

Frankie just laughed. "Maybe he came by to see us, May," she said. "Maybe he was here looking for me." She turned up the volume on the radio even louder, and stepped on the gas.

It wasn't like trying to tail somebody in the movies. It wasn't like New York City, crammed with the distraction of a hundred yellow taxicabs or like San Francisco with a roller coaster track of steep hills. Linwood was smaller than that and flatter and more open in all kinds of ways, so hanging back and trying to stay inconspicuous in that big black Lincoln Continental was not an easy thing for Frankie to do. Paul's car slowed and turned, and he pulled into the parking lot of the Eagle grocery store. Frankie glided the Lincoln right past and on around behind, and then she turned and parked on the far side of the lot where she sat with her back to the entrance so it would look like she wasn't paying any attention but she could watch him go into the store in her rearview mirror. I had to turn the side mirror and then sit close to the door before I was able to keep an eye on his car.

"If he came to see us, then why did he leave right when we got there?" I asked Frankie.

"Because he doesn't want anyone to know."

"To know what?"

"That he likes us."

I thought about that for a moment. "You mean that he likes you," I said, finally.

She turned to me. She leaned toward me and reached past me and punched the button on the glove box, popping it open. She dug around for a minute and then pulled out a pack of cigarettes and opened it and took one out and put it in her mouth and lit it.

"Maybe," she said. "Or it could be he likes us both."

Paul came back out of the store with a bag of groceries cradled in one arm and his keys jangling and shining in his other hand. He only had one bag because he was single, not a whole cartful like my mother would get, piling up dinners for the week, and snacks and pop and beer to feed a whole family. He'd stopped to pick up some pitiful bachelor dinner for himself, I guessed, the bits and pieces of things that you see single men buying—a can of soup and a bottle of bourbon, a head of lettuce, a tomato, a wedge of cheese, and a small loaf of white bread. He shifted the bag to his other arm and dug down into his pocket and gave some coins to an old woman in rags who was standing there next to the newspaper stand.

Frankie clucked. "Well anyway, he's generous," she said. "That's good."

He was looking over toward where we were, and that made Frankie squeal and slump down in her seat, but I stayed put, because I figured that trying to hide would only make us look like we were guilty of something and anyway Frankie's car all by itself would have given us away if he'd seen it, although I couldn't exactly tell whether in fact he had.

He crossed over to his own car and put his sack of groceries in the back, and then he got into the front and sat there for a moment before he turned on the ignition and backed out of the lot. Frankie pulled out and started following him again, staying just far enough behind to hope to continue to go unseen. She had to run a red light at Twelfth Street to keep up with him, and an old woman honked at us and shook her fist.

"Fucking witch," Frankie said, but she hadn't seen the lady's face, all soft and wrinkled and brown as an old potato. Probably she was just concerned for our health. Probably she saw two reckless young girls in a car that was too big for them, and she didn't want us to kill ourselves, or anybody else either.

Paul's car was climbing up the hill at First Avenue and he stopped at the light before he turned right onto Crescent Drive. He pulled up to the curb and stopped.

"Don't look!" Frankie cried.

So we both went stiff in our seats and just stared straight ahead as we sailed on past, hoping he didn't notice, or that if he did see us he wouldn't recognize that it was us, that he'd think we were somebody else, somebody he didn't know and had never seen before. Frankie turned off into a driveway at the end of the block and stopped there. We both slumped down into our seats this time. We watched him get out of his car and pick up his sack of groceries again, plus a black leather briefcase, and lock his car doors and walk up to a white apartment building. He put his key in the lock in the front door and opened it and was swallowed up inside. A woman with a German shepherd on a leash came out of the house where we were parked and stopped in the yard and stared at us.

"Want to go inside and see him?" Frankie asked.

"No!" I blurted, shocked, imagining what that would be like, climbing the stairs, knocking on his door, and then he'd answer and he'd be looking at us with a question in his eyes, surprised and bewildered, asking what are you doing here?

Frankie was crushing her cigarette out in the ashtray.

"You sure?"

"Let's go home, Frankie," I said. "My mom'll be mad."

The shepherd had begun to bark at us, and he was straining on his leash, pulling the woman toward us across the lawn.

"You're a real baby sometimes, May," Frankie said. "You know?"

I didn't know what to say. She reached out and brushed my damp hair back from my face. "I'm just gonna have to teach you some things, that's all."

She revved the engine and waved at the woman and her dog and shifted into reverse and lurched backward into the street. As we passed the building again I saw Paul. He was standing at the window in the second-floor front apartment, looking out, so maybe he'd seen us following him after all. The sliding glass door opened, and he stepped out onto the deck and leaned against the railing. Then we'd rounded the corner, and we were out of his sight.

"I think he saw us, Frankie."

"We should have gone inside."

"What would we have said to him?"

"Hi. How are you. Nice place."

I shook my head. "He would have thought we were crazy."

Frankie laughed. "Well, hell, May. Maybe we are."

So we're rolling along through the shade under a canopy of big trees on a street that's just around the corner from Paul's apartment, and then Frankie steps on it, and the Lincoln lurches forward and coasts through a yellow light just at the moment that it's turning red, soaring right across traffic abruptly enough to cause a pickup truck to screech and skid and honk, and she lets out a loud whoop at the thrill of risking her life and mine, too. We're heading down the hill then, toward First Avenue, which ribbons into town, flying past the billboard where a chisel-faced policeman cradles an unconscious child—a young girl in a plaid shirtwaist dress with a white collar and white anklets and black strapped shoes—on the shelf of his bent arms, and beside him the red numbers that tally up how many people have been killed in car accidents on the roads in and around Linwood since the beginning of the year.

"Get me a cigarette, how about?" Frankie asks, so I open up the glove box, and I dig around, and I'm expecting to feel that cold black metal of the gun that I know is there but Frankie doesn't know I know it's there and, in fact, it isn't there anymore, just papers and gum wrappers and her pack of cigarettes. I take out two and I put them both in my mouth and I light them with the car's lighter, and I hand one to her and I keep the other one for myself.

We smoke for a while. There's no music on the radio, only talking.

Finally, I come out with it. I ask her, "Where is it, Frankie?"

The car slows, and she looks at me. "Where's what?"

I smile. I'm thinking maybe I'm one up on her for once.

"Oh, come on," I say. "You know what."

She shrugs, frowns, shakes her head.

"No," she says. "I don't know. What?"

And then I say, "Your gun."

"My gun?"

She's turned onto Brand and is heading toward Broadview Avenue. We're passing by the Mannings' house with its broad green front lawn, and there are some kids there in shorts and bare feet trying to play a game of badminton with tennis rackets and a volleyball net.

"I don't have a gun," Frankie says.

I laugh. "Well, you did have one. It was in here. I saw it myself."

She stops the car in the middle of the street. She turns to me. A rosy flush has begun to bloom in her cheeks, and I can see the pulse that pounds through the blue smudge of soft skin at her temple.

"What are you talking about?" she asks.

And then I don't know what to say. The silence wells up between us like night, like the emptiness in my hand that had been there when I'd held that gun.

A horn honked behind us. Frankie jerked the car forward, and we sailed in that silence all the way down Forest Street to Grove and across Vernon and onto Tyler Drive. She pulled up and stopped in front of my house. She turned to me again, and she was frowning. She reached out and touched one cool fingertip to my cheek.

"You look hot, May," she said. "Not coming down with something, are you?"

Then she opened her car door, and she slid out and left me sitting there by myself, and she didn't even look around to see if I was coming, she just walked right on up to the house and went in. I opened the glove box again, and I searched through it again, but there still was not a gun of any kind there. She'd hidden it someplace else then, I thought. Inside the house, probably. In her room. In the back of her closet maybe, in a shoebox or inside a boot or under her clothes, or in a jacket pocket or in her jewelry box behind a secret door, inside one of those secret drawers, with the pills and the diamonds and the red and blue stones, although I knew that this would have been impossible, because that box was way too small to hold anything that was close to the size of that gun.

I decided I was going to have to make a search through her room sometime, when she was out and nobody else was home. I'd shuffle through her things, just to get to know her a little bit better, maybe, just to see whatever I was going to find. I knew that this was something she would think to do herself. Had probably already done to my own room and my parents' too, in fact. And the truth is I was gratified to find that I was actually beginning to think in a way that was reminding me of her.

Chapter Seven

I SAW A HOUSE BURN ONCE. MY FATHER took me downtown with him to watch it; it was an old house in a neighborhood that was being developed with apartment buildings, and they were going to tear it down, but then they decided to burn it instead to give the fire department something to do. I'd never even begun to guess at what was going to be the greed and the strength and the sincerely wild ferocity of the kind of fire that burns when a whole structure is consumed. My father didn't prepare me for it, and maybe that was because it took him by surprise, too. The first flames we saw weren't much more than just a soft glow against the downstairs window glass, but then their colors deepened and they became as orange as a bright sunset, but it wasn't a mere reflection, it was a real gathering of flame that was shining at us from the inside out. And then the fire started to thrash out over the front porch boards and to lap up against the eaves. Flames crackled through the house's pretty gingerbread trim, they licked up and down the trellises and over the scalloped wood siding, the porch posts and the railings and the roof's thick shake shingles and the windows' painted frames and the carved, solid oak doors. An ember wafted off and caught in a treetop; it was snagged there like a loose balloon, and it burned the whole ball of branches, like some tremendous torch. Then a smoke tornado, a furious black snake of wind and fire, was whipped up by the heat, and it spun off toward the hoses, throwing off its big embers that sizzled in the water and, finally, died.

It was magnificent.

I can picture the whole whorl of Linwood's neighborhoods, all of them burning that way, all of them in flames, just like that, all of them going down, house by house and tree by tree, lamppost by lamppost and street by street. Not just that one old house all by itself, but altogether the entire town. The whole state, for that matter. Or even the whole world, flaming up completely, like one big blast furnace, an absolute inferno that would be burning out of anyone's frantic attempts at control.

And I can see the familiar figure of Paul Gerald rising upward inside those flames. Like the Viennese devil puppet, he'd be ugly and he'd be beautiful, both at the same time—ash-faced, black-haired, bare-skinned, with his legs hanging and his arms outspread. Like an ember, he would be buried in my mind this way, and in my dreams for years his image would continue to burn and seethe and glow.

June 2

Dear Vivienne,

I thought I would drop a few words to say hi to everyone. How are you all doing? I hope you are doing fine. I'm okay so far. All things considered that is.

I guess you must be wondering why I haven't been writing to you lately, but everything's been pretty hectic in my life lately and I just haven't had the time to sit down and put pen to paper. From now on I promise I'm going to write to you every month. I think that's the least I can do, don't you? Since after all you are the best sponsor that anybody ever had. You know how much I appreciate the gifts you have sent me over all the years. THANKS A BUNCH!

Right now I'm lots better than I was you'll be glad to hear. As it is my arm is broken in a couple of places, but that's about it. The doctor's saying I'm young and strong so before I know it I'll be as good as new again. If it wouldn't have been for my boyfriend's help I probably would have been killed for sure. Thank God for Creighton. He just about killed my uncle Elgin that pig.

Well I'm getting tired again now so I'll get some rest and let you go for now. Take care and be well. Until next time when I write I'm still—
Yours truly,
Frankie Crane

THAT SUMMER WHEN FRANKIE WAS IN LINWOOD, MY PARENTS HAD BEEN married to each other for twenty years. It was an amazing thing to me then, that the simple chance of their happening to have met was what had come together out of nowhere to make me. That with a different pair of parents, I would have been somebody else. Maybe I'd have been tall and thin, a willow with long dark hair, like Frankie's. Or wide-hipped and cheerful, with rosy cheeks and round calves and heavy breasts. Or maybe I'd have been a boy. Or maybe I wouldn't ever have been born into this world at all.

My mother liked to tell the story about how before she met my father, she'd been in love with and then had had her heart broken by a boy in her high school named David Welch. He'd been tall and thin and blond. A dreamboat, she said, with deep green eyes and straight shiny hair and hands big enough to palm a basketball. He and my mother had been the one couple in their senior class that everybody was sure was going to get married first, but then David Welch went away on a basketball scholarship to a college in Colorado, and my mother stayed in Iowa, and when he came back home at Thanksgiving, instead of making a reality the romantic reunion that she'd been dreaming up and looking forward to, he dumped her. He wanted his freedom, he said. He needed a chance to flex his muscles and test his wings. They'd been parked in his car at the dead end of a lane that forked off Old Highway 18 past Grand Haden's house and then stopped there just short of the creek. She'd gazed out at the frozen cornfield and listened as he explained that he'd thought about it long and hard, and he'd come to the serious conclusion that it would be best for them both to make some new friends and do some new things before they decided, finally, to settle down in Linwood, where they already knew everybody worth knowing, where they'd already done everything worth doing, where they'd both been living for all their whole short lives. He wanted to get some experience before he settled down, he told her, without blinking, without smiling even, she said. And then once he'd been some places and done some things, maybe he'd want to come back to her, and maybe he'd be happier for it by that time, too. He didn't want to tie her down, he said. But if she decided that she wanted to wait for him, that would be all right. Or if she didn't, he'd understand. Either way, he told her, it was up to her.

David Welch had pretensions, my mother said. He had big plans. And he sure did know how to kiss a girl, too, in just the right way to make her feel warm and short of breath. It was almost as hard for me to imagine this—my mother as a young girl flushed and panting in some strange blond boy's long sinewy arms, fogging up the ice-crazed windows with the exhalations of her own hot breath—as it was to picture her in bed as an older woman, huffing and puffing and bearing up beneath the straining, determined weight of my dad.

What happened was, David Welch went off to see the world, and he left my mother behind. He joined the army and went to war, then came back to Linwood again five years later and married Carla Fassler. Some big world, my mother said. Carla Fassler had been just as much of a local girl as Vivienne Haden was, but she was worse because she'd been wild, besides, and not even a little bit respectable, with her head of bleached white hair and an admittedly shapely body that had been handled and mishandled both, by just about every boy worth looking at in the whole high school.

My mother went to a reunion not quite ten years after that, and she saw David Welch again for herself there, and she was happy to notice that he'd ruined his knees and put on weight and was even beginning to get a little bit bald. By then he and Carla Fassler had already been divorced for more years than they'd been married. Lucky for my mother, she reasoned, or she'd most likely have been a divorcée herself.

She could smile and be superior about it all well enough that summer, with Frankie and me all ears, but while it was happening to her, my mother hadn't been quite so philosophical or so smug. Her heart had been broken, all right, and she'd pined about it through the rest of that cold fall and then the whole frozen winter and on into the spring. To distract herself she'd thrown herself into her studies at school, taking only the hardest courses she could find. She liked to brag to me about how smart she'd been during that one year of college, because she really had applied herself for once and had been given the highest grades in return.

"My teachers all thought I was a grind. A real intellectual. Can you believe that?" she laughed. "Me?"

And it was hard to fathom, because my mother didn't look smart, and to my mind she didn't act particularly smart either. She just looked like everybody else, I thought. All the other mothers were the same as she was, worried about their hairdos and their children and their husbands and their houses and their gardens and their clothes. And she just acted like herself.

But she'd hardly ever gone out at all that whole lonely year, she told us, and lucky for her it was too cold that winter to do much of anything anyway, and there was no place to go, be-

sides. She'd just stayed tucked in snug in her dorm room, reading and studying and writing papers and preparing for tests.
Eating popcorn and drinking lots of coffee and letting her short
hair grow out long. She took classes in religion and philosophy
and literature, not a bit of which she could remember anymore
all those years later, except maybe an odd word for the Sunday
crossword puzzle every now and then. That had always been her
biggest shortcoming, she told us, that she had no retention. A
brain like a sieve, she said. All that high-mindedness went in her
one ear and then it spilled right out of the other. And when it
was gone, it was gone for good.

It was my father, good old plain and simple Calvin Caldwell,
large, friendly as a dog, harmless and kind, who'd had what it
took, finally, to snap my mother back to herself and bring her
around again to her truer, more boisterous and outgoing self.
He was a couple of years older than she was, but he was no
college kid like that dreamboat David Welch. Cal Caldwell had
been a working boy, with a job in a landscaping business where
he worked putting in gardens and laying sod and planting trees
and building retaining walls out of brick and limestone and
wooden railroad ties. He'd had a room in an old farmhouse that
he'd been sharing with a bunch of his friends. One night they
threw a party out there, and one of my mother's old high school
pals, back in town for the summer vacation, asked her if she
wanted to go, and she went, hoping, fearing, that maybe she'd
bump into David Welch again there, not knowing exactly where
he'd gone, that he was thousands of miles away by then, fighting his way through a booby-trapped jungle in some strange
place on the other side of the world. So she didn't run into

David, but she did meet my dad. He was sitting on the back porch when she came outside for a breath of fresh air.

It was late and dark by then, and she couldn't see him very well, and, she said, that was what she liked about him best, at first. That he was only a sound, just a stream of words, a voice without a body, as impersonal and therefore safe as the paragraphs on the pages of the books that she'd been burying her nose in all through that year.

There had been the burning tip of his cigarette, a spark that moved with his hands as he talked, and the muddy soles of his big work boots, and his smell—of moss and dirt and Old Spice, which he still wore all those years later. There had been his outline—the huge ponderous shape of him, massive and shadowy, like a secret, there in the dark. It had been impossible for my mother to tell in any clear way what he looked like, whether he was handsome, whether he might have been another dangerous dreamboat, or not. They'd both been drinking, passing a green glass bottle of red wine back and forth between them. After a while, he leaned over, and he kissed her, and she kissed him back. Just like that. Then my mother's girlfriend called out that she was leaving, and my mother stood up and said goodbye, and she went home without ever having seen Calvin's face or having heard his name or having had any idea at all who in the world he might have been, in case she'd wanted to find a way to look him up or at least inconspicuously bump into him again.

At first she'd consoled herself by assuming that he must have been someone ugly and unwanted, that there'd been something awful and offputting about him—a bad complexion or a big nose or crooked teeth and an unattractive smile. Then she'd started to fret in the opposite direction, supposing that maybe he was really handsome, after all, when all she needed was another dreamboat, somebody who was going to take one look at her and decide she was the one who was disappointing, too plain and too short and too stocky for his more glamorous taste. The best thing for her to do then, she decided, was to just forget all about this man altogether. In one ear and out the other. No connections, no retention. Gone for good. A one-night summer fling.

She'd been at the store, working, when he came in. She'd heard his voice, and she'd recognized it right away as the same one in that night in the dark out on the farmhouse porch, and she went to peek, and sure enough, there he was, Cal Caldwell in the flesh, sitting in a chair outside her father's office, filling out an application for a job on the truck.

My mother liked to say that Dad had no idea of what he was getting into, that he hadn't known that Grand Haden was her father or that she'd been the girl he'd kissed out on the back porch of his house in the dark that summer night.

Later, Grand couldn't talk enough about the new young man he'd hired, that fellow Calvin Caldwell, who was such a hard worker, a kid who wasn't expecting the world to be delivered to him on a silver platter like just about everybody else in Linwood seemed to believe they somehow deserved just by virtue of the fact that they'd been born and brought up there. But Cal wasn't like that. He was different. Better. Cal Caldwell was dedicated and reliable and mature, said Grand.

It took her more than a week, but my mother finally gave in

and showed herself to him. She screwed up her nerve and let him have a look at her, presenting herself but keeping quiet because she didn't want to give away the secret of who she was too soon. Let him get used to the sight of her first, she thought. In case he was picky and he decided he didn't like what he saw. He'd guess she must be playing her part as the boss's daughter, superior and aloof, nodding at him but never saying anything, steering clear of all the boys in the stockroom, including her younger brother Brodie, and his friend Paul Gerald who would have been beneath her, too.

My father thought of her distance as a personal challenge to himself and what he recognized were his most personable and proven charms, and he decided to take her up on it. One day he was waiting for her, leaning back with his feet crossed and his arms folded, against the back fender of her car. They talked, he told a joke, she smiled, he laughed, and then, finally, he asked her was she hungry and did she want to go out? It was over hamburgers and milkshakes at the Flame that she said enough words to him all at once for him to recognize her voice and understand who she was, and he still liked her anyway, and it all turned out even better than she'd hoped.

He told the story differently. Listening to his side of it, you got the idea that he knew who my mother was all along. That he'd seen her earlier in the evening that first night, inside the house, where there was still some kind of light. That she'd been pale and small and fine-looking, with long bushy blond hair that had made her look like a scatterbrain, but then he'd been pleasantly surprised when she came outside and he found that she was of so much seriousness, talking intently about religion and philosophy and what was real and what was not and how would you be able to tell the difference between being awake and dreaming if something terrible happened and you were all of a sudden made blind? He'd gone outside to the porch for a smoke, and he'd seen her come out sometime after him, and he'd just wanted to get to know her better, so he struck up a conversation and he started to like her and then he kissed her. He might have been sitting in the shadows, dark and massive and unknowable in an irresistible and tantalizing way, but she wasn't, not quite, and he could see her, all right, her face as pale and white as the moon bobbing in the dark. And that was why he went to the store for that job. It wasn't that he didn't like the landscaping business, or that he was dying to drive a furniture truck instead. It was that after that night he'd kept on thinking about her, and he hadn't been able to shake off his impression of her, and he'd only wanted to get to know her better, just to see whether she was someone who was going to hold up over time, and so he'd offered his services to my grandfather down at the store.

My mother never did believe his side of the story. It wasn't in her interest to for one thing. She never did like his version of what had happened nearly as much as she liked her own.

Then, that summer when Frankie was in Linwood living in our house with us, after having been married to each other for the length of twenty years, my mother and father were just about the only couple among all their friends that they knew of in town who were still together with the original partner that they'd started out with, and everybody was always looking to them, Cal and Viv Caldwell, pointing to them and holding them up as the perfect pair, still in love with each other after so many years. Look at the Caldwells, their friends would say. They're happy, aren't they? Even after so much time together? And they even had to work with each other every day, besides. How do you do it? they wanted to know. The women asked my mother this question as if they believed that there was some secret that my parents were keeping and would maybe share if only they could be persuaded to be generous enough to do it.

MY MOTHER CAME HOME AFTER ONE OF HER PROLONGED FRIDAY AFTERNOON lunches with her girlfriends—vodka martinis and crabmeat sandwiches down at the Pickwick Bar—bristling with the grand idea that she and my father were going to throw an extravagant bash, an anniversary celebration, out at Grand Haden's house. It would be just like old times, she said. They'd invite everyone who was anyone in Linwood, and it would be a party to end all parties, a glorious kickoff gala for the summer. It might even be just what Meems needed to bring her back again to herself.

And how was my father going to talk her out of it? What could he have found to say? It was as if she were testing him somehow. What about the expense? he asked. And why do we have to? he wanted to know.

"I love you, Viv," he told her, "can't that be enough?"

But no, in my mother's martini-bleared eyes, it couldn't. Not nearly. Not even close. And in the end, just to keep the peace, he had to say yes, finally, or it would have come out looking as if his reluctance only meant that her suspicions had been confirmed and he maybe didn't love her very much, or at least not as much as he should, after all.

While my mother was fretting over the guest list and the band and the invitations and the decorations and the food, for me and Frankie the big question was, what to wear? Frankie didn't have a dress and she didn't have any money to buy one with, and I only had the red velvet jumper that I'd worn at Christmas when what I needed was something summery and chic. We went to Meems's closet after work.

Brodie was outside on a ladder, stringing twinkle lights up in the trees. Grand was on the back porch, mucking around with his clay. Meems was in her room, staring at the TV.

Frankie's body was long-waisted and slim. She wore silky pink underpants and a lacy white bra. She caught me looking at her in the mirror, and she smiled. She turned to the side, and pressed her hands against her flat belly. I let my jeans puddle on the floor at my feet. I was doing my best to hide myself from her—hoping she wasn't going to mind my cotton underpants and my thick-strapped padded bra.

We tried on a pile of Meems's old dresses. Fluffy chiffons and square-shouldered silks. A gold-threaded black evening gown, a lilac shift, a high-collared sleeveless suede blouse and long straight skirt.

Frankie settled finally on a short dark blue dress—several inches shorter on her than it had ever been on Meems—with spaghetti straps and a big red satin bow that nestled in the curve at the small of her back. Later my mother went out and bought her a pair of red high heels to go with the dress, and a red beaded necklace and a bracelet and a pair of dangly silver earrings.

And my dress was a long white sheath, strapless, with silver threads and a deep slit that ran up one side and ended with a crushed satin blossom near the middle of my thigh. We found some silver shoes, too, and on the night of the party, Frankie brushed and curled my hair.

MY PARENTS STOOD TOGETHER IN MY GRANDFATHER'S LIVING ROOM, GREETING their guests. My mother was in a pinkish gown that was soft and airy, all puffed out around her body like a cloud of sticky cotton candy. My dad had on a tuxedo with a peacock blue cummerbund and bow tie. His large hand was reaching out to grasp hers, and she was holding on to him hard, as if she didn't want to lose him or she was afraid that she might be going to faint. She tottered awkwardly on the heels of her shoes because she wasn't used to wearing them so high.

It was so romantic, everyone said later, sipping their champagne, when my parents turned to each other and kissed—she on tiptoe, he bending over to meet her. Frankie had taken a place just in front of Brodie, and anyone who didn't know better would have thought that she was one of the family. Except that everyone did know better. They were curious about Frankie and what she was doing there with us. Everybody wanted to meet her.

Brodie was wearing a tuxedo, too, and his hair had been trimmed short, almost to the scalp. The scar across his forehead gleamed in the bright lights that my mother had set up so that one of her friend's sons could take pictures of the party. Meems was right there with us, with her wheelchair rolled up to one side of my mother, and she moved her fingers and nodded her head, as if she understood what was going on, and Grand was standing next to her, as tall and sturdy as a big tree, with one hand on her shoulder. He looked uncomfortable, because people kept coming up and trying to talk to him, asking him how he was, and how was Meems, as if they couldn't take a look at her and see for themselves that she was just fine in one way and as bad as ever in another, both at the same time. That nothing had changed, and she was still the same, not getting any better, but at least she wasn't getting any worse. Those people were only trying to be nice, and Grand should have been gracious and tried to understand that their intentions, at least, were good. They were only offering him their sympathy, and that was kind of them, but of course it was just exactly what he hated more than anything else anybody could have done.

This was the night when Paul Gerald and I danced.

IT WASN'T A SURPRISE TO ME THAT AFTER A WHILE, GRAND DISAPPEARED. HE WAS standing there behind Meems's chair one minute and then when I looked again, he was gone. I found him alone in his study. He was sitting at his desk, looking at a map.

I looked over his shoulder. It was a map of Minnesota, and he'd marked a route across the state, northward up to the town of Ely near the top, with a yellow highlighter pen. The green splotch of Quetico Park over the border in Canada was roadless and splattered with small blue lakes. Grand and my dad were going to rent a canoe and spend two weeks alone in the wilderness, fishing, cooking over campfires, sleeping in tents. Grand had made up a list of provisions, too, what little of absolute necessity that they could carry with them on their backs and in their canoe.

In the dim lamplight I could squint and blur my vision and guess at what my grandfather must have looked like when he was a young man—his strong jaw and the curve of his ears. His blade-nicked fingers rubbed his chin.

"You hiding back here, Dad?"

We both looked up at the same time to see that my mother was standing in the doorway. She blustered in, scolding Grand and trying to urge him up out of his chair and out into the party again.

"Do you want me to bring you a drink?" she asked.

"No, I don't."

"Some food?"

"No."

"You have to eat something."

"I will. Later."

"Let me get you a plate."

"I don't want anything now."

"May, go get your grandfather his dinner."

"May, stay where you are."

"Dad, you don't have to come out. You can eat it back here if that's what you want to do."

"What I want to do is not eat, Vivienne."

"But we have all that food."

"I'll get some later."

"I don't see why you can't go out there and be with your friends for a while."

"I can't do it, Vivienne, because I don't want to."

"It might cheer you up."

"Why do you think I need cheering up?"

"Because you're off here by yourself locked up like an old hermit."

He looked up at her, his face calm, smooth as stone.

"This is still my house, Vivienne," he said. "And I would like to be able to do what I want to do when I'm in it. I don't feel like talking to my friends, if that's all right with you. I'm not hungry. And I already have a drink. Okay?"

"But what about Mother?"

"What about her?"

"Maybe she needs you."

"She doesn't need me."

"How do you know that?"

He stood up then. The map slid to the floor. His fists were curled at his sides.

"What exactly do you think your mother wants to do, Vivienne? Dance? Tell some jokes? The woman is paralyzed. She's in a wheelchair. She can't move. She can't talk. I'm not even sure, half the time, whether she even knows who she is. Or who I am, for that matter."

The anger was raw in his face, his jaw was hard, his hands clenched.

This was what she did to us: my mother moved through our family like a small storm, rustling up feelings, blowing through and past and around us, making us say things we never meant to say and do things we never meant to do.

She studied him for a moment. She knew better than to try and press him any further just then. She shook her head, turned on her heel, and left. Grand looked over at me, his eyes steady, and then he picked up his map again, ignoring me, as if I hadn't heard anything, as if I weren't there. Even in Meems's beautiful silvery dress, I had become invisible; as usual, I was a mist.

I drifted outside to try and find Frankie, knowing that if anybody could do it, she was the only one who would know what to do to snap me back to myself and make me feel real again.

There was Brodie lying back in one of the redwood lounge chairs by the pool. He was cradling a brown bottle between his hands against his chest.

"May," he said. He liked to say my name.

"What are you drinking, Brodie?" I asked him. He thought about it for a moment, then handed the bottle to me. "Beer," he said. I sat down at the end of the chaise near his feet and sipped at it. I was considering what it would be like to climb up onto the high dive and jump off into the pool. To make myself into a jackknife; to take a swan dive down.

At the edge of the trees there was the red glow from a cigarette. And a shadow, a tangled moving shape that separated and broke into two and became Frankie and somebody else. A boy. Not a party guest, apparently, he was wearing a brown jacket and a white T-shirt and ragged blue jeans.

She went up on tiptoe and kissed him on the cheek. He

looked down at her and touched her face with his fingertips, and then he flicked the cigarette off toward me. It sailed into the pool, where it hissed and died.

Frankie pushed him away. He backed off a few steps, and then stopped. He said something to her. She was tugging at the hem of her dress and trying to straighten the red bow at her back. She gestured him away, waving her hand for him to go. He shook his head, looked up at the twinkle lights in the trees, and then, with his shoulders shrugged and his hands shoved down into his pockets, he turned again, and he walked off toward the woods.

Brodie was sitting up. He put his hand on my shoulder and hefted himself to his feet.

"Frankie," he said, as she approached us, her feet moving over the damp grass, leaving a trail behind her, slick and shimmery.

She reached up and tousled Brodie's blond hair.

"Hiya, Brodie," she said. She turned to me and grinned. "Some party, isn't it, May?"

Brodie grinned. "Some party."

"Who was that guy, Frankie?" I asked her.

She shrugged. "Who was what guy?"

Her face was pale, her lipstick rubbed off. She was holding Brodie's hand, fiddling with his knuckles while he gazed up into the twinkle lights in the umbrella of tree branches arching overhead.

"That guy you were talking to. Him." But by then he wasn't there anymore; he was gone.

Frankie took the beer bottle from me, put her head back, and drained it. Then she wiped her mouth with the back of her hand and grinned.

"Maybe you're seeing things, May. Maybe you've had just a little tiny bit too much of this to drink."

She tugged at Brodie's hand, and he looked down at her and smiled. "Frankie," he said again.

The band was playing on a platform near the pool. They picked up their pace, tumbling off into a boisterous dance song. Old man Bell lunged into a jitterbug with his daughter-in-law. Steve and Patty Raymond started to toss each other back and forth. Frankie pulled Brodie out of the shadows and onto the pool deck. She shimmied toward him, then bucked away. He stood with his hands hanging at his sides and his knees bending and locking and his head bobbing up and down while Frankie lurched and swayed around him, her hair flying and her mouth open and her head flung back and her face thrown open to the sky. They were dancing.

And there was Paul Gerald watching. He leaned against a tree off to one side, behind the band, with one hand in his pocket and the other holding a drink. He'd combed his hair back against his head. He was wearing a light, loose-fitting summer suit, a white shirt, a bright green and blue tie, shiny brown shoes. He took a sip of his drink and then he looked up, and he saw me watching him, and he smiled.

"You like to dance, May?" he asked.

"No," I told him. "Not much."

"Too bad," he said.

And I was thinking, had he just asked me to dance with him? Was that what that was? And I'd said no?

"Well . . ." I began, intending to move away from him, to glide off gracefully, as if I'd known all along what I was doing, moving through the crowd, mingling, as my mother put it, but then there was a pause in the music, and a moment of silence, while Frankie fanned herself with both hands and Brodie mopped at his face with his sleeve. And then when the band began to play again, Paul was reaching for me, he took my hand and pulled me toward him, and I could feel the warmth of his breath in my hair and the curl of his fist against my back, and he was stepping into me and moving me to one side, first, and then the other and then back again. His chin rested against the top of my head. He pulled back to look at me and smile. I could see my parents dancing past his shoulder, my mother pressed against my father, her cheek against his chest and her eyes closed, and then there was lightning and a sudden crash of thunder, and it started to rain.

All the lights were knocked out as the wind whipped through the trees and brought down some power lines. My mother's paper lanterns were shredded, the branches of the trees were thrashing like angry old women, and the rain came pounding down so fast and hard that everybody just had time to scurry inside. The guests all gathered in Grand's living room, with flashlights and candles. It was a ghostly scene, one that everybody liked to talk about and tell about for a long time afterward.

I was thinking about how that boy who had been talking to Frankie was all by himself out there in the woods, slogging his way back into Linwood to wherever it was he knew to go. He might have made it to the road and put his thumb out for a ride, but who would stop for him? He could have taken cover in a culvert. Or maybe under the bridge at the creek.

I went to the window and looked out, and in a lightning flash I could see that Brodie hadn't come in. He was still outside, all by himself, poised at the end of the high board, bobbing and bouncing on his toes, with his head thrown back and his jacket flapping and his arms outstretched to embrace the full fury of the storm.

MEEMS WAS AT THE BACK OF THE HOUSE, ALONE, IN HER BED, IN THE DARK, HER eyes wide with surprise and fear because of all the racket from the storm. She was staring at the ceiling and flinching at each smash of thunder and every lightning strike.

I sat there with her, and I held her hand until she started to calm down. She pressed her fingers against mine. She closed her eyes. Her breathing deepened and slowed. Her face relaxed so that the smirk was softened, almost gone. I took a pack of matches from the basket, and I lit one and thought about burning myself. I thought I knew then what it would feel like to be dead: that it would be something of a relief. Just like what Paul Gerald said he felt when his wife walked out on him—it would seem like a release. I'd be floating off like a lost balloon, wafting, bobbing. Maybe I'd come back to Linwood if I could, and I'd hover like a blessing over Grand Haden and Brodie and Meems. I'd make it my business to watch over them, like the cherubs in Meems's wallpaper. I'd be a guardian. I'd be something like my old self again, in fact, invisible and accounting for nothing, a ghost that wandered her way through that big old house, something drifting in the hallways, a haze that hovered over the floors like a smoke, that settled on the window panes, that rose like heat and gathered in the highest corners of the rooms. I could have been like Meems, and Brodie, too—I could have been there but not there. I could have been elsewhere.

But even then I realized that the truth was if I really were dead I wouldn't be an angel or a ghost. I'd just be gone, I'd be out of myself, I'd splinter off, like the black circle that closed up at the end of Meems's movie. Like the TV turned off, down to the last blip, the white dot that comes before the nothing. Like an airplane in the sky, slicing toward the blue through a wedding cake stack of white clouds. Like a car on a straight road, like a black Lincoln Continental slipping out of sight at the far curved horizon, soaring off into nothingness, becoming nobody, turning into emptiness, vanished, merely gone.

And that was when it came to me, a faint flickering of memory, like the quick silent flash of lightning, still far away, that darts out just at the start of a storm.

There had been another party, earlier, when I was still small. I had come along with my parents. I rode in the back seat of my father's car, looking out the window at the trees. And Brodie was there, too, with April Delaney and Paul Gerald and all their other friends.

There had been a band playing outside on the grass. Brodie had danced with April, and so had Paul. My mother had danced with my dad. There had been champagne in tall glasses served from silver trays. There had been candles floating on the surface of the water in the pool. There had been white twinkle lights in the trees. Cars were parked in the driveway and in rows across the front lawn. I'd moved among the grownups in my best party dress—dotted swiss with a crisp petticoat that scratched at my legs underneath. And my best party shoes—black patent leather with a strap on top and one pearl button on the side. And thin white socks with a delicate lace trim.

There had been a lot of people, and they were all dancing and drinking and talking and laughing. My mother tucked me in bed in Meems's bedroom at the back of the house. I remember the cabbage roses. I remember the cherubs. And the soft yellow satin sheets. I woke up later, forgetful, not sure of where I was. I wandered through the house, looking for my mother, but she wasn't there. The living room was littered with half-empty glasses and full ashtrays and crumpled napkins and plates smeared with the remains of food.

I went through the whole house, but there was no one home. I looked out the window, and there was Brodie, with Paul and April, outside on the front lawn. He and Paul were arguing. Paul backed away from Brodie, but Brodie followed him. April reached for Brodie's arm, but he shook her off. I started to open the window; I wanted to call out to them, but then Paul had turned to Brodie and Brodie was bringing his fist back. He swung and hit Paul square on the jaw, so hard that Paul's head snapped back and he stumbled, then sagged to his knees. There was April's outraged cry. And the swirl of her sky blue skirt. And the storm of her waved red hair.

Paul stood up. He smoothed his hand over his hair. He brushed off the knees of his pants. He straightened the cuffs of his shirtsleeves, and then he turned, and he walked away.

Chapter Eight

"I DO IT," FRANKIE SAID, "BECAUSE I CAN."

She pulled a stolen lipstick out of her pocket and handed it to me. Rosy Satin Pink, it wasn't Frankie's color—she preferred the deeper reds for the way that they would make her mouth shine in bright contrast to her creamy complexion and waves of dark hair. For Frankie, the business of shoplifting was just as simple as she said it was. The girl was a thief, and she'd been helping herself to whatever she felt she was in need of for all her life.

"If I don't help myself," she reasoned, "then just who do you suppose will?"

I didn't have an answer for that at the time. Myself, maybe, I thought. I might have helped Frankie, if I'd known how. My mother had already, in a way. But that was about as much as I could come up with off the top of my head. Which made Frankie smile and nod with the satisfaction of having shown me that she'd made her point, and that her point was right.

And then she'd taken it further and turned her own logic and philosophy around and aimed it back at me in the form of some warm and friendly, big-sisterly advice.

"You have to help yourself, May," she said, but she didn't mean it in the same way that my mother did when she mentioned self-help.

What my mother was talking about was self-reliance. She meant shouldering your own personal responsibility for your own personal life. What Frankie was talking about was, simply, theft.

"It's their own fault," Frankie said, meaning the myopic clerks and the preoccupied cashiers. The stupid women with their plastic nametags and flowered dresses and thick-lensed glasses hanging around their necks on silver chains and bobbing against the broad shelves of their breasts. The foolish men, swaggering the aisles in their heavy shoes, flirting with Frankie while I pocketed a plastic lighter and a pack of peppermint gum.

"They make it too easy for us," Frankie said. "So easy it's almost not any fun."

I was the best at it, because I already had the built-in advantage of being invisible. Frankie was the distraction, and I became the thief. We made such a superior team, Frankie said, because I was a natural. If those clerks all unquestioningly trusted Frankie—because she had a good smile and a friendly face and a way of opening up a conversation that was just about impossible for anybody to ignore—they looked right through me, or if they did see me, they forgot about me again the minute that I'd passed out of immediate view. I moved along in front of Frankie as if I was maybe not myself at all, but only Frankie's faintest shadow, cast forward just ahead of her across the floor. A glimpse, a smudge that Frankie's actual dynamic presence was quick to erase. I became Frankie's second self, a fainter version of the grinning and outgoing girl that she could be. We weren't sisters, we didn't even look at all alike, but we were a pair, in our way, nevertheless. Peas in a pod, as my mother had begun already by that time to say. We two girls seemed to be two of a kind.

Except that Frankie was prettier than me. There was never any quarrel, everyone was in agreement about the fact of that. Maybe it was only that she was older and more grown into herself than I was then, but I never minded it anyway. Isn't there an unspoken rule that says that between two girlfriends one will be pretty and the other one will be plain? Frankie had dark hair that curled at her temples and bright eyes with heavy lashes and milky skin on a heart-shaped face that might have been seen as sharp-featured if you were looking at it in the wrong light—her cheeks too stark and her chin too small and her lips drawn together too thin. She could look mean and parched if she wasn't careful, and there was also a hint of coldness that rose in her eyes sometimes, an icy flash, a glimpse of razor blade that might have been expected to come over her more often and more powerfully as she aged and hardened with time, if she ever got that far.

Frankie was prettier, and I was plainer, and all of us said so and knew so, even Paul Gerald. He told me as much himself, after things had gone so far that he could say such things, but it didn't hurt my feelings the way it might have, because I could see that he was trying to turn his own words around backward to make them come out sounding like he was not criticizing me, but might be paying me a kind of a compliment instead. Backhanded or not.

"Frankie may be better-looking than you are," he said. "She's got flair. But you, May, you've got depth."

THAT SUMMER, WHEN WE WEREN'T SWIMMING AND SUNNING OURSELVES OUT ON the deck at Grand's pool or working on the files in the basement of the furniture store, Frankie and I roamed through Linwood's shops together, on the lookout for liftable loot. We were petty criminals, Frankie liked to say. Two teens with ten sticky fingers each—quick hands and fleeter feet—we dedicated ourselves to the swift sneaky pleasures that came to us by way of misdemeanor.

"Doesn't hurt anybody," Frankie claimed, "but it sure does make a girl feel good."

Well, it didn't hurt anybody much. We weren't stealing national treasures, after all. Nothing that we brought home was ever of any value, not even to us. The feeling good part was what came with the quick flush, the hot rush of blood brought on by a pounding fear, the quickened pulse and the shortened breath when we slipped out the door again, our purses or our pockets filled with our mostly worthless plunder.

The thrill of it was irresistible. I could no more have gone into a store without taking something that summer than I could have passed by one of Meems's blooming rosebushes without pausing for a whiff. I was drawn, helplessly and hopelessly. It felt to me as if the objects that were out there on display on the shelves in the aisles of Linwood's shops took on a life of their own. I couldn't have explained it, then. It was wordless, like magic; in my presence, things just seemed to come somehow alive. They'd throb, with light. There'd be a humming sound going on inside my head, too. An object would catch my eye, and it would pull me in, like a magnet. A whirlpool. The drain at the bottom of the deep end.

A plastic coin purse, a piece of costume jewelry, a stick of eyeliner, a record or a paperback book, even a child's toy. These things beckoned to me—they glowed, and they made sounds, whistly whiny droning buzzing noises that drew my hand down toward them, wrapped my fingers around them, and then brought my closed fist back.

It was a magic that wore out fast, however. After I got the stuff back home, safe and sound, I'd inevitably be disappointed, shamed, to find that something essential about it had died. Like a firefly in a mason jar when the next morning you go to look and you see that the glow is gone and it's only the bare brown body of a dead bug. In my room, afterward, the goods I'd got always looked cheap and worthless to me. They were nothing that I'd ever wanted. Fingernail polish the wrong color. A pencil case plastic and scratched. A carved wooden box with a broken hinge.

But that wasn't the point, Frankie said. The point was in the taking. The point was in the act; the purpose was captured somewhere there inside the doing of the deed itself. She was sitting on the rug on the floor in my bedroom, with a stick of incense burning in an attempt to cover up the smell of her cigarette. She cradled a can of beer that she'd swiped from the kitchen refrigerator, counting on the fact that my father would have lost track of how many of them he'd already had for himself.

"It's just like sex, May," Frankie explained. "You don't do it to be done with it, you do it to be doing it, and then when you're done with it, after a while, you're all hot and bothered and ready to do it all over again."

BUT WHAT DID I KNOW, THEN, OF SEX? JUST THIS: THERE HAD BEEN CARMEL Thomas in the sixth grade, braced inside the pale cement circle of the culvert out on the far side of the playing field behind the school. With the muddy rainwater running in a rivulet between her spread feet, she'd unbuttoned her blouse and shimmied herself free, exposing the pasty white pillows of her bare breasts, letting one boy touch her with his fingertips first, then daring another, the one that everybody already knew she really liked the best, to go ahead and do it, to touch her there, too, with the tip of his tongue.

And after I gave Jamie Foster my hand to hold in the dark under the train table in his father's basement, then he'd unbuckled his belt and drawn down his zipper and shown me the firm stem of his penis, like a slim cream-colored mushroom, a blooming white insistence that was poking itself up out of the shadowed vale of his lap.

I'd kissed another boy named Reed Wicker inside a closet at a party once—holding my breath and tightening my lips and feeling his cold smooth face rub against my own until I had to pull away from him and wrench myself free and stumble out into the light again, gasping for air.

Floating on a raft in Grand's pool with Brodie sunning himself on the chaise, I had managed to position myself just right so that I had a glimpse of the darkish tender crumple of his testicles pressed against his leg far up inside the folds of his shorts.

And later, with Paul Gerald, there was more than all of that, there was almost everything, but the truth was that for me the before was better than the during. What I loved about it was the way that he had turned to me. The way that he had reached for me, as if it had hurt him to do it, wincing as if he might have been the one who was in real pain. The way that he'd touched me, the way his fondlings had molded me, as if I might have been taking form right there, brought into being by the slow smooth movement of his hands.

GRAND AND MY FATHER PACKED UP THE OLD STATION WAGON WITH THEIR sleeping bags and their camping equipment and their fishing gear, and they took off north toward Minnesota, heading into Canada for two weeks of fishing the linkage of lakes in the Quetico. We were in the driveway, me and Frankie and Brodie and Meems, waving after them as they backed away—Grand at the wheel and my dad right next to him, his big head bent over the map that he'd unfolded and opened up on his lap. He waved his one large hand out the window at us. There was a flash of sunshine glinting against the bumper as they backed onto the gravel; there was the crunch of tires and a thick billow of white dust; then it settled, and they were gone.

My mother was inside the house, giving instructions to the nurses—one fat and frowning, another thinner and happier, a third with quick efficient hands and awkwardly splayed feet—that Grand had hired to come in and live in his house with Brodie and Meems, looking after the two of them for him, cooking and cleaning and seeing to their every need, trading off shifts so there would always be someone else there, around the clock, in case . . . well, just in case.

Frankie went inside then to change into her swimsuit, but I was already wearing mine. I wheeled Meems over to the screened porch, and we waited together there, listening to the shrill sound of my mother trying to explain things clearly to the nurses in the kitchen, asking them questions, pointing things out, making lists and going over schedules. And it was then that I noticed that Grand's statue of Meems's head wasn't there under the damp cloth and plastic on the sculpting table anymore. He'd given up, then. You can fiddle with a thing too much. You can overwork it, and then it starts to change and before you know it it's been spoiled. Maybe it had been too hard for Grand to make Meems look more like what she once had than what she now did. Maybe he'd let that drastic difference between the then and the now—the was and the is, the could have been and the will be—discourage him. Or maybe it was as simple as that he just could not remember well enough anymore. Maybe he'd been unable to keep what used to be in his head long enough to make it come out through his fingers when he went to shape and form his mound of damp gray flexible clay.

I took the lid off the barrel and peered down into its cold, moist depths. I thought about how that gray clay had held a certain shape and form at one time, how it had once retained beginnings of the smooth and flawless contour of Meems's younger face, or at least of Grand's memory of Meems's younger face, or at least of Grand's rendering of his memory of her face—three times removed from the reality of it, three giant steps back from the truth—and that although the face wasn't visible in the clay now, wasn't it still somehow a part of it, nevertheless? And wouldn't it be the same for me, later, after Frankie left, as I knew she inevitably one day would? Her imprint would have been left there on me, and even if Grand were to take that clay, to dig it up out of the barrel and sculpt it into something else altogether now, yet whatever that something else was, wouldn't it always and forever still have to hold something of what he'd already done, what it had already been, even if nobody knew that but him? And me?

GRAND AND MY FATHER BEING GONE CAME AS SOMETHING OF A SURPRISING relief to all of us. Frankie was in the pool, lying on her stomach, drifting in a circle on a spotted rubber raft, trailing her fingers in the water, her chin resting in the crook of her other folded arm. Both of us girls were feeling languorous and lazy, smashed flat by the weight of the humid midsummer heat. I was up on the chaise, lying flat back with my eyes squinted shut just enough to make the sunlight sparkle through my lashes, creating an interesting stream of white and blue and brown and green stripes that I watched for a while until it started to make me dizzy, and then I had to open my eyes again and glare back up into the blinding blueness of the cloudless July sky just to get my balance back. The sun's bright heat was enfolding me like a blanket, it pressed down on me, like some feverish embrace. A dribble of sweat trickled over the curved surface of my side, and I could feel it crawling on me like a spider creeping across the surface of my skin, but it wasn't enough of a discomfort to make me want to move.

I began to drift. I was rising, leaking upward and outward, away from myself, spilling over. I was a spreading stain, like ink. I was separating myself from inside myself, and I was rising off my own body, and I was floating away. I was soaring out and coasting off, like a kite, like a speck of splinter, just that far away, just that small.

Brodie came around the corner on the mower. The rubber tires bounced off the driveway and careened onto the lawn. The sound of the mower's engine brought me back—its murmur reeled me in, and I opened my eyes and slipped back into myself again. I sat up to watch Brodie—in his straw hat and his jeans and his brown boots and his faded plaid flannel shirt with the shirtsleeves rolled up past his elbows, the sunlight shining in the gleam of his blondish hairs, as he rode the tractor mower back and forth over Grand's broad lawn, looking over his shoulder to watch the grass cut in a curving swath behind him, wrenching the wheel with both hands to draw a tight, precise circle around the base of an inconveniently placed tree. In the pool, Frankie's raft turned. She looked like she might have been asleep. Behind me, the house was as still as if there could have been nobody home.

And then Brodie braked and stopped, and without killing the engine he stood up in the seat and took off his hat and, grinning happily, he waved it and hollered hello toward the house.

Where the tall, thin, dark mirage of Paul Gerald shimmered on the hill. He was smiling, He called back to Brodie and waved. He had on dark green swim trunks and brown leather sandals and a white rayon shirt that was unbuttoned halfway and hung all the way untucked, and he was coming toward us, down the limestone steps to the pool. Frankie was awake, after all. She saw Paul, and she gasped and rolled off her raft, slipping into the water with a vague splash.

My mother had on her skirted old-fashioned black bathing suit—it fit her like a corset, with a tautened, tapered waist and a firmly boned brassiere. Below the skirt her bare thighs were heavy and puckered with fat; they wobbled as she plodded along just after Paul. She was carrying a tray with iced tea in a blue pitcher and four red plastic glasses. As she set the tray down on the white iron table, I closed my eyes again and willed the others to believe that I was asleep. I could hear the deep murmur of Paul's voice as it blended into the drone of Brodie's mower, broken only by the shrill of my mother's eager laugh.

"May?" Frankie was at the edge of the pool, grinning at me. She turned her head and squinted through her lashes at Paul. He'd taken off his shirt and was kicking off his sandals. I saw him set his car keys down on the table. He was accepting the glass of iced tea that my mother was handing him. He sipped at it, and he smiled with some gentlemanly graciousness at her and then he peered off toward Brodie as the mower came around and crossed the lawn in front of him, moving from one side and off toward the other again.

Frankie pulled herself up out of the pool and sat on the deck with her knees drawn up to her chest. Water drained off her body; a puddle darkened and steamed on the pavement in a circle around her. Her skin shimmered, gleaming with streams of moisture and suntan oil. Her hair was black and wet and curly. I could see that Paul's bare chest was shadowed by a pelt of fine brown hairs that straggled down over his belly and then funneled into a delicate dark line that dipped out of sight under the waistband of his trunks. He put down his glass and sat at the edge of the pool. He waggled his bare feet in the water.

"Hi, May," he said. "How you doing, Frankie?"

Frankie stood up. "I'm doing just fine, Mr. Gerald," she answered, even though he'd definitely told her already that she should feel free to call him Paul.

"Been getting yourself a beautiful suntan out here?" he asked.

She looked down at herself and poked a fingertip at her shoulder, feeling for tenderness and wincing when she found it.

"More like a beautiful sunburn, I guess," she answered.

"How's the water, May?"

I looked at him, my face flaming. "I don't know. I haven't been in it yet," I said.

"Well, I sure have," Frankie laughed. "And it's cold, that's what." Goosebumps shivered over her legs. She hugged her arms around herself.

He smiled. There was a glint—his white teeth, small and sharp. "That's good," he said. "That's fine." He tipped his head back then and his neck arched as his throat extended. He closed his eyes, and he turned his face upward toward the sun.

My mother was just easing herself into the water at the edge of the shallow end of the pool. She squeaked and shivered, and the skirt of her bathing suit wafted out around her hips. Her breasts bobbed. Frankie stood on the deck, with her hands on her hips. Her own girlish legs were long and slim and smooth; the leg holes of her suit rode up high on her muscled buttocks. She turned then and grabbed a towel, and she skipped off up the steps toward the house.

"Frankie?" my mother called out after her. But Brodie's mower had turned and was swinging past the pool again, and the sound of it drowned her out, so Frankie didn't have to hear and so she didn't turn, and she disappeared into the house.

After a while she came back out again. She was wearing a frog green sundress over her suit and a crumpled white canvas hat on her head. Paul turned toward her.

"Hand me my sunglasses?" he asked.

She picked up his shirt and fumbled through its breast pocket until she'd found the glasses there, and then she pulled them out and handed them over to him. When he put them on, his eyes were hidden, and it became impossible anymore to tell what he was looking at or what he might be able to see.

"May," Frankie said. "You hungry?"

I didn't move. "I might be," I answered. I wasn't sure what

Frankie was getting at yet, or what it was I was supposed to say. Was I hungry or wasn't I?

"You could make a sandwich," said my mother.

She'd climbed up onto Frankie's raft and was drifting through the oblong shadow of the high dive.

"How about we go get us some ice cream?" Frankie asked.

I sat up and looked at her. Frankie shifted her weight and opened her palm behind her back so I could see then that in her fingers she was dangling Paul's ring of keys.

"Ice cream sounds good, I guess," I said, swinging my legs over.

"Okay with you, Vivienne?" Frankie asked, turning toward the drive. "It'll be my treat."

I was on my feet. I pulled on my shorts and my T-shirt, and I slipped into my thongs. Paul was reaching for his tea again. He sipped at it, but behind the dark lenses of his glasses it was still too hard for me to determine the exact focus of his eyes.

My mother, dozing, hummed her approval. "Mmm-hmm," she murmured. Paul put his glass down. He bent forward and dipped his fingers into the pool. When Brodie rode by on the mower, Paul looked up at him again and waved.

I found Frankie waiting for me in her car. The engine was running, and the top and the windows were down, and the radio was on. When I got in, Frankie turned and grinned at me.

"Okay," I said, "now what?"

"Well, now what do you think?" Frankie asked.

I shrugged. "I don't know. You tell me, Frankie. What?"

Frankie smiled. She licked her lips and jangled Paul's keys. "Well," she answered, "how about let's just go have us a little look-see at how that old boy lives."

She parked the Lincoln across the street from his apartment building, in the cooler shade. I looked up the street to check on whether I could see the woman with the shepherd dog again, but that house was still, shimmering in the heat, its windows blindly reflecting back the sun.

"I'm not sure we should be doing this," I said to Frankie.

She looked at me and smirked. "Oh, don't be such a baby, May," she said.

"But what if somebody sees?"

"Sees what? What exactly is there to see?"

Two girls sitting in a car, discussing this. One of them worried-looking and fearful, the other one sarcastic, smirking and painfully brusque. Two girls getting out of the car. The pavement, white, baking. Heat waves moving in the trees, like a shimmer of fire. One girl following along after the other one, up the walkway to the building's beveled glass front door. One girl, still fearful, in spite of herself, turning to look back at the street, in case anybody out there is watching, in case they understand, in case maybe they see; the other girl preoccupied with the business of the moment, fumbling to find the right key. She tries one, then another. Until the door opens up. The one girl's proud smile. The other's still anxious frown.

"Easy as pie," Frankie said. "Musta been meant to be."

She held the door open for me, and I looked at her, and she nodded toward the inside of the building, and so I stepped forward, finally, and so it was me who was the one who led the way in.

Because what was happening was this: there were two things at work inside my mind. One was just a simple schoolgirl curiosity, gnawing at my insides like a timid little mouse, benign and wondering, asking, well, I wonder what does it look like here, in this place, in these rooms where this man lives? And the other, it was that same dreadful thrill of danger, that same all-consuming and exquisite fear that I only just that summer had begun to get to know.

There was an elevator first, that carried us upward to the second floor. The building was still, hushed, apprehensive, a private sort of place, where adults lived quiet and unruffled and intimate lives. There was a hallway, dimly lit. There were doors on both sides, with brass numbers. Frankie stopped at 6, and then, again, she was fumbling through Paul's keys, trying one first and after that another, until the lock tumbled and her wrist turned, the knob revolved, the door opened, and this time she didn't wait for me, but led the way inside herself.

Paul had pulled his window drapes shut against the heat; his rooms were cool and clean, sparsely furnished and dimly lit. The air conditioning hummed, fanning a chill breeze around us. I shivered at it, at the cold and at that same enthralling fear. There was a smell of cigarette smoke and coffee and lemon furniture wax. Books and magazines had been arranged in two tidy piles on a polished glass tabletop. A white leather sofa curved around a corner and against two walls. The pale hardwood floor was bare beneath a scatter of patterned wool rugs.

There was a wall of books, in cases that rose up from floor to ceiling. A telescope at the window. An upright piano with a cluster of small, framed photographs arrayed across its gleaming top.

Among them I found one of Paul Gerald and Brodie Haden and April Delaney, from all those years ago. The three of them had been posed in the doorway on the back porch at Grand Haden's house; they were standing side by side and arm in arm, with April in the middle, her look pensive between the eager faces of the smiling boys.

"Let me see it," Frankie whispered.

I handed it to her, and she studied it for a moment, frowning, and then she turned, her eyes bright and quizzical.

"That's Brodie?" she asked. "Old Humpty Dumpty himself?"

I nodded.

"Well, he was sure something cute at one time in his life, now wasn't he?" she said.

I nodded again.

Frankie touched the glass with her fingertip, polished just that morning to a deep, bloody boysenberry blue.

"And who's this?" she asked, pointing.

"That's April," I told her. "Delaney."

And looking over Frankie's shoulder at that snapshot just at that moment, I could hear April's laughter, and I knew just exactly how she would, in a minute, throw her head back to howl at something clever that Paul or Brodie had said. I could see the wild flame of April's coppery hair as it tossed, and her lovely freckled face, half in shadow, and her green eyes, suddenly closed.

Frankie put the picture back. I followed after her, down the hallway, to the bloom of the master bedroom at its end. There were bird paintings on the walls—tentative watercolors, Audubon prints. Frankie grinned at me and then she whirled and dropped and fell backward, bouncing, onto the mattress of Paul's broad bed. She rolled over and rummaged in the nightstand. She found a dirty magazine there; she pulled it out, and we flipped through it, gasping at the photos, of glossy tongues and rolling breasts and gleaming penises.

There was also this: Frankie's smile in the darkened room, floating. Around the corner, the bathroom where Paul's toothbrush and his razor rested, poised. The dark curl of a hair against the porcelain edge of the sink. A pair of boxer shorts hanging on a hook at the back of the door. My own fist clenching, crushing them, running their silkiness between the press of my finger and my thumb. A smell of shaving cream and citrusish cologne. A glass ashtray balanced just so on the fiberglass bathtub rim, with one cigarette in it, half-smoked, in a bed of ashes, crushed.

And all of that was really nothing more than this: evidence of the man. Traces of his warm flesh. He was there, in all of his things. There was the leathery, lemony smell of him, the feeling of his presence, of himself, wearing those boxers, leaning forward over that sink alone, solemn and silent, shaving with that razor, scattering exactly those loose splinters of his beard.

I looked in the mirror to see Frankie framed in the doorway behind me. She was smiling, twirling her finger in her hair.

"What?" I said.

"Seen enough?"

I shrugged. She turned away. I looked around the room. The bed was rumpled where we'd rolled on it. I bent to straighten it.

"Frankie," I called to her. "Wait." When she came back, I said, "We don't want him to know we were here, do we?" I put the magazine back in the drawer. I moved to cover what I could see of our traces, our presence there left behind.

"But why?" she was asking.

And then Frankie was moving through Paul's rooms with a purpose of her own, replacing things and shifting them, turning them askew, just so. A chair placed there, in its opposite corner. The bed, left undone, sheets mussed and rumpled and, seemingly, used. A closet door, hanging open. A cupboard door, ajar.

"Just to make him wonder," Frankie said, grinning. "Just to throw him off."

She took a piece of paper, Haden letterhead, from under the phone on the counter in his kitchen, and she wrote on it: "Dear Paul, I'll love you forever. Guess who." And then she pressed it between her lips, embossing it with the perfect full circle of her kiss. She folded it and took off her hat and left them both there on his pillow for him to discover later, a mysterious romantic sort of surprise.

ON THE WAY BACK TO GRAND HADEN'S WE STOPPED AT THE DAIRY QUEEN TO make it look as if we actually had gone someplace, after all,

Frankie said. Soft-serve dip cones, one brown butterscotch, the other pink cherry. Frankie pulled the Lincoln up next to Paul's car in Grand Haden's driveway. She skipped over the hot pavement in her bare feet. She sat in one of the iron chairs near the pool, pulling her knees up and lapping at her cone. I fed mine to Grand's old yellow dog, and my mother scolded me for that. She was lying on a chaise, her skin greased, browning, because, she said, she looked thinner when she was tan. She had wads of cotton on her eyelids, and her hair was stiff with lemon juice, to brighten it. She'd been doing the same thing since she was a teenager.

Frankie smiled at me. She squinted at the swimming pool, the water flat, still, gleaming in the sunshine, throwing off shards of colored light.

"Where's Mr. Gerald?" she asked, her voice soft and calm.

My mother sat up. The cotton wads dropped into her lap. Her breasts in the black swimsuit wobbled with her movements. She bent forward, brought her knee up, scratched at the top of her foot. She looked at Frankie, blinking, then tipped her face back toward the sun again.

"He went for a walk," she answered, finally. "Paul and Brodie. Down to the creek, I think."

Frankie's fist was on the table. She opened it, and Paul's keys spilled out, jangling against the metal mesh of the tabletop.

My mother, on the chaise, looked over to see Frankie stepping out of her dress and moving with a quick skip to the edge of the pool. She dove in and began to swim her laps, steadily, back and forth.

I'd picked up Paul's watch, and I held it, palming its weight, running the links of the band through my fingers, around and around. I brought it close to my face and breathed its smell, of metal and sweat. I eyed the clear white oval eye of its face. I put it back down again, beside the keys. I kicked off my thongs and stepped out of my shorts and shucked off my shirt. I climbed to the top of the high board, and I stood out there at its precarious end, bouncing, until I saw Paul Gerald coming out of the woods with Brodie, and then I plunged off.

WHEN I GOT HOME LATER, I WENT TO MY ROOM AND CLOSED THE DOOR AND turned the lock, and I couldn't help it, I kept feeling that there was something about it not quite right, something out of place, something dislodged, something mussed and shuffled. I felt as if my own life, my own self, had been disturbed and stirred up, somehow. Standing there in my room, looking around it, it felt as if there'd been some kind of a change. A slight shift in the arrangement of my things, and I was at first afraid that maybe my mother had become suspicious, maybe she'd done a search of my room, maybe she'd found what I'd hidden away in the dust-furred murk under my bed. But when I looked I was relieved to suppose that because the individual items of my stolen stash still all looked to me to be the same—piled up in the same haphazard and unpredictable way, thrown there and then abandoned, left untouched and unchanged and unmoved—that my mother must still be in the dark about me and what I'd been up to and all that I'd recently done. So, that part of me was still safe, at least, it was still hidden and still secret and still merely mine.

And what about Paul? Had he come home and found that the things in his apartment had been changed? Had he seen Frankie's note, and her hat, and had he recognized them as hers? Had he realized what we'd done, and had it made him smile, and did he wonder, why?

Chapter Nine

MY MOTHER LEFT FOR CHICAGO THE NEXT day. She needed a vacation, she said. She owed it to herself. She worked too hard, and she'd earned the right to treat herself to something for herself and no one else—why should she have to stick around all on her own all summer, she wanted to know, when my father was off having a good time, doing what he liked to do, and so was Grand, so why shouldn't she be able to pack up and go off and enjoy herself for once, too? It was the Fourth of July weekend, after all, so the store would be closed anyway. No business lost, if that mattered to anybody. The nurses that Grand had hired seemed to know what they were doing. My mother needed a break, she said. She just wanted some time of her own. It would be good for her, she reasoned, good for everyone, in fact, if we would just let her get away to be by herself for a couple of days.

If Frankie and I would be all right by ourselves, that is. She chewed on her lip, considering. She stood with one hand at her thick waist, and she regarded us, trying to find a way to sum us up, squinting as if that might help her see more clearly what we were all about and whether we could be trusted alone and on our own.

Frankie was fast, as usual.

"Now you know we're going to be just fine, Vivienne," she said. "Don't you worry. We're almost grown, and we can take good care of ourselves."

Frankie talked my mother into feeling comfortable about doing what she wanted to do anyway, she coaxed her toward it, urged her into making up her mind. She deserved it, Frankie said. She should do it, it would be good for her.

My mother stocked the refrigerator with frozen dinners for us, and Frankie laughed at that and said, don't worry, we'll make salads for ourselves, because Frankie was on a diet anyway. I said we'd go out for hamburgers sometimes. We'd be just fine.

My mother looked at me, doubtful. She brushed my hair back from my face. And I looked right back at her. I squared my shoulders and lifted my chin, trying to present myself as grown up and self-assured, because I knew that if I looked as if I could trust myself, then my mother might begin to believe that she could trust me, too; if I looked as if I wasn't worried, then my mother wouldn't be worried either; and if my mother wasn't worried, then she'd let go and go away. This was something that I had never even dared to dream about, being left at home alone. All right, with Frankie, which was just as good as being alone. Mrs. Alt would come in the next day, to clean, and then we'd be completely on our own and in charge of ourselves for four long days.

She made up her mind and went upstairs to pack. Frankie was standing there in the kitchen, washing the dishes, and she kept telling me what to do without even bothering to look at me, acting as if all of a sudden she was going to be my mother or something, she was going to be responsible, she'd be the one who was in charge, a babysitter, and I was still just little helpless May, a kid who couldn't be trusted to know how to take care of herself.

"Clear the table, May," Frankie said. "Take the trash out. Put these placemats away. Get your hair out of your face."

I got mad after a while. "Take it out yourself, Frankie," I said. "You're not my mother."

My mother was standing in the doorway, with her bag in one hand. She was wearing a linen suit with a red skirt and a blue jacket and red, white, and blue shoes and silver earrings that were shaped like stars. Frankie turned to her and smiled.

"All set?" she asked.

My mother looked at me and her eyes questioned mine, and I answered her back with a smile, not so big that it might scare her, but small, sweet, confident, and self-contained—the look of a girl who was growing up into herself, who was sure and secure, who knew what she was doing, in charge and in control, without a care in the world.

My mother pursed her lips in resignation then, and she took a deep breath, and she answered Frankie.

"Yes," she said. "All set."

All around us the house loomed, quiet, empty, and waiting. There was a gone-ness about it—everything was neat and tidy and in place because Mrs. Alt had been there all day already and now she was almost done. She was upstairs folding clothes, and so the tabletops sparkled, and the rugs had been vacuumed, and the floors were polished. Behind me, a fly was buzzing at the screen door, frantic to get out. I heard the soft pop of a firecracker exploding in some boys' driveway down the street.

Frankie was posed with one leg outstretched, her bare foot on display on the kitchen table. She was painting a new coat of that red polish on her toenails. She had the radio playing; she wagged her head and whistled through her teeth and grinned at me.

I stepped past her and opened the refrigerator and peered inside. I took out a beer and opened it. Frankie looked up at the sound of it, and she smiled, then went back to working at her toes again.

"You want one?" I asked her. She shook her head no. I stood at the door, looking out, drinking my beer, while Frankie polished her toes. When I finished that one, I went back to the refrigerator again, and I helped myself to another. The music on the radio sounded good. The air outside was hot, but that felt good to me, too. Around my face and at my temples my hair was damp with sweat and starting to curl, and my cheeks were burning and my head was buzzing, and all of it felt good to me, better than much else that I'd ever been.

FRANKIE HAD A THEORY, ABOUT HOW MY MOTHER HAD GONE TO CHICAGO because she was having an affair, and she tried to get me to believe it.

"Why does that bother you so much, May?" she asked, smiling.

Her eyes sparkled at me, full of the fun of trying to tease up a little trouble for her own amusement. She'd popped an orange capsule filled with tiny white and yellow beads—to help her diet, she told me, to keep her from always wanting to eat. It made her drum her fingers and wiggle her toes and swing her leg back and forth. She chewed on the inside of her cheek. She twirled a bit of her hair around and around her fingers. She asked me if I wanted some, but I was nervous enough already, I told her. I liked the flat purple tablets that looked like gems better. The ones that made me sleepy, that drew the curtain down and left me drifting in the dark.

It bothered me, I told her, because I couldn't picture it, that was all. I couldn't conjure up the image of my own mother sitting on a stool in a hotel bar, all by herself, fluffing her hair with one hand, tugging at her skirt, clasping her handbag in her lap, ordering a drink, catching the eye of a stranger and smiling, then talking to him, then letting him buy her a drink, then letting him touch her hand, then letting him reach and brush her hair out of her eyes himself, with his own flat thumb. She smiles at him, and then she drops her eyes when he tells her how pretty she is when she smiles. When he suggests that she should find a way to smile more often.

"Maybe if you had something to smile about?" he asks her.

While my father is sitting across a campfire from Grand, drinking brandy from the glass lip of a leather-jacketed flask. He stares into the fire, and the flames glow inside his eyes. Lake water behind him ripples, its waves lap at the mud shore. Bats swoop through the trees. As it gets dark, my father and my grandfather sink further into their separate silences, until they've become large, unmoving shadows, as still, as dumb, as inert as two big rocks.

While my mother stands at her hotel room window in her bare feet and her slip, with one arm crossed over her breasts, her hand clasping her shoulder. She looks down at the traffic that crawls along the maze of lighted streets. She makes up her mind and turns back toward the bed. When he reaches for her, she rolls toward him; his arms are out, he catches her.

FRANKIE FINISHED WITH HER TOENAILS AND GOT UP FROM THE BREAKFAST TABLE. She picked up her keys, and she tossed them over to me.

"About time you learned how to drive, May," she said.

I got into the car on the driver's side, a change that in itself felt strange because I'd never done it before. I had to slide the seat all the way forward, which I could see was cramping Frankie's legs, but there was nothing I could do about it, and anyway, she didn't complain.

"It's not that hard, May," she said. "You just put it into gear and then . . ." She frowned and stared out through the windshield, thinking. Chewing on a stick of peppermint gum. She shrugged, finally. ". . . Well, then you just, I don't know. Drive."

Frankie took a lot for granted sometimes, and that angered me. She had trouble making herself see how things might seem from some other person's point of view, and it was hard for her to understand that somebody else didn't always feel exactly the same way about things as she did. Not everybody was brave the way that she was, I told her, but she just laughed at me. Frankie assumed too much, sometimes. She expected me to be able to do things that I wasn't sure at all that I would ever be able to do.

But that time I knew what I wanted. And that time I was determined to make it mine. If Frankie believed that I could drive, then so did I. I put my hands on the wheel. That was the first thing. And then we just sat there, while I worked at talking myself into it, silently. It was hot inside the car. Frankie cranked down her window and spat out her gum.

"You have to turn it on, May," she said finally, reaching over me for the key.

But I batted her hand away. I could do it myself. "Just give me a second," I said.

Mrs. Alt came out the back door of our house just then, and she trundled down the driveway, carrying her big purse under her arm, to her car. Before she got in, she turned to look at us, peering. Then she shook her head and looked away. She got into her car, pulled away from the curb, and was gone.

I turned the key. The sound of the engine seemed to surge up through me, blowing off the heat and my embarrassment, and Mrs. Alt's disapproval and my own fear. I shifted into drive, and gripping the steering wheel with both hands—at ten o'clock and two o'clock, Frankie said—I pressed against the accelerator with my foot. And the car lunged forward. Then I hit the brake too hard, and it jolted to a stop, rocking Frankie. She braced her hand against the dash. She turned and smiled and told me it was okay.

"Just be easy with it, May," she said.

I took my foot off the brake again, and then we were creeping forward, inching around the high curve of the driveway toward the house, skimming past the front porch and rolling downward into the street and across and then up into the driveway again. I pressed on the accelerator, and we gathered some speed and did it again and again, moving around and around. My heart was pounding. I squealed with the pure excitement of it, and Frankie let go of the dash and clapped her hands. That's how easy it was, to move the Lincoln along that one long swooping curve, from the driveway up toward the house then down to the street and over and up into the driveway again.

Frankie was grinning. "You're a natural driver, May," she said.

And she was right, I did get the hang of it right away. I slowed and stopped, not so suddenly this time, at the top by the house.

"Hang on," Frankie said. She bounded out of the car and skipped up the porch steps and disappeared into the house. I stayed put in the driver's seat, with one hand hanging on the wheel, as relaxed and casual as if this were something that I did every day, had been doing all my life, in fact. A girl with wheels. I was as pleased with myself as I'd ever been, breathless, the wind knocked out of me by the unfamiliar satisfaction of my own accomplishment. I'd done it. You did it, May, I told my-self. I reached forward and fiddled with the radio. I leaned my head back and closed my eyes, drummed my thumbs against the steering wheel, pressed down on the brake, holding back the huge weight of the car, keeping its power in place with only the gentle pressure of my foot, and I let the soft purr of the engine thrum through me. I could drive. I was in charge. We'd be going where I decided, this time. Our destination would be my choice, my whim, now.

And then, something stirred. There was a rustle of leaves, a crunch of gravel, a footstep, a finger tapping at the glass. I opened my eyes and sat up, startled.

"Frankie?"

I looked toward the house, but the front door was still hang-ing open just past the screen, precisely as she'd left it when she'd slipped inside.

And then, there was a movement. There was a shadow that shifted, just out of sight, just behind me, and a boy's voice was asking, again, "Frankie?"

I turned, and he was there, the boy, and when he saw that it was me and not Frankie, his smile faded. He put his hands in his pockets and tucked in his chin and stepped back.

We gazed at each other that way, for a moment. Neither one of us knew what to do. His eyes were hooded, dark, his hair was tangled, his forehead was smudged with dirt, his chin was furred by a scraggle of youthful beard. He shifted his weight from one sneakered foot to the other; he dropped his shoulders, and he turned away.

"Wait . . ."

I started to go after him, to stop him and ask him, what? who? why? But I'd forgotten about the car and that the engine was still running, and when I moved my foot off the brake the Lincoln lurched forward. I slammed the brake back on, and the car shuddered and stopped with its front left fender just short of the edge of the porch steps.

There was Frankie backing out of the house with a bag of our swimsuits and towels; she was closing and locking the door after her; she was tumbling down toward me again. She opened the door and leaned in.

"Okey-dokey, May," she said, "you're driving. Let's go."

When I didn't respond, she lifted her head and looked over the top of the car, and she peered into the shadows of the trees beside the driveway until she saw him. He was there, he hadn't moved, he was half hidden in shade, still with his hands in his pockets. He was smiling now, hopefully, at her.

Frankie ducked and climbed into the car. "Don't look at him, May," she said. She pulled the door shut and settled in her seat, waiting for me to drive off. I watched him frown and lift his hand to brush his hair back from his face.

"Drive," Frankie said.

"But . . ."

"Jesus! Just do it, May."

And when I still didn't respond, she brought her own leg over, muscling mine aside, and she stepped on the gas and the engine roared.

"Drive, goddammit!" she cried. "Now!"

So I did. I shifted into reverse and took my foot off the brake, and we lurched backward toward him, and over my shoulder I saw him lift his hands and jump away, and then I shifted into drive again, and we were bounding forward, we were careening around the curve of the driveway, and bouncing down into the street. Another car was coming just then, but I wrenched the wheel and turned in time, and the guy honked and screeched, but by then we were already sailing away.

Frankie threw her head back and howled.

"Who was that?" I screamed at her. My hair was flying, we were flying, skimming through the streets I'd walked down all my life.

She turned to me and grinned. "Look at you, May. You're driving this car as easy as if it's something you've been doing every day."

I'd turned onto Brand and was climbing the long slow rise toward Forest Hill. I looked in the rearview mirror, half expecting to see him standing there in the street, or running after us, or flying along on his pink girl's bike, pedaling hard to try to keep up.

At the entrance to the park, I stopped, put on the blinker, and turned. I cruised past the playground, pulled around behind the baseball field and, finally, slowed and stopped. I shifted into park. I sat back to catch my breath.

"Okay, Frankie," I said. "Who is he? What's going on?"

"Who . . . ?" she started, but I reached over and clasped her arm and squeezed it to stop her.

"Don't do that," I said. "Don't fuck around with me anymore."

Her gaze was solemn, like a child, spanked.

"Creighton," she said. I let go of her. She rubbed her arm.

"Creighton?"

"My old boyfriend. And I mean, old. As in, not anymore. As in, once upon a time. As in, over and done with and leave me goddamn the fuck alone."

There was a shimmer of tears in her eyes. She took a deep breath. Her face had tightened, hardened, sharpened.

"Why is he here?"

"He thinks he still loves me."

"How did he know where to find you?"

"Good guess, don't you think? Where else would I be?"

I thought about that for a minute. Hadn't she said she'd gone to Chicago first? That she was only on her way out west?

"I didn't want to scare you," she went on. "I don't know what to do to make him go away."

"He followed you all the way here?"

She shrugged. "I guess."

"What does he want?"

She smirked. "What do you think he wants?"

"What will you do?"

"What can I do?"

"Tell him to go away."

"Well, hell, I've done that already. He won't."

"Can't we make him?"

"It's a free world, isn't it?"

I stared at Frankie. "But . . ."

She glared back at me. "Listen, are we going to sit here and talk all day, May, or what?"

I squeezed the steering wheel with both hands. "Where do you want to go?"

"I don't know. You're driving. You decide."

I shifted into gear again and pulled off and kept going. We could head in whatever direction I decided on, if I'd known where I wanted to go, which I didn't. I just let the streets take us, in their circles; I let the Lincoln follow along the spiral of Linwood's fingerprint, looping around and around and across and over and back again.

When we got to the top of the hill by Paul Gerald's street, then Frankie sat up.

"Turn here," she said.

"What for?"

She smiled at me. "Let's just see if he's home."

"Frankie, I don't think . . ."

She put her head back and closed her eyes. She took a deep breath, then turned to me.

"Come on, May. What the hell are you afraid of?"

So I turned onto his street.

And then Frankie said, pointing, bouncing, "Look, there, a parking space, right out front. See, May? In the shade and everything. That's a sign, don't you think?"

I pulled over and parked. I sat back and looked up at the white slab of his apartment building. I wiped sweat from my lip and the back of my neck. Frankie was out of the car.

"Frankie?"

"Come on!" And then she skipped off, her skirt fluttering prettily around her slim bare legs.

So, there was me behind the wheel of the Lincoln, and there was Frankie tripping up the steps to Paul Gerald's apartment building in her short skirt and her white sandals and a pink and green flowered blouse. She pressed the buzzer and turned to look at me, with her hands on her hips. She turned back toward the speaker again, because he must have answered, and she leaned closer and spoke into it. She turned back to me again, smiling now. After a moment she was pushing through the front door, and then she'd disappeared inside as the door swung back behind her and shut.

I didn't know what to do. I sat in the car. I waited, to see what would happen next, but nothing happened. I looked up at his window, but the curtains were drawn and there was no movement, no signal, no sign of Frankie, nothing.

Finally I turned off the car and got out and locked it after me, taking my time, in case she came back. I walked up to the building, and I was just reaching forward to press the button that would ring his bell, when an old man came out. I smiled at him, and he held the door open for me, and I slipped inside and down the hall, to the elevator and up and down the hall again and then I was standing outside Paul's closed door. I listened, but there was nothing. A woman came out of the apartment across the hall. She looked at me curiously, and I smiled and turned to the door again and knocked.

Frankie opened it.

"Well, it's about damned time," she said, lowering her voice so Paul wouldn't hear.

He came out of the kitchen and stood behind Frankie. He was holding a glass, ice and amber, bourbon on the rocks.

"May," he said. "Is that you?"

Frankie stepped aside.

Paul smiled. "Well, well, well," he said. "Isn't this a nice surprise." He turned to Frankie.

"We were in the neighborhood," she said. "And we thought about you."

Frankie crossed the room and plopped down on the sofa. She fanned her face with her hand and picked at the front of her blouse.

"Well, I'm flattered, I guess," Paul said. He reached past me and closed the door. He touched my elbow and I moved away from him, farther into the room.

Frankie had one arm stretched out across the cushions of the leather couch. Her legs were crossed at the knee. She swung her foot back and forth prettily. She kept grinning at me.

"Can I get you anything, May? A soda? A beer?" Paul asked.

Frankie jumped up. "We'll have a beer if you've got some," she said. "That be okay?" And as she passed me into the kitchen, she wrinkled her nose and reached out and flicked her finger at my breast.

I followed her. She turned and stooped to peer through the opening of the kitchen's pass-through window at Paul.

In the refrigerator there was a jar of olives and a package of sliced cheese. A full carton of milk and an opened can of to- mato juice. And a six-pack of bottled beer. Frankie took one for herself and handed another one to me.

"You're from Kentucky?" Paul was asking her.

She laughed. "Don't go calling me a hillbilly if I say yes, all right?"

232

He smiled. "Got yourself a boyfriend there?"

"Well," she told him, "I used to, I guess."

I was at the window, looking out through the curtains at Frankie's car parked down there on the street for anybody to see. Near me was his telescope. I bent and looked through it, but whatever was there was just a smudge of something, out of focus and blurred.

Paul had come up behind me, and he leaned over to fiddle with the lens, and I could feel him then, his warmth, and I could smell the mintiness of his breath.

I turned to see that Frankie was watching us. She raised her eyebrows and rolled her eyes.

I took a sip of my beer. It was so cold that it seemed to knock the wind right out of me. My eyes filled with tears. Paul had turned, and he was gesturing toward the window.

"There," he said. I bent and looked into the telescope at a tree in the distance; its branches squirmed with a gathering of black birds. I turned to him. He was so close, his face so near that I could see the lines, the pores, the flecks of color in his eyes.

Frankie was at the stereo, fiddling with it. She turned it on, and the music blared out, too loud—a piano piece. She looked at Paul, and laughed, soundlessly. He walked over to her side. He changed the tape to something jazzier, and Frankie closed her eyes, moving to it, swaying from side to side. He watched her, smiling. Her bare feet stepped and crossed and stepped. Her polished toes glimmered like stones in the carpet. I walked over to the sofa and sat down. My beer bottle left a ring of water on the glass-topped table. I dabbled my fingers in it.

I took another sip of beer, wincing. Frankie still swayed. She walked along the bookshelf, peering up at his books, running her fingers over their spines, pulling one down and looking through it and putting it back and taking down another.

"You like to read, Frankie?" Paul asked. His words sounded slow, drawn out, deepened.

"Aw naw," she told him, turning again to flash him a smile. "Not so much, I don't guess."

She'd pulled out a photo album with a black leather cover, and she carried it over and sat down with it on the sofa next to me. She opened it up on her lap, and began to leaf through it. There were black and white farm landscapes. And strangers' faces—a boy and girl looking out a window, a man standing beside a dilapidated barn, a snaggle-toothed youth in overalls leaning on a fence, a woman in a flowered dress hanging sheets up on a clothesline in the wind. And Brodie. And April Delaney. And me.

"You took these, Paul?" Frankie asked.

"Most of them I did."

"They're beautiful," she told him. She elbowed me. "That you, May?"

I nodded.

"Would you take a picture of me sometime, Paul?" she asked.

I stood up. "I have to go to the bathroom," I said. My head was spinning.

"May, are you all right?"

"I'm fine."

I stumbled down the hall and through his bedroom and into

his bathroom. I closed the door behind me and locked it and turned on the light. I studied my face in the mirror and felt as if it belonged to a stranger, somebody I didn't know, someone I'd never met. Like the pictures that Paul had taken, of people that he happened to see. I touched my face, patted it. Paul's boxer shorts were still hanging on the hook on the back of the door. I turned, and I buried my face in them, breathing in his smell. His razor was still perched at the edge of the sink. I picked it up and turned it, drawn to its glint. I thought about lying in his bed. About cutting my wrists and spreading my arms and letting myself bleed. About my blood, a dark stain spreading out of me, and soaking through the mattress and dripping onto the floor. I looked up into the mirror again and I saw my plain face framed there, with Frankie's coral-colored lipstick smeared on my mouth, and I turned and vomited into the toilet. My own bile burned in my throat and my nose and my mouth.

When I came out of the bathroom, Paul was sitting on the sofa next to Frankie. The photo album was on the table, closed. I watched him touch her face and take her chin and pull her closer to him and kiss her. Frankie had her leg up over his lap. His hand was sliding up under her skirt. She opened her eyes and saw me, and she winked. She pulled away abruptly, and stood up, tugging at the hem of her skirt.

"Well, we gotta get going now, Paul," she said.

He stood up next to her, awkward, unsure of where to place his hands. "You just got here," he said.

"That's right, we did, but now we gotta go." She reached up and ruffled her fingers in his hair.

His face was flushed red. "All right," he said. "All right."

Frankie laughed and tossed her head. "But we'll be back, Paul," she said. "We surely will. Won't we, May?"

And then she turned and was out the door, and he was stepping toward me, about to say something, with his hand outstretched. His shirt was rumpled and half undone, and his hair was mussed.

"May?" he said.

But I was already out the door and running down the hallway, after Frankie; I was bursting out into the blinding bright light of the summer afternoon outside.

Frankie was in the driver's seat, waiting for me. I handed her the keys, and she revved the engine and peeled away. I looked back behind us, and there was Paul Gerald standing outside on his balcony, leaning over the railing to watch us as we went.

"We left him in a hot spot," Frankie said, and she hooted loudly again. "He's probably in there beating off, right now, even as we speak."

And I leaned back and closed my eyes and took a deep breath of the fresh summer air, and I thought about his hands in Frankie's hair and his mouth moving over hers, and his fingers sliding up her leg, and what I imagined for the moment was that he'd been doing those very same things to me.

WE HEADED OUT TO GRAND'S. I COULD SEE THAT BRODIE WAS THERE, INSIDE HIS room, standing at his window, placed just so between the folds of the opened curtains, with his hands in his pockets. He was looking out, watching. He may have been watching for Grand, wondering where he'd gone. Wondering, maybe, when he was going to come back.

We put on our suits and went swimming. Our bodies moved through the water, back and forth, over and under, and Brodie's eyes followed. He brought out a box of sparklers, and then we sat wrapped in towels in the lawn chairs that I set up side by side all in a row just so at the edge of the pool. Frankie lit the sparklers one at a time, and we watched them burning in our hands.

The splayfoot nurse was on duty, and she rolled Meems outside in her wheelchair, and put her near us to marvel over our bright fiery display with her hands clenched in her lap and her face screwed up into its smirk that looked like it might have had some pleasure in it somewhere. After a while the nurse went back inside, and she took Meems with her, rolled her through the house to the back bedroom, where she sat in the lamplight and read out loud to Meems for a while from her magazine.

When the real fireworks started, Brodie went inside, but Frankie and I stayed put. We sat there in our dampish suits, and we watched the sky as the rockets sliced through the haze just past the trees and then burst, great flowers of color that soared up from the fairway of the Linwood Golf Club out off Vernon Road and bloomed in the black sky above our heads. And left spider webs of smoke behind.

Brodie didn't like all the noise. We saw the light go on in his bedroom, and his shadow crossed back and forth over the window, cast against the drawn shade. Then his light went back out again, but that didn't mean that he wasn't still awake, Frankie said, or that he wasn't still watching us. She struck a match and lit a cigarette. She handed it to me, and then she lit another one for herself. We smoked, in silence. She bounced her foot and studied her polished toes and fiddled with her hair. Her face looked like a pale mask there in the dark, shadowed and hollowed and pinched.

I looked up at Brodie's darkened window and wondered whether he really was still standing there, just there, on the other side of the glass, peering out, his hands clapped over his ears.

"Did you ever try to kill yourself, Frankie?" I asked her, still squinting at the house, sucking on my cigarette, blowing a stream of smoke. She picked a bit of tobacco off her tongue. She leaned back in her chair and took a deep breath and shut her eyes. She had a Coke in a bottle, and she'd spiked it with some of Grand's bourbon from the bottom drawer of the desk in his study, and every now and then she'd tip her head back to take a sip, then pass it over to me to do the same.

What was it that I wanted her to tell me? Just what exactly did I want to know? Whether she really was so much like me? Spirit sisters? Two of a kind?

A stream of gold and silver sparkles boomed and bled across the sky.

But "No," Frankie answered me at last. "May, have you?"

I might have tried to kill myself a few times, I said, as a blue and silver stream of stars spewed and spilled above my head. Maybe I had, I told her. Maybe I'd wanted to die one time or more. But I hadn't been able to do it, I had to admit that. An aerial bomb blew, a hard bright flash of light followed by a solid singular emphatic boom.

"Did you ever try it, Frankie?" I asked her again. "Did it ever get that bad for you?"

She laughed at me. "Never had to, May," she answered. "Had plenty of people ready and willing and almost able to do it for me all by themselves. Didn't need any of my help at it."

The color bombs were exploding out beyond the trees, their sounds delayed by distance, thunderous serious afterthoughts thrown at us from across the smoke-filled sky. Frankie's voice drifted toward me; it seemed ghostlike and disembodied in the surrounding dim.

She told me that after her father died his three brothers moved back home again with the excuse that they were just there to bury him. But one after the other they made themselves comfortable and moved in and settled down. And one after the other one figured out a reason that it would be best for him to stay.

It turned out to be Elgin who was the one who took a shine to Frankie. It was Uncle Elgin, the youngest of the Crane boys, whose black eyes followed her wherever she went, when she was within his reach. He was the one with the money. He was the one who brought gifts. He sat on the porch step, and his hands moved on his knees, gripping them. He smiled at Frankie; he bought her a bracelet; he let her go for a drive in his car. When he asked her to kiss him, just a little peck, he told her, just a nip to let him know that she was grateful to him, she had turned her face away, and that had made him mad, so he'd whacked his hand out at her, and his fist had grabbed hold of her wrist, and he'd turned her around and twisted her slender arm up so high behind her back that after a while it gave way and snapped.

Frankie stood up from her chair, too fast. She spilled her Coke, let it fall out of her open hand and roll away on the grass. She bent to get it and staggered so the lawn chair wobbled behind her and tipped over backward. She dropped her towel and tugged at the straps of her suit.

"Frankie?" I stood up and reached for her, but the beer and the bourbon and the purple pill I'd taken had all worked together to turn the world into a soft blur for me. The edges of things seemed smudged, boundaries between were merged and bleary, like watercolors blooming and bleeding and seeping into each other.

"Frankie?"

"Come on," she said, her voice coming to me like a glass shard, hard and sharp and clear.

But then she was off. She'd molted out of her bathing suit, and her bare-skinned body was straying over the grass—she'd become a wisp, a trail, a trace of palest smoke. She flew toward the pool, and then, with a soft splash, she dropped off the edge and was gone.

Clumsily, I tried to follow her. It was important that I keep up, I thought. I was struggling with my own towel and wet suit and stumbling over hers. Then I was standing on the hard cement deck, naked, with my toes curling over its lip, watching Frankie swim, an energetic streak across in one direction and then back again in the other, her pale flesh gliding through the inky surface of the pool like a pure white shimmering fish. And then she stopped. Someplace in the middle. I wobbled at the edge, flailed for balance. She'd turned, and she was floating on her back, with her hands skulling at her sides, and her bare breasts flattened, and her knees softened and parted, and her feet dangling down.

Over our heads, the golf club fireworks continued to burst. Their stream of colors was reflected off the water, they shimmered over Frankie, their lights glowed against her. The sound, a stutter behind the light, rebounded through the trees. I stood there at the side of the pool as if frozen in place on its edge, looking upward toward the sky and then down again at the water and then back up again into the sudden violence of the brightened sky.

Frankie was flailing to upright herself. And she was pointing upward, but away, behind me, toward the darkness that was looming like a blanket above the thrusting top twigs and branches of the trees.

I turned, staggered, caught myself, shaded my eyes, as if against the sun, to see, swinging along and seesawing out of nowhere and down toward us, a parachute that had separated from the last color bomb and materialized in the sky above our heads, wayward, wafting on the lift and drop of the breeze, heading through the darkness toward me.

Frankie was at the edge of the pool, her hair dark, wet, slicked back against her head and shoulders and down her back. She elbowed herself up and stood on the deck beside the straddled legs of the high dive, her body sopped and glistening, a rainbow of bare flesh. She raised her hands, reaching skyward toward the scrap of floating white paper. I stepped across the deck, onto the lawn, felt the grass sink beneath my feet, cooler and softer. Frankie was beside me. We stood shoulder to shoulder, and I could feel her shiver. Then she was off, chasing after the parachute, laughing, howling, and I was running after her. I pulled her aside to pass her. Frankie cried out my name and sprinted after me. The paper parachute floated toward the back of Grand Haden's house.

Meems's windows were dark; they watched us like a pair of black blind eyes. She might have seen us. Maybe she was still awake, and maybe she happened to be looking upward and outward from her bed just then, toward the window. Maybe she saw the flash of the fireworks and the tease of the parachute, and us two girls, nymphish, bare-bottomed, bare-limbed—May and Frankie, tumbling crazily this way and that way across the expanse of the back yard.

Had Meems's hands clawed and clutched at the brown and yellow blanket trim? The fireworks flashed, splattered colors against her window glass. The great booming noises shook the panes and echoed out over the long sprawled fields. The angels on the wallpaper shifted with the roses in the changing light. Meems's thin limbs strained, her stringy muscles tightened and loosened and then tightened again and stayed that way as she closed in on herself, contorting inward, contracting down, a spasm of unexpected strength, and her whole body was drawn in, as fierce as a clenched fist.

And, in the next room, what? The hired nurse paused. She looked up from the glossy pages of her magazine, she listened for a sound, something, she turned her head, and she listened, and then she heard it again, a whimper, a squeak, the whistle of a breath sharply indrawn. She set the magazine aside. She stood up and crossed cautiously toward the door.

Outside in the high sky another explosion of color burst to inflame the angels, and they leered and leaned outward, reaching for Meems in her bed. The nurse stepped into the room. She flicked the switch, and the ceiling light streamed, and there was Meems, flat on her back on her aluminum-framed hospital bed, and her face had softened back into its real beauty again, and her mouth had slackened toward her youth, and the smirk was erased, it was, finally, gone.

Then what? The nurse looked up, pursed her lips in her dismay that this had chanced to happen during her shift, wasn't that just her luck, and such a nice lady, too, and such a nice house besides, what a damned shame it was, because this had been a good job, not too demanding, pleasant, even, and she looked out of the brightened bedroom windows and first what she saw there was only her own reflection, the ghost-white shape of her own uniform shining back at her, and then, beyond that, there was more, there was a movement somewhere outside in the swarming dark, near the hovering loom at the edge of the trees. There was the pale white mist of two girls' bare bodies, romping, chasing, at play and careless, wildly careening here and there across the flat breadth of Brodie's new-mown lawn.

All the house lights went on, suddenly, one after the other, and the house seemed to accordion outward from Meems's room toward the front, as the nurse walked through it from room to room, flipping switches as she moved, her great flat feet slapping over the bare wood floors. Frankie stopped, breathless, frozen in light. I ducked, gasping, and huddled downward toward the ground to cover myself. I felt a shadow of warm black dread, like oil, slipping over me; it seemed to come closing in on me from all sides as if it would blot me out. Blind, I crawled over to the edge of the pool. I found my towel first and then my suit, and I struggled into it, and then I went into the house.

The nurse was in the kitchen, talking into the phone. Brodie was standing in the hallway.

"What?" he kept asking me. "What?"

Another firework exploded outside, and he cringed and ducked and clapped his hands over his ears. When I pushed away from him, he began to whimper, keening as he rocked forward and back, and after a while the sound of his cries blended in with the siren that came wailing toward us from a distance outside.

The ambulance threw blotches of red light over the grass. Frankie had wrapped a towel turban around her wet hair. I was shivering in my bathing suit. The nurse was on the phone again, trying to get hold of my mother in Chicago, finally leaving a message for her at the hotel desk, and Frankie looked at me with raised eyebrows, as if to ask, where was she then, if she wasn't in her room at that time of night? Brodie was sitting at the kitchen table with his head in his hands. I was standing outside in the driveway, hugging myself, watching the ambulance pull away. And after it was gone I looked up into the trees to see the parachute, waving like a scrap of cloud.

Chapter Ten

IF YOU WERE TO WALK OUT THE BACK
door of the screened porch on the side of Grand
Haden's house, over the limestone patio and down the
steps and along the walk, past the pool and across the
back lawn, through the gardens, over the fence, beyond
the roses and into the woods, you might be lucky to
find there the winding path that leads through the
brush and past the trees and on down farther, all the
way to the creek. I'd walked there plenty of times as a
child, sometimes with Brodie and sometimes by myself
and sometimes in the company of one of my grandfather's slavering yellow dogs. I'd waded out over the
stones in my canvas sneakers and stood in the running
water, and more than once I'd wished for a friend to
come out from the cover of the mottled shade and find
me there.

She'd be a strange girl, I imagined, and wild in a

way, an animal child, raised by woods creatures, maybe. She'd be the opposite of me, that's what. She'd have snarled dull hair and a dirt-smudged face, ragged worn-out clothes, tough-soled bare feet. She'd be shy in one way, wary and on her guard, but friendly in another, lonely and love-starved. It could turn out that she'd find something in me that she liked. We'd get to know each other. I'd bring her food wrapped up in a square of blue bandana—biscuits and cheese and apples and cookies—and a sack of clothes, crisp and clean, without holes or tears, and a pillow to put her head on when she slept, and she could be my own secret single friend. I'd meet her there in the woods whenever I could, and sometimes maybe I'd bring her an extra-special kind of a present, too, something pretty, something frivolous, like a mirror or a marble or a piece of sparkling glass, and no one would suspect a thing, nobody would even know about her except for me.

Of course she'd be glad to see me. She'd get so she was hoping for me, expecting me, waiting for me to show up, sometimes. We probably wouldn't talk to each other much, at first. We'd have a secret, silent understanding between us, a mutual acknowledgment that made it so we wouldn't have to. Maybe she couldn't talk anyway. Maybe she'd have been living on her own and alone for so long that she'd invented some crazy language for herself, with words and phrases that only she could understand, and then she'd have to teach all of it to me, and I'd be quick to learn. We'd be so close, though, that for the most part we'd each one know what the other one was thinking, even before she spoke. Of course we'd like all the very same things.

Of course we'd always want to do the very same things. So we'd go climbing trees and walking along through the shallows of the creek bed together. Sometimes we'd hold each other's hand. We'd have made a plan to meet on such and such a day at such and such a time, and then I'd find a way to slip away and come down to the creek, with a bag of sunflower seeds so we could sit with our feet in the water and crack the seeds and spit out the shells, and she'd turn to me and tell me in her own way about how glad she was to have me with her there.

Of course none of that ever happened, really, but after a while, anyway, it got so I was, in spite of myself and my knowing that it was only a dream and never likely to in any way come true, longing harder and harder for the sudden appearance of this singular girl. I did my best to wish her into being, because it seemed to me that that was all that I could do. Standing under the trees, in the cool dappled summer sunlight, with the birds and squirrels and whatever else there was around me that made the noises of the woods that came together to create what was a silence of a kind at the same time, I'd gaze into the shrubs and seem to see her there, a girl shadow moving, and I would wait for her to step forward, in her blue jeans and her sneakers, with her hair tied up in the back just exactly the same as mine. I'd hear the sound of a footstep, maybe, a rustling of leaves that was more solid than only the wind. And there'd be her voice in my ear, and my own name spoken—May?—and I'd turn around, fast, fully expecting to find that she was there, watching out, waiting for me to see her. But she never was. Or, anyway, I never did.

November 16

Dear Vivienne,

*Hi! How is everybody, anyway? I am doing just fine.
Hope you all are doing fine. Sorry I haven't wrote in a
long time. Me and my sister were just put in a foster home
which maybe by now you already know.*

*Thanksgiving is coming up soon. I'm hoping you'll
have a nice one for yourselves. I won't be able to go home
for Thanksgiving because my social worker has said my
family didn't want us to come. Elgin in particular because
he just can't stand being around me anymore.*

*Well I'll let you go for now. So I hope to be hearing from
you real soon.*

*Your friend as always the same as ever just me . . .
Frankie*

MY MOTHER TOOK THE FIRST FLIGHT SHE COULD GET BACK TO LINWOOD
from Chicago, and Frankie and I picked her up at the airport.
We watched her step off the plane into the blinding sunlight,
with her head down and her hand on her hair to keep it in
place, and Frankie turned to me and gave me one of her wise-
guy, told-you-so, know-it-all smiles.

"She's hung over," she said. "Big night last night." She
twirled her finger at me. "Whoop-de-doo."

"You've got a dirty mind, Frankie Crane," I told her.

Which only widened her grin. She tossed her head, let her
dark hair fly. "You bet I do, May Caldwell. You just bet goddamn I do, and you should be happy for it, too."

It took Grand and my dad a little bit longer than that to get back themselves. They drove the station wagon straight home as fast as they could after the news of what had happened to Meems had finally wended its way into the deep woods over lakes and creeks and rivers and streams to them, in their fishing boat, lines cast. They showed up at the house in the middle of the afternoon two days later, both of them unshaved and unwashed, groggy, sunburned, smelling like wood smoke and whiskey and sweat, their faces creased and set as hard and grim and determined as flattened dried gray dirt after a rain and then a day or more of good strong sun.

We'd kept the store closed, and someone with good intentions had gone down and hung a black wreath on its front door. Out of respect, my mother said, trying her best to dredge up an understanding smile. It was a kindness, she explained, a gesture of decency, and they'd meant well. But she sure didn't want Grand to see it, because we all knew it would only be something else, one more thing on top of a thousand others, that was going to end up making him mad. Bad enough that his wife of almost fifty years had died, and he hadn't been there to hold her hand and help her through it, without adding on to that a bunch of people who were as good as strangers to him all making too much fuss and too much noise, all having to ask questions and give advice, all offering their particular condolences and just generally stirring feelings up inside him that he would have preferred to keep covered over. He just wanted everybody, even us, his own family, to go away and leave him alone so he could savor his pain in silence and solitude, like a cat that crawls down under the house and hides there in the dust and the darkness until she either gets better or she doesn't and she dies.

But Meems had been too well liked by too many people for any of that, and nobody was going to let her go on out of this life and into another one without an acknowledgment of some kind, and they were not going to abandon us to our grief, either. They dropped by at the mortuary for the viewing on the day before the funeral—droves of them coming and going, all those families that Meems had kept track of and written her personal thank-you notes to over the years that they'd spent furnishing the rooms of their homes through us, and every one of them had some special little bit of business that they remembered about her and wanted to describe to one of us, myself or my mother or my father, some endearing memory that they wanted the chance to explain again to Grand.

The Tower Funeral Home was on the west side of Linwood, and its business had been in the Tower family for going on their fourth generation of sons. People liked Tower's because it was in an old house whose rooms had been converted to accommodate their mortuary needs. It felt more like someone's home than an institution, with its carpeted entryway and the framed mirrors and the paintings on the walls and the pretty print wallpapers and curtained windows and a wide staircase that led up to the second story with a broad curve of wooden banister, painted white.

Meems's coffin had been placed up on a sort of raised carpet-covered platform at the far end of the main viewing room, in front of the big stone fireplace that had, in another time, been the warm center of the room, in fact of the whole house. The coffin was closed, in accordance with Grand's tersely barked order that my mother keep the whole business as short and simple as she could.

My mother was standing just inside the outer door, greeting a steady stream of guests. She was wobbly on her feet. She wrung her hands, crushing tissues, and slowly shredding them. Brodie hovered nearby, his hands in his pockets and then out of them again, his hair cut too short, and his cheeks shaved too close. His face was flushed and shining; he kept stretching his neck and turning his head from one side to the other, uncomfortable in his tight collar and his dark suit and his wide striped tie. His shirt kept coming untucked.

Grand himself had taken cover in another more private room, one that was reserved for just the immediate family members behind a mirrored window that he could see out of but nobody else could see in. It was a marvelous arrangement, Ralph Tower took the time to boast to us, his face reddening— the bereaved could see and not be seen, he explained, so we could keep track of who was there and who was not and know that we still had our own privacy, watching them. Grand didn't care. Or at least, he never bothered to take a look. He wouldn't talk to anybody, either, not even to the ones who had been his and Meems's oldest good friends. As far as he was concerned he was the only person who had ever known her. He didn't want to share her. I didn't blame him. I felt closer to him, because he seemed to feel the same as I did and it was a relief, in a way, for me to be able to recognize something of myself in him.

He wouldn't speak, or maybe it was only that he couldn't. What words would he have had to tell anybody about how he felt? It wasn't anything that he had ever had to say out loud to anyone but her before. He turned his chair around so his back was to Ralph Tower's mirror, and he closed his eyes and sat there that way, so still that if you didn't know him you might have believed that he had fallen asleep. He endured what he had to by sucking himself down into himself, and he hunched down over himself, and he became a rock–unmoving, unmoved.

My mother said later that it was only that he was an old man, and that handicapped him so he didn't know how to behave the right way in such an uncomfortable and unhappy and public situation. He'd always had Meems there with him before, and she would have told him beforehand what he was supposed to do and how he was supposed to feel, what he was supposed to say and how he could be expected to behave, and, my mother said, we should forgive him for his hardness, because that wasn't what he meant to be, it was only what he was.

What I saw was how he looked to me in the dim evening light on his back screened porch, with the summer hovering around us outside, warm and fresh and pleasant in spite of anybody's grief, and how he'd be sitting there, listening to the comfort of the night noises in the woods, and how he'd look up suddenly, as if maybe he'd heard something; his hands would be frozen, and he'd listen. What I saw were his nicked fingers and the wood chips in his lap and the troubled dark shadow that kept clouding over on his brow.

A big part of what was making Grand so unhappy, I knew, was that he simply missed his wife. And another part, I thought, was that he couldn't help but speculate toward putting some blame on his own self for the fact that she was dead. Maybe he shouldn't have gone off fishing with my dad in Canada. Maybe he shouldn't have left Meems in the care of a stranger, a smiling splayfoot nurse.

On the wall in the hallway past the living room there was a photograph of Brodie and Grand and Meems and my mother all together, posed side by side, and in it Brodie and my mother had their arms around each other's shoulders, and all four Hadens were trying to smile and look happy—they were a family of loved ones, inseparable and undamaged still. Brodie and my mother grinned at the camera stupidly. Brodie was a boy and my mother was a girl, and he was blond and fair and baby-faced, and she was leggy and awkward and thin. On one side of the two of them was Meems, an angel sweet and small, with her hands brought together and folded at her throat and her head tilted prettily to one side. Grand stood on the other side of his children; larger, he loomed, darker-haired and deeper-browed. He had a presence that Brodie and Meems and my mother all three of them seemed to lack, a weight that made him seem more solid than they were, and next to him his children were only just pale shadows of their father's bigger bulk.

Maybe? my mother said. Maybe if you'd stayed home? Maybe if you'd locked her in a room. Maybe if there'd been no parties, no music, no laughter, no games, but only silence and stillness and solitude, then maybe Meems would have lived? But, for what?

He looked at her. He reached his hand out and folded it over hers. You know what Meems would say to that, my mother had gone on. You know what she would have said. And he'd nodded his head, and he'd sighed. He'd looked off into the trees. He still missed her anyway, he said. He didn't miss her any less, knowing that her life had been full. He wished that she was still there, with him, and he understood the honest selfishness of that desire, and he wasn't sorry for it and he wasn't asking to be forgiven for it, either.

Brodie sat in the front row of the chairs in the big room, face to face with the coffin, but he couldn't concentrate on it, or on anything. He would have rather been outdoors, I guess, riding his mower over the grass, digging in his garden, whacking a path through the weeds in the woods between the trees. He kept looking around, watching the people coming and going. He had a tightened, worried look on his face, as if maybe he wasn't really ready to understand yet exactly what was going on, as if he didn't quite know the reason why he was there, and he was going to be surprised later when he realized that what had happened was that Meems was gone. He held a thinking burl that I'd given him, and it kept him occupied, in a way, as he turned and rolled it, over and over. His eyes scanned the crowd as he squeezed the burl and rubbed it between his four fingers and the flat of his thumb.

I couldn't stand any of this anymore, after a while. Because I knew that what was going to happen next was either I was going to have to leave, just get up and walk out the door and off and away, or else I was going to have to do something dreadful, something unbecoming and unladylike, embarrassing and unforgivable, like burst out laughing too hard over nothing or break down crying too loudly over everything, or maybe I'd throw something—take off my shoe and hurl it over the heads of the mourners, toward Ralph Tower, through his marvelous mirrored glass—or else, and more likely, I'd say something that I shouldn't or I'd touch something that I wasn't supposed to, and I didn't even know what that could be. Only that when I did it, this thing, whatever it was, would have broken my spell, and I'd have changed myself by it, permanently. I'd have drawn everyone's eyes toward me, I'd have become visible to all of them, for once. They'd see me, and when they did, then that would be the end of who I was.

There was this fear, then, and it was a strong storm of feeling that was boiling up inside of me, and I didn't understand exactly what it was, and I was afraid that I was not going to be able to control it if I ever let it go too far. The way my father bit down on his anger, this was something of my own that had to be held back, or else it would get away from me, I was afraid, and then I didn't know what would happen. Anything. Everything. I'd explode, maybe. I'd burst into a million sparkly pieces. Or I'd implode. I'd come crashing inward on myself. What I wanted to do was go upstairs and open a window and climb out onto the roof and close my eyes and jump.

At the top of the main staircase in the Tower Funeral Home there was another, smaller viewing room, and its door had been left ajar, by mistake or on purpose, for air maybe, or out of carelessness, I didn't know which and it didn't matter anyway, but in the middle of the room there was an old, old man, and he was as dead as a doornail, lying there flat on his back, nestled in against the snowy white satin cushions of an opened coffin with his eyes closed and his hands folded, in peace. Somebody else's loss, a memorial service scheduled for later in the day, after the Haden funeral was over with and cleaned up after. I peeked in, and then I went in, and I closed the door after me, and I crossed the room to this dead old man, and I stood over him, and I looked down at him, and what his being dead did to how he looked was make it seem like maybe he wasn't actually real. He might have been a mannequin, or a color photograph, or an elaborate plastic doll. His skin was waxy, pasty, powdery. This is what death looks like, I thought. And the truth is, to me, it didn't look half bad. I could imagine myself lying there like him, with my own two eyes closed and my own two hands folded so calmly that way. I could be wearing the white-and-silver-threaded fancy dancing dress again, I thought, and those splendid glittery shoes.

I went to the window and tried to open it, but it was stuck. I saw Frankie outside, in the parking lot. Creighton was with her. They were having a conversation of some kind. An argument, maybe. She waved her hand at him. He kicked at a stone.

There was this: Her flowery skirt. His black sneakers. Her red shoes, which my father would comment upon later, saying they were inappropriate for the occasion, forgetting that maybe they just happened to be all she had. His long legs in torn and faded jeans. Her bracelets. His hair hanging to his shoulders, tucked back behind his ears, limp, oily, dirty-looking. His blue eyes, bright with anger. Two dime-sized circles of color in his cheeks. The sports jacket he was wearing, even though it was so hot. It was too big for him. The shoulders were too broad and square and the sleeves were too long—their cuffs hung down past his wrists. That jacket looked just like one that I thought I might have seen sometime on my father's own back. Creighton had a tie on, too, it was knotted around his bare neck and it lapped down over the front of his T-shirt like a long silky tongue. Frankie was gesturing, lifting her arms and tossing her head. No, she told him. He leaned toward her, asking again. The wind blew her hair into her face, and it swirled through her skirt. He turned away from her, then came back. He spoke to her, his lips tightened, his face reddening even more. Dimes to quarters, now. He raised his hands, and exposed his fists—empty, but knuckled and hard. She stepped back, but he reached out and grabbed her, pulled her to him, bending so his face was close to hers. She struggled against him for a moment, and when he let go of her she straightened her skirt, tossed her head, and collected herself. She glanced up at the building. She seemed to be looking right at me, and I started to wave to her, and I tried again to get the window to budge, but already she'd turned away. He followed her across the parking lot, off toward her car. She got in, and he got in, and then the two of them drove away.

July 22

Dear Vivienne,

Hi and howdy and all like that. How have you and your family been doing these days? I'm doing just fine so far. I am so sorry for not being in touch with you.

I've been going just about every day to see my uncle Elgin in the hospital and that takes up a lot of my time.

He got his arms caught in a fertilizer spreader. It took all
the meat off his arms from his shoulder down to his hands.
The doctors said they might have to amputate his arms.
He did lose a lot of blood. You've never seen such a mess I
hope and I hope you never will. But he can move his
fingers some so maybe he'll get to keep his arms after all.

I want to thank you again for all you've sent and done
for me over the years. You are the best and I mean that.
Thank you.
Well I guess I've got to go. So I'll talk to you later.
Bye for now . . . Frankie

AND THEN THERE WAS THE FUNERAL ITSELF, BUT FRANKIE WASN'T THERE.
The organ playing, a woman in a dark purple dress pumping at
the pedals with her feet. People filing in, sitting down, shifting
in their seats, leafing through their programs, coughing into
their fists. There was Ralph Tower up in front of a lectern with a
microphone, and he was speaking about Meems and Grand,
about death and flowers, about resurrection and deliverance,
about angels and roses and the bright blue endlessness of the
summer sky. There was my mother's head bowed, her face in
her hands, her shoulders shaking. There was Brodie sitting next
to me, fiddling with his burl until my father put his big hand
out finally and touched Brodie, stilling him. There was Grand
looking like he might have been hollowed out, with his hands
on his knees and his head bent and bowed, his eyes black and
blank as he stared downward, toward the toes of his shoes.
There was the ride in the limousine then, with me hungry and

ashamed of that. I saw a fast-food restaurant with a picture of a hamburger on a poster in the window, and instead of feeling sorrowful or reverent, I was only wishing that we could pull over and stop for a minute, to grab a bite to eat.

There was the constant perfumy smell of all those flowers—roses, so many roses, because everybody who knew her knew how much she'd loved them—a scent that was so much close enough to being something like Meems herself that I began to feel lightheaded and sick to my stomach, and I had to roll down the window and gasp in the fresh air. When I raised my hand to my face, my mother put her arm around my shoulders, meaning to be a comfort to me because she thought I might be going to cry, but I wasn't, I was only gagging on the smell. The smell of roses that would forever afterward smell to me like age and grief and guilt.

There was the cemetery, Linwood Memorial, a vast green grassy meadow broken by stones and angels and monuments and one great mound of upturned earth, so black and wet that it drew Brodie to it; I saw how he looked at it, with longing, and I knew that he was wanting to put his hands into it, to kneel down next to it and roll up his sleeves and waggle his bare fingers in.

Ralph Tower said a few more words then. And we each of us placed our single rose on the coffin's lid, walking up to it, one by one. We turned away from the grave, and with that, it was done. I saw that my mother's sharp high heels were sinking into the grass, hobbling her, as she moved across it toward the waiting limousine. She walked on one side of Grand, and my father walked on the other, both of them helping him as if he'd become something frail and old and huddled now, no longer his hardened, dark, and solemn self.

I looked up and saw Frankie then, which was a relief. She was standing next to Brodie, who was looking up at a black marble angel with folded hands and outspread wings. She'd changed her clothes. She was wearing torn blue jeans and an orange blouse and tennis shoes. Her hair looked tangled; there was a smudge of dirt on her forehead and a hectic flush in her cheeks.

"You okay?" I asked.

She turned to me. "Why wouldn't I be?"

"Where have you been?"

"I went for a drive," she said. Then, "What are you, my mother?"

I shook my head. "I was worried about you," I told her. "That's all."

Frankie tossed her hair. "Don't worry about me, May," she said. "All right? Worry about yourself."

"But your face is dirty," I told her.

She swiped at her forehead with the back of her hand. "Anything else, May?" she asked.

I shook my head.

She looked at her watch—leather-banded, gold-faced, she'd swiped it from the display case in the Market Jeweler's downtown just the week before. She smiled.

"Hungry?" she asked.

And I smiled back at her, relieved.

"Starved," I said.

Brodie had stepped up closer to the angel. He was reaching up, trying to touch his fingertips to its flawless face.

"Brodie," Frankie said. He stopped, with his hand still up, and turned to us. "You hungry, Brodie?" she asked him. "Want some food? Some lunch?"

He dropped his hand. He nodded. "I'm hungry," he said. He stepped toward us. "Hamburgers?"

And Frankie threw her head back and laughed. "Hamburgers!"

Brodie looked at her, smiling slightly, still questioning. "French fries?"

"Yes," she said. "And root beer. Tenderloins. Chili fries. Onion rings. Brownie sundaes."

His smile had widened. He looked at me and nodded his head, hard. "Okay," he said. "Okay, May?"

And Frankie took his hand and answered back at him, "You betcha, Brodie, my man. A-okay."

I saw my dad at the bottom of the hill, standing by the limo. Grand and my mother had climbed inside, and he'd turned back to look for Brodie and me. I waved to him. He called out to us, but I pretended not to hear him, and I waved again and turned away, and Frankie and I led Brodie down the hill toward where she'd parked her car.

First thing, Frankie put the top down. Brodie sat behind us, leaning forward with his hands on the backs of our seats and his face lifted up into the wind.

I dug in the glove box and got a cigarette and lit it and passed it to her.

"I don't like funerals, May," Frankie said. "I think I've just about had my fill of death."

"It's okay, Frankie," I told her. I took the cigarette from her.

"You shouldn't worry about me, you know."

"But I saw him," I said. "I mean, you and him. And it had me a little worried, that's all."

She smiled. "Me and him?" she said.

"Creighton."

She took the cigarette back. "Well, what about him?" she asked.

"I saw you talking to him, that's all," I told her. "Outside in the parking lot. This afternoon. Before the service."

"Oh you did, did you?"

I nodded. "He looked mad, Frankie."

She snorted. "Well, he was mad, May," she said. "He was real mad. But he's not mad anymore."

"Do you want me to do something?"

She looked at me, puzzled. "Something like what?"

"I don't know. Get my dad or something? Call the police?"

And she laughed again. She slapped the steering wheel. "God, no, May. Why would I want you to do that?"

"Well, what if he hurts you?"

"Who, Creighton or your dad?"

"Creighton. What if he, I don't know, does something crazy?"

"He's not going to do anything crazy," she said. "I can absolutely promise you that."

Then she smiled at Brodie, and he grinned back at her, uncomprehending. She turned up the radio, loud.

Frankie took us to the A & W out on Seventeenth Street, a drive-up where they brought your food to you on an aluminum tray and served it right there in your car. We ordered, and then while we waited Frankie opened up the glove box, and she brought out another bottle of bourbon, this one exactly like the first one that I'd found there, except that it was almost all the way full.

We passed the bottle back and forth, and ate our hamburgers and our tenderloins, shared onion rings and french fries, slurped at big cold mugs of root beer. Brodie ate so much so fast that I was afraid he might get sick. I handed him the whiskey and told him to take a sip to slow him down. It made him sputter. He coughed. He started to hand the bottle back over the seat to me, but then he changed his mind, and he kept it. He took another swallow, without choking on it this time, and he smacked his lips.

"You like that stuff, Brodie?" Frankie asked.

But he'd taken another bit of hamburger and his mouth was full. He nodded, chewing.

"I was starved," Frankie exclaimed, munching on a french fry. "Famished. I think I could just about have eaten up this whole town." She turned to Brodie and touched her finger to his cheek. "And you're so sweet," she said, "that I think I could just about eat you."

He pulled back from her, alarmed.

"Oh, but I won't," she said. She smiled at him. "Don't worry, Brodie-boy. I won't."

He'd spilled a dabble of ketchup on his white shirt. Frankie licked a corner of her napkin and leaned across the back of her seat to dab it on him, and Brodie pointed at the floor near his feet, where Frankie's flowered skirt was wadded up into a ball. Frankie scrambled up to her knees and bent over the back of the seat and grabbed it. "Ugh," she said. "You've made a big mess, Brodie."

She got out of the car and carried the bundle of the skirt over to a trash can and stuffed it in. She came back brushing off her hands.

"That was your skirt, Frankie," I said.

She looked at me. "I know that."

"You're just going to throw it away?" I asked.

"It's ruined, May. All right? And I never liked it that much anyway, besides."

Then she took the bottle of bourbon away from Brodie and drank from it and passed it on over to me.

WHEN WE GOT BACK TO GRAND HADEN'S HOUSE WHAT WE FOUND WAS ALMOST like a party, except it wasn't. People had brought food, and they let themselves in through the back door or stood on the porch and knocked at the front. They hovered outside in small groups, on the grass or the steps or around the pool, still dressed in their good clothes, sipping coffee or plastic cups of punch or white wine. Cars were parked willy-nilly all over Brodie's cleanly mown lawn, just as they always had been in the past, at the best of Grand and Meems's fancy parties.

But, inside the house, the gaiety was gone, replaced by an agreed-upon solemnity, broken only every now and then by someone's raised voice, a woman's brayed laughter, a door too loudly shut. Grand was out on the back porch, sitting in a chair, drinking his whiskey in a glass without ice. The half-gone bottle was on the floor near him; for once, he wasn't even trying to hide the fact that it was there. It didn't seem to be making him feel any better, though. He wasn't speaking to anybody still, he was just sitting there, drinking and staring down at the ground. People would come up and talk to him, and he'd look at them, his face empty and uncomprehending, and then they'd decide to move on. Until finally Paul Gerald and my father came, and they helped Grand up to his feet and then took him back to his room and made him go to bed.

I looked up, and there was Brodie, walking in his bare feet across the grass, in his good pants and his good shirt, ketchup-stained, and his nice tie, but barefoot. He dropped down to his hands and knees, and started to dig around with his fingers in the garden dirt. My mother got up to go to him, but Frankie put her hand out and stopped her.

"Oh, leave him be, how about?" she said. "He's not hurting anything, is he?"

I sat in a chair by the pool, watching the water and sipping at a can of Coke that Frankie had been kind enough to spike for me, until after a while my dad came down and joined me there. He sat on a chair near mine. He reached over and put his big hand on my knee. I looked at him, feeling dizzy.

"You okay, May?" he asked.

I told him that I thought I was.

And then he started talking, but I couldn't make any sense of what he was saying. Something about Meems and Brodie and my mother and Grand. His words seemed all mixed up and garbled to me, pure nonsense, but I didn't mind listening to it for a while anyway.

He'd asked me something. He was looked at me, waiting for me to answer.

"What?" I said. "What?" I tried to sit up.

And I could see the anger that was squirming in the muscles of his face, working his jaw, creasing his brow and curling his lip. He snatched my can of soda out of my hand, and at first I thought maybe he was going to take a drink of it himself; he brought it up to his mouth as if that was what he was going to do, but he didn't drink it, he only smelled it. He looked up, past me, and I turned, and we both saw that there was Frankie, standing on the hill, in her jeans and her orange blouse, and she had her hands out and her hair was flying and she was barefoot, skipping, floating down over the grass toward us. She saw my father stand up then, and she stopped.

"Frankie," he said.

"Mr. Caldwell." She grinned. She fished in her pocket for a cigarette, lit it, offered one to him. He waved it away.

"How are you feeling, Frankie?" he asked.

She looked at him, suspicious now. "Fine," she said. "Considering."

"Considering what?"

She tapped ashes and shrugged. "Considering the circumstances, what else?"

"May has been drinking," he said.

And I felt the heat rising to my face, scalding in my cheeks. I tried to get up, but I was groggy, and all I could say was, "Dad . . ."

Frankie was frowning. She crossed her arms and cupped her elbows. "Do tell," she said. She turned to me. "Is that so, May?" she asked.

I nodded.

Frankie shrugged again. "So what?"

"So this," he said. "I suspect that you're the one who gave it to her, who encouraged her to drink it, who made her think that it was something that she wanted to do."

I was standing up then. "Dad," I said, again. I stumbled toward him. "She didn't . . ."

But he put his hands on my shoulders and pressed me back into the chair again. "Sit down, May," he said. "Don't say anything. Stay put."

Frankie looked at me. "Are you going to take that from him?" she asked.

My father kept one hand on my shoulder, and he bore down on me with it, holding me in place. I tried to shrug against it, but it was as if I'd been paralyzed by him. I stayed put.

"I suggest you pack your bags now," my father said to Frankie. "Party's over. Your welcome here is worn out."

Frankie was angry, I could tell, but I wasn't sure whether it was with him for pushing her around or with him for pushing me around or with me for letting myself be pushed. I saw the fire that burned up into her face—it shone in her eyes, for a moment.

Brodie came around the corner on his mower, careening over the grass.

When I looked again, Frankie was gone.

Chapter Eleven

I LOOKED EVERYWHERE FOR HER, BUT NO-body could tell me where Frankie was. I went from room to room and outside by the pool and in the driveway and in the yard, but she was gone.

What made me mad was two things: one, that my father had said those things to Frankie and, two, that I knew that what he'd said was right. I was angry with my dad for being who he was on the one hand and with Frankie for being who she was on the other and with both of them for acting just the way that they could have been expected to act. I walked all the way through the house to what I was thinking was going to be the sanctuary of Meems's bedroom far away at the back.

The door had been kept closed and the windows shut and the air conditioning on, so the room was gloomy and chilly. I shivered and hugged myself. The aluminum hospital bed was gone. Grand had had it moved up to the attic with Meems's old mahogany frame, which probably he couldn't bear to bring back down into the house again either—one bed would have reminded him too much of the present situation and the other would have made him think too much about the past. The carpet had been recently vacuumed, and the whole room had been cleaned, so it smelled like furniture polish and disinfectant, and that rotten pondwater smell of Meems's was gone. There was the basket of matchbooks. And Meems's dressing table, still covered with her bottles and jars of cosmetics and creams. The reading chair. The chaise where Frankie had lounged, blowing on her wet nails. The phonograph and the jazz records that we'd listened to together, with Frankie standing at the window screen smoking a cigarette and snapping her fingers and waggling her hips.

She'd taught me how to shimmy. "Lean forward, May, like this," she'd said, hunching her shoulders in toward her breasts, "and then you just hang them down soft and loose, see, and you give yourself a shake."

Outside, the sun was starting to go down, and it was beginning to get dark. And I was standing there in Meems's half-empty bedroom when I felt it, all at once, a cold black dread that rose up and flooded over me. It was this: the certain knowledge Frankie was going to leave me. That it was over now, and she might, in fact, have already gone. She was going to drive off into the sunset. She'd go to Hollywood and become a movie star. Or to Arizona to live like an Indian on the flattened top of a mesa, sleeping on a blanket in the grass out under the stars. Or to New York to be a model, or to Chicago or Atlanta or Denver or Washington, D.C. She could go anywhere and become anything she wanted, she could do anything, Frankie could, because she'd spent her whole life learning how to live by helping herself.

I clenched my fists and closed my eyes. I thought I could smell roses. I thought I could hear the rustle of angels' wings. I opened my eyes again and looked into my own dim reflection in the mirror on Meems's dressing table—my face seemed a featureless blank oval, framed by a fall of plain brownish hair, as if I'd been erased, undone and unmade, like Grand's clay sculpture of Meems. Without Frankie to reflect me, I thought, who would I ever be?

I turned to run off, I didn't know where, anyplace, someplace. All I wanted was to find a way to lose myself, to escape from not only who I was, but also who I wasn't.

But there was Paul Gerald, standing in the doorway, and he stopped me. With the light shining from behind him, his whole body seemed like it might have been on fire. He reached out for me, and I fell against him. I sobbed, once. He brought his arms up and cradled me in them. His hand at the back of my neck felt warm and soft. He bent and kissed me on the temple—the touch of his lips against my skin was a swift, sharp shock, dizzying, as if a bolt of lightning had struck me in the head. I looked up at him, and his eyes held mine.

His breath was in my hair. His lips moved over my ear, a whisper, my name. May? I bent away, and I opened myself up to him. I turned my body toward him, and I found his face, and I kissed him.

I couldn't tell anymore, what was my fault and what wasn't. What was my own doing and what was the doing of somebody else. Frankie came to Linwood, Meems died, Frankie left, I turned to Paul. I could do what Frankie did, maybe. If she wasn't there, I could become her. I could be the girl that she was, maybe. I could help myself.

Paul must have known all of this, somehow. Maybe he'd seen it in me, long before. And now, he didn't seem surprised, he seemed glad. Grateful, in a way, that was all. It was as if he'd been expecting this. Or hoping for it, anyway. As if I'd made a promise somehow, and now I was keeping it, and there we were.

He closed the door and stood with his back to it. I leaned into him, with my face turned and my cheek pressed against his chest. I listened to the sounds of his body—his heartbeat, his breath, his insides moving. His voice, hollow and deep and far away.

"May."

And I reached up and skittered my fingertips over the angles of his face.

So, then, was it me? Had I been the one who'd started it? Was all of it all my fault? Had I gone out looking for something else that summer, for something more than what I'd had, and was it my looking for it that had brought that something else about, that had brought that something more into being in my life and in Frankie's and then after that in Paul's? Was I asking for it? Did I get what I'd deserved? And was it just my asking for it that came back to me and made it so? Whatever it is you want most, my mother said, that's what you have to give away. What I wanted most was just myself. And so when Paul turned to me, I gave him what he wanted. I gave myself away.

He smiled at me, and his face creased with his smile, with what I took to be the kindness and the understanding of it. His eyes worked to catch and hold on to mine, but I fought him at first, and I tried not to look back. I tried to ease past him, at first. And he almost let me go, but then something else happened, and he changed his mind, and I could feel how close he was to me—his body seemed to be pulsing toward mine, and he stepped in front of me, and I stopped. I looked up into his face. I let myself be drawn up into his eyes—green as moss, with specks of gray smoke and sparks of a yellowish flame. He touched my cheek with his thumb, and I felt an ache—it tugged at me and seemed to pull me down. He drew me toward him, closer. He enveloped me, he folded himself over me, and I could hear him moan as he held me that way, as he kissed me again, as he moved his hands over my shoulders and down my arms and pinned my hands and trapped me.

I started to pull away, and he stopped and opened his eyes and looked at me.

"It's all right, May," he said. "I won't hurt you," he told me. "I won't do anything you don't want me to do."

He reached out and began to unbutton my dress.

"If you want me to stop, May," he said, his voice deepening, "I will."

I shook my head.

He closed his eyes, and he slipped his hand inside my dress and over my breast, squeezing it, twisting its hardened nipple, gently, tugging at it with his finger and his thumb, drawing out the ache in me. He lifted my skirt. He slipped his hand up the back of my leg, his fingers slid inside my underpants, they glossed over me. He moaned again. I tried to push him away, but it was too late for that, already it had all gone too far. He couldn't stop himself, and I couldn't stop him. He was tearing at my clothes, he was pressed against me, and he was lifting me to him. With his hands under my buttocks he hoisted me closer, and then he sank himself into me, he bent me back and pinned me, he stabbed me with an exquisite shrill pain that felt as if it might be breaking me, it might be smashing me, I might be about to shatter into a million bright pieces, like Brodie's own brainful of birdshot stars.

And I arched my back and looked up past him, and there was Brodie standing in the twilight outside the window, looking in, watching us. He seemed to have become a boy again, with dirt smudged on his face and mud covering his hands. He was holding a bunch of wild flowers that he'd picked in the woods. I struggled, gasped, cried, pulled away. Paul let me go. Brodie looked at me, and then at Paul. I could see his face there on the other side of the glass, and his mouth was moving, saying my name, asking me, "May?"

I turned away then, and I ran.

I SKITTERED OUT OF THE HOUSE, ACROSS THE MACADAM, OFF THE DRIVEWAY AND onto the gravel road. My dress flapped open, baring me. My hair flew in my face and stuck there, blinding me. I was damp, hot, breathless; my body felt shapeless, loose and flowing, a waft of moist warm air; I'd become a phantom again. I stumbled along the shoulder of the road in the dark, kicking through the fine dirt, ruining my good shoes. A car sailed past, its brake lights flashed as it slowed, pulled over, then stopped. It backed up to me, and then stopped again. Inside, I could see, it was Paul. He was leaning across the seat and opening the passenger side door. He was looking up at me.

"May?" he said.

I turned away, slipped down into the ditch. I could hear him behind me. He wasn't giving up. He'd turned off the engine and was skidding in his soft shoes; he was coming after me. I kicked a can out of the way, I stumbled on an old tire, and then I fell.

Paul helped me up to my feet. He turned me toward him again. I was limp in his arms. I had no will of my own anymore. He kissed me, lightly, and then he let me go. I looked up at him, and turned away. He took my elbow and led me up out of the ditch, down the road, to his car.

PAUL DROVE ME HOME. HE TOLD ME HE WAS SORRY, AND I WASN'T SURE whether that made me feel better, or worse.

"No, it's all right," I told him.

He put his arm around me and pulled me close to him. I nestled myself up against him, and he kept bending over and kissing my hair.

"You know, I remember when you were a little girl, May," he told me. "The sweetest thing," he said, "you were always smiling, always so pleased with yourself."

This didn't sound like me. I looked at him; he saw my surprise.

"No, really you were," he said. "Sunshine. The light of day itself."

When we got home, my parents were there, waiting for us. He stopped and parked and then ran his hands over his hair, smoothing it. Then he got out of the car and stood, posed, with one hand in his pocket. I heard my mother say his name. My father asked, "Is she all right?" Paul walked across the yard to them, his shoes skimming the grass.

"She's fine," he said. "She was upset, but she'll be all right." He laughed. "Who could blame her?" he said. "It's been a long day."

My mother was thanking him. My father was reaching out to shake his hand, and then he pulled Paul closer, he hugged him, smacked him on the back, then let him go. I got out of the car and walked up to the porch. My father turned to me.

"Okay, May?" he asked. I nodded. I didn't trust myself to speak.

"Thank God for Paul Gerald," my mother said.

And then I followed them up the steps and into the house. Paul beeped his horn twice as he drove away. I lingered downstairs.

"You okay, honey?" my mother asked.

I nodded.

She put an arm around my shoulder. "Don't worry," she said. "Frankie will be back."

I nodded again. "Maybe I'll wait up for her, then."

"Not too late?"

"No."

So then she went upstairs. And then I felt the house come

closing in all around me, dark and empty, and the rooms all seemed to be folding out away from me—there was that silent house, looming and dark, and there had been my lonely childhood lived in it, with my mother busy with her business and, if Frankie was right, her love life, too, and my father self-absorbed and silent, and all the time all that quietness had kept folding over me like a blanket, smothering me beneath its weight.

I turned and went across the hall, to Frankie's room. All of her stuff was still there, just the way that she'd left it—the clothes and the jewelry box and her suitcase and the framed photograph of her dad—and I considered that to be a hopeful sign. It made me think that maybe she might be coming back, after all, even though at the same time I think I already knew better than that. I opened her closet and looked inside at her clothes, still hanging there, the bright dresses, the blouses, a sweater with a tear in the elbow of one sleeve. Her shoes were scattered over the closet floor, among them the tasseled loafers and some sandals, and the jewelry box at the back that I picked up and carried over to the bed. I sat down and held it in my lap and opened it. I looked at what she'd called her finery. And a folded strip of four shots that had been taken in a drugstore photo booth. In one of them she had an arm around Creighton, and in another one she was kissing him, and in another one they were both sticking out their tongues and screwing up their faces, and in the last one she was rolling her eyes while he lapped his tongue against her cheek, and in all of them she was wearing what looked to me like one of Meems's old flowered hats.

I searched Frankie's room then, the drawers with her clothes, socks and underpants and shorts and T-shirts, until finally I found it, under the mattress, her gun.

I held it in my hand, and as I looked at it there was, in my mind, a flash, a spark of recognition, of recalling not what had been forgotten but what had only been unremembered. And it was this: the pool party, at Grand Haden's house, with Brodie and his friends and my parents and theirs when I was six years old, little May Caldwell in my stiff blue dotted swiss party dress and squeaky black patent leather shoes.

April had let me sit next to her in a webbed chair near the pool. She gave me a small sip of her champagne. She fluffed my curled hair with her fingertips and smiled and told me I was pretty. She and Paul Gerald danced, and I stayed where I was so I could watch them, and then April danced with Brodie, and then with Paul again, and I took another sip of her champagne and after a while I dozed off and fell asleep, and then my father found me there, and he picked me up and carried me off to the back of the house, to Meems's room, to put me to bed. That was how it always had been, and I was used to it. There were the same cabbage roses and the same satin sheets and the same laughing angels, all looking down and watching over me. They chortled, they smiled with their fat faces, they squeezed their own dimpled knees.

There was Brodie. There was April. And there was Paul.

Everybody drank too much.

When the party was over, my parents went home, and they left me there, sleeping, but after a while, I woke up. I wandered through the house, looking for Brodie, but I couldn't find him.

I looked out the window, and I saw him hit Paul. Then Brodie was in the kitchen, with April. They were arguing. She was angry. He reached for her, and she pulled away.

There was me, poised in the doorway, in my lilac cotton nightie, calling out to them. Not calling, screaming Brodie's name. My small hands were on the door frame, scrabbling. And there was April, gasping. And there was Brodie bellowing as he hobbled toward me, and there was his hand on my arm, lifting me off my feet, like a hard sweep of wind that turned me and hurled me, weightless, away.

I ran back to my grandmother's bed, and I held my breath, and I looked at the angels, and I heard April scream again, and then the back door slammed as she ran away from him, out of the house and into the back yard. I could see them through the window; they were outside near the pool. He was holding her, and she was trying to get away from him, but he caught her and hit her and her neck snapped back and he hit her again. Brodie stepped away from her. April wavered toward him. She slumped forward and fell to her knees and then to her hands, and then she tumbled over sideways in the grass.

"Brodie?" I whispered. He was standing in Meems's bedroom doorway, with his head resting sideways against the doorjamb. His shoulders were slumped. His hands were hanging at his side. His hair was mussed. His face was smudged with dirt. His shirt was rumpled. He was barefoot. There was mud on the cuffs of his pants.

"Brodie?" I whispered again.

He raised his eyes to look at me. His face was flat, his look solemn, and absent-seeming, somehow. He winced, seeing me, and then with what looked like great effort, he straightened. He stepped forward into the room. He crossed to the bed and sagged to his knees near me. I reached out, and my fingertips brushed the fine blond strands of his hair, and he looked at me and smiled, small, pained. I touched his face, and he turned his cheek against the flattened palm of my hand. He laid his head down on the bed near me. I patted him, like a dog. I palmed his jaw. I fingered the silken softness of his hair.

"Brodie?" I whispered his name again.

He staggered up then, and, groaning, he rolled onto the bed beside me. He moaned and reached for me. He took me into his arms, and he held me against him, blanketing me with his smell, his pulse, his warmth. He was clinging to me. And once more I whispered, "Brodie?"

He pulled back to look at me. He smiled again, and shook his head. He rolled away and lay on his back, with his hands folded behind his head, gazing at the ceiling. The distance between us then was vast and cold. There were crickets outside, creeching. An owl's deep hoot. The flap of heavy wings. I curled into a ball and snuggled against my uncle Brodie. I thought then that everything must be all right after all, so I closed my eyes, and I drifted off, and I let myself fall asleep.

I dreamed about swimming, and I dreamed about trees. I dreamed that I was standing up on top of the high dive and I was looking down and there was Brodie's body—strange and pale, bare except for the bright flowers that bloomed in the heavy fabric of his swimming shorts, his long thin limbs awkwardly outflung against the cold blue bottom of the deep end of the pool.

And then an explosion, like thunder, only closer and louder and harder and sharper, jolted me awake.

THERE WAS ME, SITTING UP IN BED, EYES WIDE AND FRIGHTENED, BECAUSE I didn't know where I was at first, or what was what. There were the angels' faces, unchanged and frozen and gazing down at me. The satin sheets were cold; crumpled, they seemed to lap at my legs like the shallow water in the creek. I was alone.

There was me, and I was running through the house to find him. There were my girl's bare feet on the hardwood floor. My girl's small toes in the carpet. There were my own small arms wrapped around myself, hugging me.

There was Brodie's bedroom. There was the shotgun in his hand.

"I'll kill that old snake, before it bites you, May," he'd told me, brandishing the gun. "I'll shoot it in the head; I'll blow its slimy snaky body into smithereens. For you."

There was Brodie, my uncle Brodie, and he was looking at me, his favorite little girl, and he was not looking at me, too, both at the same time.

There was me, May, and I was calling out to him.

"Brodie? Brodie?"

There was my uncle Brodie, and he was struggling with himself, he was trying to pull himself up. There was Brodie's face, his blond hair fallen forward, his fair face drained white, as white as a billow of summer cloud. He was looking for me, I thought. When he opened his mouth to speak, something dark spilled out; it was a blackness, thick and seeping, and it flowed out over his chin, and it surged down toward his chest.

There was me, May, and I was leaving; there was me, and there was the darkness that was closing down and in and around and over me, and I was lifted out and up and away from myself. There was me, and I had become a speck; I was me, and I was not me.

There was me not me crying out, "Brodie? Oh, no! Brodie?"

Smithereens, he'd said. For you.

What had he done?

There was a little girl in a big room, and there was a young man on the bed near her, and he was trying to sit up, and she could see that he was hurt in some way but in what way was not exactly clear to her, and neither was why, only that it had something to do with a gun and something else to do with his mouth, because he seemed to be bleeding, and he seemed to have a question in his eyes, but he didn't seem to know just what it was, and neither did she.

But she kept calling out to him anyway.

"Brodie?"

She went into the bathroom, because she wanted to help. Her bare feet pattered across the cold white tiles. She opened the cupboard and stood up on her tippy-toes to reach a towel from the lowest shelf. She brought the towel to him, and she handed it to him, and he took it from her, and he looked at it first, puzzled, and then he held it to his face, darkening it, and then he fell back against the pillow, groaning, and his eyes rolled in his head.

There was a smell that wafted up to her. A poop smell that she recognized, and it embarrassed her. She turned away from it; she wrinkled her nose at it; she covered her face with her hands and gagged. He was struggling again, and his hands were scrabbling at the bedspread, he was sitting up again, and he was reaching out for her.

But she was gone. She was running, again. This little girl, only six years old, in a lilac flowered nightie, in bare feet, with snarled hair and chewed nails and skinned knees, is frightened in the deepest part of her, and she's trying to find a way to get away, because she knows that what she can't be anymore is herself. She understands that something terrible has happened, the worst thing, and that she's somehow in it, just because she's seen it, and she's wondering whether it might have even been her fault somehow, because she knows that she should never have been here and she should never have seen this, that it is something that is too far beyond her, something that is too much greater than she is, something that is too deep and too cold and too dark for her, and so she runs away, and she tries to find some safe place to hide.

I HUDDLED IN MEEMS'S CLOSET FOR THE REST OF THE NIGHT, UNTIL THE ROUND window at its end was shimmering with sunshine—another day of sweltering late summer—and then I heard the sound of somebody moving outside in the room.

I got up, and I opened the door, and I peered out through the crack to see that it was Brodie fumbling around, searching for something, it looked like, but I couldn't imagine what. And I wondered whether maybe nothing so bad had really happened to anybody after all, and maybe it all had only been nothing more than a bad dream. His movements were slow and awkward and disjointed-seeming. Puppetlike, and comical in a way. He'd take a step, then stop and look around, thinking, then take another step. And he was naked; his penis was a strange pale stem in the deep shadow between his legs. The hair on his belly was blond and softly curled, something to nuzzle, I thought. But his eyes seemed strangely blind, dazzled-looking, dazed.

The phone was ringing, and I darted out and dashed through the house to answer it, but by the time I got to the den, whoever was calling had hung up, and the line was only dead.

I put on my bathing suit then, because what we'd planned was to go swimming together that day, April and Brodie and me, and maybe Paul, too, and I was hoping that everything still might be going to be all right.

I heard our car pull into the driveway, and then my mother was coming in through the front door. Her voice rang out, calling our names. His first, then mine.

I could hear my mother close the front door after her. She jangled her keys in her hand as she walked into the house, her heels clacking over the hardwood floor, then silent on the carpet, then clacking on the floor again, across the entryway, into the dining room, into the kitchen and out, down the hallway, toward the bedrooms and back, and then, finally, through the living room.

She was calling out our names again. His first, then mine, and with more urgency that time.

I SAT ON THE GUEST BED WHERE FRANKIE HAD SLEPT, AND I HELD HER GUN IN MY hand. I savored its weight, so serious there. I cradled it in my palm, and I saw again that blackness, too, that blankness, that nothingness, and it seemed to close in over me—a cloud, a mist, a shade drawn down. I raised my hand, and I settled the barrel inside the warm, moist circle of my mouth. It clanked against my teeth, and I thought of Brodie, doing this, and I thought maybe I could understand something about the sense of it, finally; at least I thought maybe I could understand what he had thought was going to be the sense that it could make.

Then, after a while I squeezed the trigger, but nothing happened, I wasn't exactly sure why.

Chapter Twelve

FIND CREIGHTON TEMPLE, THEY SAID knowingly, to us and to the press and to each other, and that's where you'll find Frankie Crane. What they reasoned was that Creighton must have taken her, somehow. That he'd kidnapped her, probably held a gun to her head. Or something.

Yes, I told them, she had had a gun. Yes, I said, I had seen it. I thought it was a revolver, isn't that what it's called? It was smallish, black. About so big. But, no, I had never seen her use it, and, no, I didn't know whether she even knew how.

My father watched me, and he listened to my answers, his jaw working, his fists clenching and unclenching, until after a while they asked him, would he mind stepping outside for a moment? Might make it easier for me, and for everybody else, too. Have a cup of coffee, a smoke, relax a little bit, if he could.

The gun had been in the glove box of her car, I said.

I'd seen it there that very first night when she was here. It had been raining, in spurts. I'd been sent out to the car by my mother, to bring in the bags while Frankie took a bath.

But then, later, when I looked for it, the gun was gone. Why had I looked for it? I didn't know. We'd been driving around, and I'd reached into the glove box to get Frankie a cigarette, and that was when I realized that the gun wasn't there anymore. When I asked her about it, she pretended not to know what I was talking about. What gun? she'd asked. She'd been mad at me for bringing it up. Maybe she was still trying to protect him then, I suggested. Seemed like she didn't want me to know that he was there. He'd been an embarrassment to her, that was why. She didn't want to put my dad off any more than he already was, I guessed. If he'd known there was a boyfriend who'd been following her, he'd have kicked her out of the house for sure. That kind of trouble, he would not have wanted. He wouldn't have stood for it, that much had been clear.

And what about the note in Paul Gerald's apartment? I shrugged. Maybe she liked him, I said. Did they have a relationship? Could have. Did Creighton know about it? Yes, probably he did.

What they assumed, then, was that Creighton must have forced Frankie to go off with him. That he'd somehow been able to get his own hands on her gun. That he'd taken her away, and then maybe after that he did something to her, in anger, to shut her up—and not one of them wanted to dwell too long on or think too hard or talk too much about exactly what. He'd destroyed our furniture store first, and then he'd abducted Frankie Crane, and then he'd driven her away, and finally he'd abandoned her car on that dead end street in a rundown neighborhood someplace in downtown Des Moines.

Her car? they asked me. Had she told us that it was her car? I answered, yes, she had. That her uncle Elgin had given it to her. Given? they asked. I nodded, yes. It was a gift, I said. They'd looked at each other. Frankie hadn't been given that car, they told me, she'd stolen it and used it to run away with her boyfriend. Elgin had had some kind of an accident; he'd been laid up in the hospital and hadn't even known that his car was gone until several months later when, both his arms having been amputated, he was released and sent home. I shrugged. I didn't know anything about that, I said.

When they asked me about Creighton, I told them that, yes, I'd seen him. That he'd been hanging around all along, right from the beginning and even before, asking for money first, then showing up outside our house or Grand Haden's every now and then. That we'd even called the police about him once. That what Frankie had told me was that he'd followed her here all the way from Kentucky. Or, not followed her, but preceded her, because he'd known that this was the most likely place she'd come. But we'd all of us known that much from the start— where else but here had Frankie ever had to go?

I told them that I'd seen Creighton on the night of my parents' anniversary party and then again a while later in my own driveway and also in the parking lot outside the funeral home on the day that we'd buried Meems. That Frankie might have been arguing with him about something that last time. That he'd been dressed up, as if he'd been expecting her to introduce him to us, finally. That she'd seemed like she might have been afraid of him, maybe. That she'd told me more than once that Creighton Temple was crazy, it was one of the things she'd liked about him, in the beginning, and she wasn't sure what he might do, or to what lengths he might be inclined to go to get her back and keep her for himself.

My father was outside in the hallway, pacing, smoking, growling. They asked him to come in and sit down again, then they asked him, do you mind, sir, answering a few questions about this girl?

Nothing that I told them was actually a lie. It was what I didn't tell them that maybe made what I said turn out to be something other than exactly the whole entire truth. There was more, but no one ever came out and directly asked me, what? So if they didn't know everything, how could that have been turned around and blamed on me?

Find Creighton Temple, they all told each other, so sure of themselves.

But what I knew was this: that Creighton Temple was gone. And then some.

Smithereens.

It was on the night after Meems was buried that Frankie left us for good. I'd changed into a pair of jeans and a T-shirt and a sweatshirt from her closet, and I'd put her gun in the front pouch pocket, because it felt better to me to have it than not to have it, even if I didn't use it, even if I couldn't use it, even if I didn't know how. What I liked was that I could feel its presence there against my middle, as if it were a weight, grounding me, holding me in place and making it so I didn't drift off.

By that time it was already deep in the middle of the night, and my parents were upstairs, asleep together, zonked out after the funeral, in their bed. My father's car keys were on the counter in the kitchen, near the phone, where he always left them. He was a man of habit, and his habits could be counted on. The back door squeaked, no matter how slowly and carefully I opened it. My sandals slapped the pavement in the driveway, resounding it seemed to me, no matter how silently I tried to walk. The garage door creaked, rising. The car's engine roared to life when I started it. I backed it out and rolled it down to the bottom of the driveway, and then I sat there, peering up through the windshield at the house, with my heart pounding in my ears, and I was expecting at any minute to see a light go on upstairs or my mother's face, pale, framed in a window, peering down, or the front door banging open and my father blundering out. But there was none of that. There was nothing. They didn't know what I was up to. They hadn't heard a thing.

So I was still their invisible daughter, after all. I was still their imperceptible ghost girl, stealing away from them, unnoticed and unheard.

At least I still had that.

I waited until I was at the end of Tyler and veering over onto Broadview before I turned the headlights on. And then there was nothing stopping me; I was as good as gone. I could have headed off for any place I wanted to, but at first I was happy just to prowl the streets in my father's car. At first, that was enough.

More than. Enthralled by the novelty and the naughtiness of it both, I haunted Linwood, cruising through the neighborhoods that I knew just about as well as I knew my own self. I wound around the spin of those circular streets, aimlessly, without any purpose or destination, really; my only plan at that time was plainly not to have a plan. I was going to let those wheels of my dad's lead me off wherever they wanted to, carry me away to any place they would. Through the park, which was deserted at that late hour of the night, except for one car that had been parked all by itself behind the baseball field—not Frankie's Lincoln, it was something smaller, with, I supposed, a pair of lovers in the front seat, kissing. Past the car lots out by the highway, all brightly lit, gleaming glass and chrome—wheels. Around by the high school, dark and empty-looking like some dead bug's abandoned shell.

I came up the hill at First Avenue, glided past the solemn faces on the traffic death toll sign, and surfaced at the top, on Crescent Drive. When the light changed I turned off onto Paul's street.

The trees on either side bent their branches over me, forming a bower of broad leaves. I pulled up to the curb across the street from Paul's building and stopped. I could see that the light was on inside his apartment. So, maybe he was awake then. Or maybe he couldn't sleep either, any more than I could. I wondered whether he was thinking about me and what we'd done.

I imagined Paul on his back in his bed, propped on pillows, with his legs spread out over the watery surface of his sheets. He might be watching television, smoking a cigarette, sipping at a glass of whiskey and ice. Or maybe he was lounging on his white leather sofa, leaning back with his feet on the table, crossed at the ankles. He might be leafing through a magazine, pausing for a moment, looking up and listening, but hearing nothing after all, turning back to his reading again. Or maybe he was lying in his bed, with the television turned off and the light turned off, too, with his eyes closed, maybe he was hoping to be able to sleep, maybe he was holding on to himself, maybe he was trying not to think anymore about me.

I thought I saw his shadow move across the white screen of his curtained window, but then I thought, maybe not. I pictured his telescope, set up there, and I realized that it was possible that he could have been looking through it just then, at me.

The other houses on the block were all dark, closed up tight, all the people in them sleeping. A car came by, its headlights skimming me, but that one wasn't Frankie's Lincoln either.

I coasted down to First Avenue again; then I turned south toward the river. I thought about what it would be like to drive off the bridge into the water, to be carried away by it, so much worthless debris. I could see the HADEN'S sign there among the other buildings, the black and gold letters spelling out my grandfather's name against a glowing bright white background. It seemed to be beckoning me.

So I turned into the parking lot, and I coasted around to the back and stopped.

My father kept his keys all on that one single ring. I let myself into the store through the back door, and then I stood there in the empty showroom, and I felt its silence slide down over me. I was surrounded by furniture, upholstered pieces all waiting to be bought by somebody, sometime. Beds for couples to make love on, couches for husbands to take naps on, tables for families to eat dinner from, or maybe to quarrel over, lamps for them to turn on or off, or maybe to pick up and take aim and throw.

I went into my father's office, and I found the bottle of scotch that I knew he kept in back of the lowest drawer of the filing cabinet behind his desk. I opened it and took a sip. Gasped and winced and took another. I sat down in the padded leather chair. Under the glass of the top of my dad's desk were all the snapshots that he'd collected over the years—photos of me as a little girl, and of my mother and my dad, of Brodie and Meems and Grand, and of all of us together, a family, posed in different ways and placed just so at different times. Paul Gerald was there, too, in one of them. He standing next to Brodie, with his arm around his shoulders, like a best friend, like a brother.

I took another sip of the scotch, and then I picked up the phone, and I called Paul. Listening to the distant ringing in my ear, I pictured him—his hand smoothing back his hair, his bare feet on the carpet, the glint of his watch, the opened collar of his shirt.

"Hello?"

His voice, deep and hollow-sounding, was something that I was not prepared for. It brought him to me clearly, and I remembered him, pulling at me, tugging.

My own silence felt like something dark and deep welling up around me. And he said "Hello?" again. I could hear him breathing. I could picture the knuckles of his hand, his long fingers curled around the curve of the receiver. And then he said, "May? Is that you? May?"

He was drowsy, sleepy-sounding, his words were slurred. He'd been up all night drinking, I thought. What he sounded like to me was drunk.

I looked down to see my own face grinning up at me from a snapshot trapped underneath the press of the desktop glass, but all I could see was the look on Brodie's face, as he stood there at the sink in Meems's little bathroom.

I was thinking about how Brodie had loved April. About how he'd tried to keep her for himself. About how they'd danced at a poolside party and then afterward they'd fought, and she'd told him about Paul, and he'd been angry, and he'd hit Paul.

And I was seeing this, too, outside, in the pool: April Delaney's battered body, face down and floating, turning there below the shadow of the high dive, with one arm outflung, riding the water's wind-rippled veneer. Her fingertips dangling, dipped gracefully down. Her skirt hiked; one bare buttock bobbing. April's hair fanned out, spread like a wet flame, billowing. The swell of her dress flowering out around her, like a blossom set afloat.

"May?" Paul was asking. His words were slow. "Is it you?"

"It's me," I told him.

"May," he whispered, his voice hoarse, "where are you, May?"

"I'm here, Paul," I said. "At the store."

Then I reached forward slowly, and quietly, carefully, I settled the receiver back down into its cradle on the desk. I picked up the bottle of scotch, and I carried it with me through my mother's mocked-up rooms. I was thinking about how I could pretend to be someone in them, that I could walk into one and find a life for myself there—reaching into a crib for my baby, climbing into bed with my husband, setting the table for an important dinner with my boss. I walked out toward the storage room at the back of the store, then down the back steps to the basement underneath.

Light from the streetlamps was spilling in through the wired glass panes of the window well, illuminating Frankie's typewriter, still sitting right there where she'd left it on her desk. I reached out, plunked one key, and then another, but the sound of it was too loud, and it frightened me. I took one more sip of my father's scotch, then capped the bottle and set it down.

I leaned against the bare white limestone wall and closed my eyes and let its hard lumps press against my back. I turned around and spread my arms out and felt the wet coldness of the basement walls seeping into me.

I'd stood in the creek behind Grand Haden's house, and I'd peered out into the woods, searching for the wild girl who was going to show up there and step out from the shadows to become my friend, my other self. But she had never done that, she'd never come, she'd never been there, and I'd always gone home disappointed and alone. Until Frankie. And after Frankie, then everything was different. After that then everything, including me, was changed.

Maybe I was the one who was drunk.

What I felt then was a coldness, like a shadow, drifting over me. I opened my eyes, and lifted my head and looked up and saw, in the window well in the wall above me, a movement.

There was a scuffling sound, like the furtive scrabble of a rat, and then a pair of feet, in tennis shoes, appeared. I watched as the latch turned and the window opened, and then, feet first, someone was slipping through and dropping to the floor, falling forward and catching herself with her hands. She stood up, and brushed her palms on her jeans. She turned around, and seeing me, she yelped.

"Jesus Christ, May," she said, flattening her hand against her chest. "You scared me just about more than half to death."

I didn't know what to say to her. "I'm sorry," I said.

Because there was Frankie, back again in front of me, face to face: the exact thing I'd been wishing for, conjured up right there in the flesh, in her bright orange blouse and her faded blue jeans torn in the knees and patched over with faded bits of calico and flowered print cotton cloth. I wanted to throw myself on her, to hug her, to kiss her.

"What are you doing here?" she asked.

I looked around the room, at the dank of the basement, the filth of it, the wet and the chill. And I realized that standing there in it was something close to what it would feel like to be buried alive. I thought of Meems, and tears stung my eyes.

Frankie was pulling her hair back out of her face. She put her hand on her hip and waited for me to collect myself.

"Well?"

"Me?" I asked her. "What are you doing here, Frankie? That's what I would like to know."

"Oh you would, would you?"

I nodded. "Yeah. I would."

My eyes were burning, and my throat was clogged, and I hated that. I rubbed the back of my wrist across my face, fast. I was mad at myself for being such a baby. I tried to square my shoulders and shrug my feelings off, but Frankie saw it, and she knew.

"May?" she said. She took a step toward me, cautiously. "You okay?"

I couldn't talk. I shook my head. She opened her arms then, and she took me into them, she gathered me up and held me and I felt myself opening, and all that blackness and darkness that had been in me seemed to come spilling out, all of it at once, like ink, leaving behind a light that was white and bright enough to blind me.

Frankie held me. She patted my hair, and she caressed me, and I breathed in the smell of her. She rocked me back and forth like a child that way, and she hummed and hummed, soothingly. After a while, she felt me soften and sigh, and then she let me go. She pulled back and held me at arm's length and looked at me. She touched my cheek, licked her thumb, rubbed a smudge of something off my forehead, peered into my eyes. I shuddered, pulled myself together.

"I thought you'd left me, Frankie," I said.

She smiled at me for a moment, then shook her head.

I sniffed. "What?" I asked.

She looked down at herself, fiddled with the buttons on her blouse. "Well, this," she said. She peered up at me, squinting. "May Caldwell, you are just about hopeless, you know that?"

"What's that supposed to mean?"

"You still don't get it, do you?"

"Get what?"

"Get anything. You're still just little old May Caldwell, one big nobody, wandering around in the dark like the world's only something that's been happening outside of you, and it doesn't have anything at all to do with who you are."

And I wanted to tell her then that she was wrong. That I had changed. That I was not the same girl I'd been before, that I was somebody else now. That I'd been with Paul Gerald, for one thing. That I'd stolen my father's car, for another. She'd said she wanted to teach me some things. Well, I'd learned them, hadn't I?

"What are you saying, Frankie?" I asked.

"Nothing new. Nothing that hasn't been said already before, May. Nothing your daddy hasn't already pointed out to you himself."

"My daddy?"

"He's a smart person, that man. Sees plenty. Understands a lot. You gotta give him credit for that, at least, I think. He saw what was what just about right away, didn't he?"

She turned, and I was afraid she was going to leave me again.

"No, wait," I told her. "Don't go."

I was begging her, and I hated myself for that, but I couldn't help it.

She looked back at me, over her shoulder, and she squinted and smirked and shook her head in that infuriating way, and then she turned away again.

"Frankie," I said. "What are you doing here, Frankie?"

"What do you think I'm doing, May?" she asked.

"I don't know," I said. "I have no idea."

She was standing in the shadows in the far corner of the basement, where the old incinerator loomed.

"Frankie?"

"Come over here, May," Frankie told me. "Come closer, okay? Just take a little look in here."

She had bent over and was tugging at the levered handle of the iron door, but it was stuck. She stood back and kicked at it. Then when she pulled at it again it screamed and turned, and the door's hinges screamed, too, as she hauled it open on a black hole, yawning into an empty space that smelled of dirt and ash and oil and smoke.

"Come here, May," she said.

I stepped toward her. "Why?" I asked.

She stood back. She rubbed her hands against her pants, and it was only then that I looked, and at first I wasn't sure what I was looking at. A bundle of something dark on the incinerator floor.

I turned back to Frankie, but she was still shaking her head at me. I looked closer, and it was only then that I finally understood. I could just make out the boyish face, and the hammer with its claw end slickened and shiny with blackish blood. The boy's feet, in their torn sneakers, were awkwardly placed one on top of the other.

"It's Creighton," Frankie told me.

And it was, and he was there, and he was dead.

———

"He wanted me to go with him," Frankie said. "He said, 'Let's get out of here. I love you.'"

She told him she wasn't going anywhere. That she'd learned to like it here.

"But what about me?" he'd asked her.

And she'd looked at Creighton Temple—in his jeans and his T-shirt and the plaid sports coat that was too big for him and the necktie that he'd knotted at his throat. He'd wanted to impress her, she said; he'd hoped she would invite him in to her new life, in Linwood, with us, the Caldwells and the Hadens and our friends. She'd looked at Creighton, she'd sized him up, and then she'd answered him.

"What about you?" she'd said. With her hand on her hip. With her lips curled up into a mocking smile, maddening him.

He'd taken off his jacket. He'd stepped toward her. He'd grabbed her arm and swung her to him; he'd held her there close against him, she said; he'd backed her up to her desk, and pressed his body hard onto hers, grinding his pelvis into her, digging at her with the buckle of his belt. She'd relaxed in his arms, and he must have thought that meant that he'd won her, after all. She'd let him kiss her. Let him tell her how much he needed her. Let him lift her skirt and tear her panties, let him shove himself deep inside her, while he held her head in the vise of his flattened palms and gazed into her eyes.

"I love you, Frankie," Creighton had told her. And maybe, she said, he did.

She'd gritted her teeth and closed her eyes. And then when he was finished, when he'd turned away, she picked up a hammer and she stepped up behind Creighton and she swung her arm back. He'd sensed her movement and he'd turned just in time to see it, just in time to know, she guessed, but then the hammer had caught him, and then it had slammed him down.

"He was my scout. He came by your house to get a feel for the lay of the land, see?" Frankie had gone back to her desk and opened a drawer and got out a cigarette and lit it, and she was pacing nervously now, back and forth, gesturing as she came and went. "To consider the prospects. While I waited around the corner, out of sight, in my car. And what he found out? Only good news, May. Only the best. They're generous people, all right, those Caldwells, he said. Good sponsors, we already knew that. Kind and caring and living in a big white house up there on Tyler Drive in Linwood, Iowa. Ask them for some help, and they'll probably be glad to give it to you, without too many untoward questions asked."

She blew smoke, folded her arms, then unfolded them again.

"Your mother gave him ten dollars, May," Frankie said. "Not only that, but she even followed him, she went looking for him, and when she found him she stopped him, and she gave it to him, and she told him to take care."

And after that Frankie knew it was going to be safe for her to show up in person on our doorstep, too, and when we invited her to, she moved in and then she got to liking it and then Creighton wouldn't do what she was asking him to, he wouldn't leave her alone, let her be, go away.

I was still looking at Creighton, at his folded hands, at the silver ring on his finger. At the watch on his wrist, gold like

Paul's. The necktie around his throat. That madras plaid jacket, a wadded-up bundle like a pillow near his head.

"What are you saying, Frankie?" I turned away from him and raised my eyes to look at her. My anger had come boiling up so fast it dizzied me. "That everything you did here was a lie?"

She shook her head. "Well, not all of it wasn't, May. The part about my uncle Elgin was the truth. And about my daddy, too. But the rest, well, hell, what can I say? We came here together, just to see what we could get, I'm admitting that. That was all it was at first. Stabbing in the dark. But what we found here turned out to be a lot. A lot more than I ever expected, in fact, and I give your mother a whole lot of credit for that."

"He wasn't crazy?" I asked.

"Well, he was crazy all right, I guess," she said. "That was why I liked him, I think."

"But he wasn't following you? I mean, you knew he was here. He was here with you?"

"For a while he was, yes. But then, I don't know. I got so I was starting to like it some, I guess. Is that so bad? Are you surprised? And I wasn't sure anymore about whether I wanted to stick with our plan. Oh boy, did that ever make him mad."

She dropped her cigarette and stepped on it.

"Your plan?"

"To get what we could get and then get gone."

She was smiling at me again. Smiling and shrugging and shaking her head.

I wanted to slap her.

"What about me?" I asked. And she answered me just the same as she'd answered Creighton.

"What about you?" Frankie said. Her green eyes, looking at me, made me feel my old self, worthless and stupid and ridiculous and dumb. Her mouth was twisted to one side. Her eyes were narrowed, foxy, sly, and critically regarding me.

Anger seethed through me, the same as in my father—it grabbed and shook me, and I wasn't able to resist it; I stepped into it, and I reached out, and I grabbed Frankie. I tried to drag her down; she struggled against me, and we tussled there, our feet slipping on the damp linoleum floor. I had a handful of her hair gathered up in my fist, and I was yanking on it. She clenched my shoulder, dragging at me, trying to throw me off balance and knock me down where she could sit on me and hold me and pound on me until I was still. One way or another. I realized then that she could just as well be trying to kill me, too, just the same as she'd killed Creighton already.

"May," Frankie growled. And then she swung one hand back behind her, and she brought it around, and she hit me with it, hard, on the side of my face. I reeled back, blinded, stunned, partly by the fact that she'd struck me and also by the fact of being struck. She stood back and looked at me, panting, with her head dropped forward and her hands on her hips. She blew out, hard, and shook her head.

"Dammit, May," she said. "Now why'd you have to go and make me do that?"

But already my hand was in my sweatshirt pocket and already I had the gun in it and already I was lifting it and holding it and pointing its black barrel straight over at her.

Her face was clouded over with disbelief.

"May?"

I didn't say anything, just looked into her face. I wiped at my nose with the back of my hand. There was a heavy, broken feeling in my face.

Frankie stood up straight, and she folded her arms over her chest.

"So now you're going to kill me, is that it?" she asked. "You guess you'd like to shoot me? After everything I did for you?"

She knew I'd never do it. That even if I'd known how, I didn't have it in me, even if she did. She turned her back on me, and she walked a few steps away, then swung around to face me again.

"Look at what you were before, May," she said. "And then take another good gander at who you think you are now. That's something, you gotta admit that. You're standing there wearing lipstick, holding a gun, about to shoot me. Me!"

The gun trembled in my hand. She stepped closer and reached out and took it away from me.

I USED TO DREAM THIS: THAT I WAS ASLEEP, AND I COULD NOT WAKE UP. THAT I was drugged and drowsy, shaking myself, but I was still not able to come all the way to. I used to do this: burn myself with a match tip. Slice at my leg with a razor blade. The skin would graze off, only so deep, and the blood would bead up, and then it would start, finally, to sting. The relief for me came when I felt the pain. It was a reassurance, then. A sign that I was there. Like pinching yourself to see if you're awake, except harder, much harder, you have to pinch yourself until you're bruised. To cut yourself until you bleed. Blood that would be a miraculous thing for me to see, welling up and seeping out and letting me know for certain that there was after all something of substance inside of me, that there was a fullness, I was brimming over with it, and I was not, therefore, a hollow, intangible girl.

FRANKIE WAS LEANING BACK AGAINST THE SIDE OF THE INCINERATOR WITH HER feet crossed and her arms folded over her chest. She looked at me and shook her head.

"You know, May, if you think this is bad, you should have seen my uncle Elgin," Frankie said. "You would have felt sorry for him even more, I guess, lying there on the ground, spreading his shredded arms. But you know what? I should have left him to bleed there in the dirt, but I didn't. He deserved it all right, I should have walked off and left him there to die." She looked into the incinerator at Creighton. She turned to me. "May?"

And with that I came swooping back.

Everything around me seemed too loud then, and too bright, too. I could hear it all too clearly and see it all too sharply: the rustle of her fingers against the fabric of her jeans, digging in her pockets, coming back with her lighter, blue, plastic—she flicked it, and its flame surged upward, hissing. The sheen of her polished nails. The straight line of her nose, shining, her nostrils, her lips, slightly open, the wet gleam of her teeth. My own breathing. My own pulse.

My face, where she'd hit me, ached and throbbed.

"I think maybe you broke my cheek," I said.

"I didn't break your cheek, May."

I sobbed.

"You've got to pull yourself together now. Get a grip, all right?" Frankie said. "I'm gonna need your help."

She had her lighter, and she was playing with it, flicking it on and off, staring at the flame.

"I don't know, Frankie," I said. "I don't know what to do."

She was still staring into the lighter flame. Then she let it go out, and she turned to me and smiled.

"We're going to burn him," Frankie said.

"Are you crazy?"

"Set him on fire. Ashes to ashes, see?"

The incinerator was just like a wood stove, she explained, only bigger, that was all. She'd had one in the kitchen of her house back in Kentucky, she told me. You open up its belly, she said, you put the wood and the kindling in, you light it, you close the door, and then it burns up what's inside and it warms the whole house at the same time. She spoke as if we were going to light a barbecue.

"Back home we had to use sticks and paper for our kindling. Here," she said, "there'd have to be gas. So, all we have to do is figure out how to start this thing."

There was some kind of a contrivance of knobs and pipes and levers to one side of the opened door, but they didn't any of them mean anything to me.

"I don't know," I said again. My voice was too loud, and it echoed away from me. "I don't know how to do this," I whispered. Frankie closed the door and locked it, and she bent closer to peer at the dials. She turned one, then another, stood back, listened. She opened the door again—every time she moved it, it screamed, sending shivers through me. I clapped my hands over my ears. She stuck her head inside and sniffed. She flicked her blue lighter and held it out, but still nothing happened. She went to her desk and got a piece of Haden's letterhead stationery out of the drawer; she rolled it up and lit one end and poked it into that black hole, but still nothing, no gush, no whoosh, no flare of a sudden larger flame. The paper flared and smoked, and then it went out.

"Shit," she said. She kicked at the contraption with her foot.

"They must have turned the gas off, Frankie," I told her, still whispering, "when they put the new heating system in."

She reached in through the door and took hold of Creighton's hand, and she yanked at him. Grunting with the effort of it, she tried to haul him back out. But it was too late for that. Creighton was in there, and he was dead, and there was not going to be any bringing him back.

Frankie closed the incinerator door, and again its hinges screamed. She turned the lever, and she sealed it shut.

I could feel that blackness seeping over me.

"I need some air, Frankie," I said. "I think I'm going to faint."

She followed me up the stairs and out the back. And then we were standing under a tree near the river, and I could imagine that we must have looked like two girls standing there in the early morning with nothing better to do than share a cigarette between us, as if nothing in our lives had ever begun to go wrong.

———

For me, it was just good to be with Frankie right then. I tried to forget about it all. I only wanted to pretend just for that minute that everything was still all right, that this was just us, me and Frankie, standing around before we had to go in to work, kicking at the dust, waiting for my dad to show up to open the store. Beyond the river, the morning daylight was beginning to brighten the sky. The streetlights on the bridge all sputtered off, one by one. There was the sound of boyish laughter—young fishermen up at dawn.

But then that moment was gone, and Frankie was stepping on her smoked cigarette butt as a car pulled up into our lot. It was Paul, out in front and stopping there. Frankie grabbed me and drew me away, and together we ducked behind the tree, then craned around, two pale faces, to look. To see: Paul Gerald, stepping out of his car and closing the door and walking up to the front of the store.

This was a different Paul Gerald than any one I'd ever known. This man had wild hair and rumpled clothes. His shirt was unbuttoned and untucked. He wavered when he walked, weaving and staggering. He looked like he must be drunk. He fumbled through his keys, dropped them, stooped to pick them up.

"What's he doing here?" Frankie asked.

I shrugged. "I don't know," I told her. "Maybe he's going to work."

He found the key that he was looking for, he unlocked the door, and he let himself into the store.

I was thinking that my father would be waking up soon. That

he'd be taking his shower and knotting his tie, stepping into his shoes, sitting on the edge of the bed to tie them, thundering downstairs, pouring himself a cup of coffee, lighting his first cigarette. Trying to find his keys. Noticing that his car was missing. Finding out that his daughter was gone.

"What'll we do?" Frankie said.

"He won't go down into the basement," I said. "And even if he does, he won't look in the incinerator."

Frankie moaned. Her hand was on my shoulder, squeezing it.

The light went on in the basement. Frankie had turned away from me. She had her arms folded, hugging herself. She paced a few steps away from me, turned, paced back.

"What's he doing in the basement, May?" she asked.

"I think maybe he's looking for me," I told her.

I tried to picture the caged elevator, gliding upward between the floors, stopping at the top, creaking open. He's stepping out onto the showroom floor, I thought. He's wandering through the furniture, staggering, steadying himself with his hand on the back of a chair.

The lights in the first-floor windows came on, and then we could see Paul. He was walking through the furniture showrooms like a ghost, haunting them. He moved along from one room to another, passing the windows, disappearing for a moment, then showing up again in an altogether different setting.

He was calling out to me, I thought. I could almost hear him saying my name. May? May? But I wasn't answering, so he stopped, and he sat down on a chair. He collapsed there. He leaned back, closed his eyes. I could see then that he had a bottle in his hand. That he was fumbling in his pocket and that he'd put a cigarette in his mouth.

I looked up to see that there were boys in jeans and T-shirts, leaning over the railing with their lines cast, fishing off the bridge. Their laughter drifted toward me. Their lines shimmered, pulled straight and taut as the water flowed away from them, sucked off by the strength of the river's current, all but carried away.

Then it happened: the scrape and flare and hiss of Paul's lit match as he brought it to his cigarette, and it was all so fast that before he could have known what or why, the flame was sucked away from him, and it whooshed down from his hand to the heating duct in the floor and then on down farther, into the basement underneath the store. The gas from the incinerator, not turned off, only slow to start, had begun to seep away from Creighton and upward toward Paul; it was wending its way to him, through the old heating ducts.

A pause.

And I was crying out, "Paul!"

And then, it all of it exploded. And everything, the store, Linwood, the world, seemed to be on fire.

Frankie's eyes were brightened by it. Her astonishment glowed in her face and softened it, like wax.

The glass windows in the store all burst.

The boys on the bridge looked up.

After that, it was only fire, burning. And Frankie in her car, driving away.

I was a girl, and my dreams were of Death. When he called to me, I wanted to answer him. When he beckoned, I tried to comply. I was tempted to follow along after him; I didn't care exactly where. Anything would be better than this, I thought.

I found him beautiful. It felt dramatic. It seemed to be clearly real.

The detectives have said that Frankie Crane is dead, and my parents take them at their word. Not Grand, though. He never will. She's alive still, he says. He's sitting in a chair under the tree near the pool in the back yard, whittling. With me on one side of him, studying the turning trees. And Brodie on the other side, rolling a burl over and over in his hands.

Grand has turned back again to the pleasure of his old habit of driving his station wagon over the back roads around us, looking for water to fish in, and sometimes when he comes home he'll take me aside and he'll tell me that he's seen her, he thinks. He'll say he's spotted her, that she is definitely still out there somewhere, that it is his confirmed opinion that the girl is not dead, after all. Far from it, he says, reaching over to lay his hand on my shoulder, giving me what he means to be a reassuring small shake. She's a survivor, May, isn't she? he asks. And when I agree with that he says it again, that she's still out there somewhere, all right, and she's very much alive. As beautiful as ever. He's seen her for himself, he says, with his own two eyes, and she's alive and well and looking like she's doing just fine.

She's been sitting in a car that's stopped at a light, or she's been riding in a truck that's turning off onto the main highway, or she's been walking down a street in a small town, or she's been inside a gas station paying the cashier, or in a bar, slipping down from a stool and disappearing, before he can get to her, out the back. He's had a glimpse of her face moving among some others in a crowd. Or her back, rounding a corner and drifting off that way out of view. He follows her whenever he can, but by the time he ever catches up with where he thinks she's been, she's always already gone.

Sometimes he means Frankie, and sometimes, I think, he means Meems.

What my mother is picturing for Frankie is this:

A girl's body, a huddled bundle dumped in a ditch. Stripped of her clothes. Battered and bruised. Picked *apart by predators, her flesh torn and chewed, her skin ripped, the muscle and the meat of her pared down to bare bone.*

Or buried.

Or burned.

Or drowned.

But I know now that death is not that. It isn't Frankie at all, in fact. It is this: it is April Delaney, floating. It is April Delaney's hair, drifting. It is Brodie Haden, sinking back on the pillow on his bed. Brodie's boyish face, uplifted in the moonlight. Brodie's bare hand, drawn back. It is Meems herself, dwindling down. It is Creighton Temple, bashed.

Or else it is me, burrowing under and cowering alone, with my head covered by my hands.

It is the me that once was, the May that used to be. It is not this, the May that I am. It is only that, my old younger smaller self, diminished, vanished and shriveled and faded and gone. Cast off and left behind.

And, finally, it is Paul Gerald. He is the devil puppet, grinning. He is Death—dark-haired and ash-eyed and fair-skinned—and he is rising upward, and he is floating off, and he is an angel, he is a saving grace above a furious roil and a cleansing conflagration, a sudden and unstoppable explosion of spark and smoke and heat and torrid flame.

Acknowledgments

To John Herman, for letting this one begin; to Lane Von Herzen, Jo Giese, Jennie Nash and Ellen Hattman, for their gracious readings; to Betsy Lerner, for seeing through to the sense of it; to Natalie Bowen, for her thoroughness and care; to Carole Abel, for her enduring belief; to Parker and Jesse, for being there; and, always, to Tom—Thank you.

STC